WITCH'S SABBATH

Recent Titles by J M Gregson from Severn House

Lambert and Hook Mysteries

AN ACADEMIC DEATH
DEATH ON THE ELEVENTH HOLE
GIRL GONE MISSING
JUST DESSERTS
MORTAL TASTE
TOO MUCH OF WATER
AN UNSUITABLE DEATH

Detective Inspector Peach Mysteries

DUSTY DEATH
TO KILL A WIFE
THE LANCASHIRE LEOPARD
A LITTLE LEARNING
MISSING, PRESUMED DEAD
MURDER AT THE LODGE
A TURBULENT PRIEST
THE WAGES OF SIN
WHO SAW HIM DIE?
WITCH'S SABBATH

WITCH'S SABBATH

J. M. Gregson

This first world edition published in Great Britain 2006 by
SEVERN HOUSE PUBLISHERS LTD of
9–15 High Street, Sutton, Surrey SM1 1DF.
This first world edition published in the USA 2006 by
SEVERN HOUSE PUBLISHERS INC of
595 Madison Avenue, New York, N.Y. 10022.

British Library Cataloguing in Publication Data

Gregson, J. M.
  Witch's sabbath
  1. Peach, Percy, Detective Inspector (Fictitious character) - Fiction
  2. Blake, Lucy (Fictitious character) - Fiction
  3. Police - England - Lancashire - Fiction
  4. Detective and mystery stories
  I. Title
  823.9'14 [F]

  ISBN-10: 0-7278-6342-8

Typeset by Palimpsest Book Production Ltd.,
Polmont, Stirlingshire, Scotland.
Printed and bound in Great Britain by
MPG Books Ltd., Bodmin, Cornwall.

In memory of Ben,
a faithful canine companion of many years,
who died as this book was completed.

One

There would be more snow before nightfall, she thought. This was a snow wind, light at present but steadily gathering strength. There had been nothing to indicate more snow when they set out. There had been only a cold hard frost and a bright low sun, pouring its heatless light over the Pennine Hills from the east, blinding at first on the white carpet which had already covered the hills. But with each of the passing hours the wind had gathered strength. Now it was blowing relentlessly over the lower slopes beneath them, sweeping in from the west, where the land dropped away to the sea thirty miles away.

There was a crust of frost on the snow that had fallen last night, so that their feet crunched through a hard top into the soft cold beneath. The snow built up on the soles of their boots until it made another sole, thicker and more treacherous, and every few minutes Dermot would stop and knock the compacted whiteness away methodically, then watch her toiling behind him, with what she was sure was disapproval of her faltering progress.

Her boots were smoother than his, worn with the miles of climbing over the Lake District fells which they had endured over the years. Dermot hadn't done much of that and he had new boots. It was perfectly logical that she should slip and slide more than he did as the ground became steeper. She wanted to tell the self-satisfied sod that Pendle Hill was a mere pimple compared with Scafell Pike and Helvellyn, that she had climbed grander hills than this in her time without breaking sweat. But she was panting too hard for anything like that, and he moved on each time she came up to him, as if to show that he was impatient with her weakness, that he tolerated it only because of his benevolent nature.

1

As they climbed higher and the wind became more bitter, she drew the string of her hood tight beneath her chin, concentrating on the patch of ground ahead of her, enjoying the fact that theirs were the first footsteps here since the snow had fallen. They were on a well-used path beneath the whiteness, but she enjoyed the illusion that they were making a new track where none had existed before, that this was somehow wilder terrain and a more individual exercise than it really was.

She watched her breath wreathing in long cones of steam as she climbed the last few yards to the gap in the dry-stone wall, where Dermot stood looking towards the long mound and steep northern end of Pendle Hill. He leant with his elbows lightly on the dark pillar of stone that marked the gap in the wall they would pass through and surveyed the ground ahead.

'"Announced by all the trumpets of the sky, / Arrives the snow,"' he said.

He liked to throw in quotations. It would have been more impressive if she hadn't known that this one had appeared in *The Times* yesterday, Eleanor thought ungenerously. And more telling if he had been able to complete it: she was sure it had been four lines in all. But she couldn't remember how it had ended either, so she said nothing, merely nodding rather stupidly and looking past him at the awesome scene ahead.

'Ralph Waldo Emerson,' Dermot added pretentiously.

She pushed past him and set out resolutely across the huge white carpet of the next rise. She knew she was being ungenerous, that she should have responded to him in some way, should have at least acknowledged the attempt at communication he had made. Perhaps this happened to others as well; perhaps this was what marriage did to you. She could remember the old, premarital days when she had loved him to quote, when she would have teased him, come back with an answering quotation of her own in happy competition. But now all she could think of was Christina Rossetti's carol,

> Snow had fallen, snow on snow,
> Snow on snow,
> In the bleak midwinter,
> Long ago.

She might have crooned it softly to him, in the days before they were married, when he had admired her warm alto voice. But now she would be too inhibited to do anything but quote the words. It would be a cliché, and Dermot would underline the fact with that small, contemptuous smile of his, which said this was so obvious that it would have been better left unsaid.

She could hear him panting a little as he came up beside her, and she kept up her brisk pace, as if it were necessary to her, not a mere substitute for conversation. And then, inevitably, she slipped, and her arms clawed wildly at the air for a moment. She saved herself from any serious injury by dropping forward on to all fours, her gloves feeling for the iron ground beneath the inches of snow. He reached out a hand to her, but she scrambled up without its help, absurdly furious with herself for this small evidence of weakness.

She looked away to her left towards where the village of Sabden lay, invisible over the slope of this winter landscape. 'This is the area where the Lancashire witches used to operate,' she said, attempting to divert him away from her feebleness.

'If indeed they were witches at all,' said Dermot, happy in his twenty-first-century scepticism.

'They were hanged for it,' said Eleanor, suddenly resentful on behalf of her sex.

'Convicted at Lancaster Assizes,' Dermot said. He sounded as if he was anxious to cap her little gobbet of conversation and tidy it away.

She was reluctant to let him have the last word, contemptuous of her own pettiness even as she indulged it. 'I read a book about it a long time ago,' she said determinedly. 'It was quite good. Brought it all to life. Gave you the flavour of the times. They were mostly just women who were using herbal remedies to—'

'*Mist Over Pendle*,' he said with a superior smile. 'I expect we all read that in our youth. Only fiction, of course.'

He spoke as if that made the book both highly suspect and not worthy of serious consideration. Perhaps he wrote off all the books she chose to read as mere frivolity. But no doubt she was just fancying that, Eleanor told herself. She

3

found it difficult to give Dermot credit for anything these days. It was as if he had forfeited her trust in all areas, rather than just one.

Somewhere over the shoulder of the hill, an invisible sheep baaed, its bleating sounding unnaturally close, carried to them from miles away by some freak of the searing wind. Both of them looked automatically towards the sound, but there was no living thing visible across this frozen landscape.

'We'd better get on if we're going to the top. The darkness will drop in early now that the sun's gone, and we want to be down by then,' Dermot said.

Thank you for stating the obvious: I've done a damned sight more walking in my time than you, she thought. But she knew that he was trying to be conciliatory, though on the face of it they had had no disagreement, and that she should be grateful to him for that. 'You'll have earned a pint by that time!' she said with a smile, and both of them thought of the lights and the welcoming warmth of an old, low-roofed pub, even though they knew that the pubs would be closed when they came down from Pendle, in the late afternoon of the January day.

They moved forward in a more companionable silence, united now in their contest against nature, concentrating on their small, safe battle against the English winter on this last outpost of the Pennines. As they turned on to the long slope towards the summit, the wind was at its keenest, hard into their faces, stinging their cheeks with the tiny fragments of ice it whipped from the waste ahead of them.

Then it began to snow. The flakes were tiny at first, a welter of painful pinpricks to supplement the icy fragments from the ground. Then they grew larger, the wind blew almost horizontally, and all landmarks disappeared. The sky seemed to be reaching down to engulf them.

It was at this point that the lace snapped in Eleanor's left boot.

She fumbled with it for a moment, then realized that frozen fingers were never going to handle the icy threads. Dermot had toiled on, head down against the strengthening wind and snow, oblivious of his partner's distress. Typical! She swore heartily after him, but he could not hear her above the torrent

4

of wind. He looked back when he reached the next wall and the next gap, to see her limping drunkenly up the slope through the white world behind him.

'My lace has gone.'

'You should have checked them before we set out, on a day like this.'

She wanted to hit him, felt a compelling impulse to swing a drunken uppercut at what little she could see of his smug face. But she knew she would miss, would lose her balance and fall on her face in the snow. She must conserve what energy she had: for the first time, she felt a little burst of fear.

She said through stiff lips, 'We can't get to the top now. Not in this.'

Dermot turned and looked towards the now invisible top of Pendle Hill. 'This isn't a blizzard. It's only a snow shower. We knew we might get one or two of these when we set out. Conditions will improve in a minute or two. We're not far from the top, really.'

She didn't believe that. But she couldn't stand still and argue, not with the snow building steadily on the front of her anorak and waterproof trousers. She caught a glimpse of what was no more than a dark, low shadow, through what this smug bastard said was not a blizzard. 'There's a building over there. I'm going to shelter for a few minutes and lace up my boot again.'

He said, 'I don't think that's a building at all. And it means losing height and leaving the path. You'd be better crouching here, in the lee of the wall. I'll help you with your lace.'

But his belated offer of help was borne away on the wind as it howled about his ears. Eleanor had set off towards her haven, setting her feet sideways and downwards into the deepening snow to retain her balance, taking tiny steps with her stricken left boot and much longer ones with her right. He hesitated a moment, bellowed a useless 'Bloody women!' into the teeth of the gale, and set off reluctantly after his wife.

It was a building all right – a series of buildings, indeed. It emerged as she neared it as the remnants of a farmhouse, deserted now for probably fifty years and more, where some wretched tenant had striven hopelessly to wring a living out of a few acres of this hostile world. Most of the roof of the main building had collapsed years ago; what was left hung drunken and dangerous from the exposed rafters.

Dermot caught up with her as she paused briefly to decide which was the best shelter to choose. 'You can't go in there. It's not safe! The place is falling apart. It'll come down about your ears.'

'I'm bloody going!' Eleanor, who never swore, found it strangely satisfying to shout the words through the gale. It was a fitting answer to the silly sod's determination that she shouldn't go into the place.

She moved past a tiny enclosure with low walls, which must once have been a sty with a single pig. She stopped in front of a low building which had been added to the end of the stone gable of the farmhouse. 'This will do.' It was better preserved than anything else in the place, because the main building had protected it from the prevailing west wind and the worst ravages of desolation.

'You shouldn't go in there. It won't be safe. There could be rats or anything!' He sounded desperate to stop her.

And the mention of rats almost did stop her. She didn't like rats, and the thought of them in the near-darkness of this hovel filled her with terror. But then she said, 'There'll be no rats here. Not at this altitude. Not with no food around.' She wished she felt as certain of that as she sounded. She lifted the remnants of a wooden door and ducked her head beneath the low stone lintel of the outbuilding.

Eleanor waited a moment for her eyes to adjust to the gloom, as her body welcomed the blessed relief of shelter from the blizzard. It felt almost as if the place was heated, such was the fury of the wind and the snow outside. She bent and brushed the compacted snow from the instep of her boot with the back of her gloved hand, then picked cautiously, experimentally, at the broken lace beneath.

She needed to re-thread the longest part of the broken lace through the top few holes of the boot and re-tie it. That would be good enough for her to get down to the valley, or even to complete the walk if the weather relented and her oaf of a husband insisted on going to the top. And it should be possible, if she could just get some feeling back into her frozen fingers. It's only Pendle bloody Hill, she told herself resolutely. Not Everest; not the Matterhorn; not even Ben Nevis.

It was whilst she was trying to motivate herself that she saw the thing in the corner.

It was against the far wall of the room, hard up against the stone of the wall, as if someone had been saving space. A long, low, indeterminate shape, only dimly visible even now, when her eyes had accustomed themselves to the semi-darkness of her refuge. She did not want to investigate it, but she felt her legs moving her towards it, even as her instinct told her to turn away.

Dermot's voice said from outside, 'It's coming fine now. I told you it would. Let's be on our way!'

The words seemed to come to her from a great distance. She wondered why he had not come in, why he had been so reluctant to follow her into shelter from that icy torment outside. She bent towards the dark shape at the far end of the small, square room, recognized what had once been clothes upon it, accepted in her mind that this thing was probably human.

It was in the darkest spot of all, in the furthest and darkest corner of the hovel, that she saw what had once been a face.

Two

Detective Chief Inspector 'Percy' Peach, reluctant to venture into the biting cold until the last possible minute, sat in the passenger seat of the police car and watched his detective sergeant donning boots.

It was a much more interesting sight than it would have been when he began his CID career. This was entirely due to the fact that he now had a female sergeant – or, to be strictly accurate, this particular female sergeant. Percy Peach was only thirty-eight, but that made him an old sweat in police terms. DS Lucy Blake's calves, even within the close-fitting blue trousers which passed for plain clothes, were infinitely more attractive to Peach than the long shanks of DS Bert Collins, which had once walked beside him on journeys such as this. That long streak of discretion, as Percy had been used to calling him, had displayed solid police virtues; but DS Blake had other qualities altogether.

DCI Peach decided that there was a lot to be said after all for the modernization of the police force.

He pulled on his well-worn wellies and set off in single file behind his younger colleague on the route to the spot where the corpse had been found. There were plenty of tracks ahead of them in the snow, but single file seemed safest in these conditions. The fact that it enabled him to study DS Blake's perfectly rounded rear on the way to the ruined farmhouse was purely coincidental.

The police surgeon had gone through the ridiculous formality of pronouncing what was left in the outhouse as dead and gone on his way. But the Home Office pathologist was there when Peach and Blake arrived, the funnels of his breath interweaving with those of the civilian scene-of-crime team as they went quietly about their business under the direction of Sergeant Jack Chadwick.

Within the crime-scene area cordoned off from a curious public by police plastic ribbons, there was normally a professional cynicism. The members of the team liked to show that they had developed a professional carapace in relation to blood and gore and the whole business of death. They would make tasteless jokes about corpses and their degeneration, asserting their familiarity with death, reminding their colleagues that they were old hands in these things.

On this occasion, it was different.

They spoke to each other in low tones, almost in whispers. It might have been the still, biting cold in the place, which seemed to cut through even the thickest of garments. It might have been the isolation of this derelict building, which seemed even more isolated from the rest of living, human life in the snow and frost of the winter landscape. But Peach was certain, after a swift, appraising glance round the stone-walled room, that it was the thing that lay in the corner which was stilling the normal robust exchanges.

Even the pathologist seemed to be affected by the atmosphere. But his frustration at being able to do so little here probably contributed to his terseness. He nodded to Peach, acknowledging that they had met before, with each encounter overshadowed by a death. 'It's a difficult one, this one. Difficult for me, I mean. Maybe not for you.'

Peach forced a bitter smile. 'It won't be easy, I'm sure. They never are, when we don't find the stiff until well afterwards.'

'She's been gone a long time. Been here for months,' said the pathologist tersely.

It was a female, then. You couldn't tell even that from the blackened oval that had once been a face. Peach moved across the crowded little enclosure and stood looking down at her for a moment. Most of the flesh had gone, but the skin was still stretched like dark parchment over the bones. He said aloud, 'We'll get them, love. Whoever did this to you.'

Then, as if embarrassed by this tiny eruption of emotion in one who was supposed to take these things in his stride, he lifted his eyes to the wall above the body and said gruffly, 'Young, was she?'

'I think so. I don't want to disturb any more than is strictly necessary. I'll cut away her clothing when I get her into the lab.'

There was a moment's silence. He didn't need to explain himself. Everyone knew that what was beneath the soiled garments might be brittle, might break whenever it was moved. Whatever it could offer in the way of evidence would be best contained within the clothing until that could be cut away and the contents exposed upon the stainless-steel tables of the laboratory.

'How long ago?'

'Months rather than weeks. Maybe longer than that. But you could have deduced that for yourself. I'll give you some-thing better in due course.'

'You'll make it a priority?'

'Yes.'

'She's quite probably a missing person, you see. It'll be difficult to pin her down, until we have some idea how long she's been dead.'

Peach realized that he was going through the motions, talking for the sake of it, doing anything to lower the tension in that grim and freezing place. If this proved to be one of the thousands of people who went missing in Britain in every week of the year, they would probably need to know exactly when she had died even to identify a victim. He was assuming already that it was murder, that no one would have come out to this bleak place to end her own life.

As if he followed this train of thought, the pathologist said, 'I'm not even sure how she died, yet. There's nothing obvious from what we can see and I don't want to run the risk of contaminating the evidence by interfering with the clothing. You'll have all that soon enough, once I get her on the table.'

Lucy Blake forced herself to go over and stare down at the very dead thing in the corner which was to become a part of all their lives, and of hers and Peach's in particular. It was an absurd part of working in what was still essen-tially a man's world: she was the only woman in that crowded, icy room. She had to show them that a woman could look down on a thing like this without puking, without showing a weakness which would be entirely human. It was ridiculous and probably out of date; perhaps she was the only one present who felt that she had to show a male toughness in the face of a shocking sight.

DS Blake had learned early in her days in uniform that young male PCs were far more likely to throw up than she was when they attended a gory road accident, but she had always taken it as a sign of humanity in them. And you couldn't win in the canteen culture: if you showed yourself to be tough, the diehards would decide you were probably a dyke.

Her eyes seemed reluctant to transfer their gaze from that awful blackening face, with the lips almost completely gone and what was left of the mouth twisted into a ghoulish leer, which no living face could have carried. She forced her focus away from the face, saw for the first time long, dark hair, which might in life have been lustrous. It was dry and soiled now, but the only thing about the corpse that looked as if it had been recently alive. She knew that it was a myth that the hair and the nails went on growing after death. She was suddenly certain that this had been beautiful hair when the woman had been alive. But that was probably only because she wanted it to have been so, wanted this relic of life to have once been splendid, as some compensation for having died in a place like this.

If indeed she had died here: the CID professional asserted itself in her. The probability was that the woman had been killed elsewhere and merely dumped here to guard against the quick discovery of her remains. Lucy resolved that she would get the man who had done this – she was already sure that it was a man; and with that determination, she felt the hunter stirring within her, the love of the chase that Percy Peach said was an essential part of any CID officer. Even here, in the presence of death and its grisly residue, she felt a guilty excitement. Grim mysteries like this were what she had joined for, were what had made her and others want to be part of CID.

She moved a little, transferred her gaze to the other end of the body. The feet looked pathetically small in their trainers, which shone unnaturally white and clean in the arc lamp the

11

SOCA team had rigged up with a battery to assist their work. She thought how inadequate such footwear was, then remembered that this woman might have died in the summer, when the sun had shone through long days and the weather had been warm, even up here.

'So you've no real idea how long she's been lying here?' she said to the pathologist, repeating Peach's enquiry just because she wanted to say something, anything; knowing even as she completed the question that it was naïve: he'd have told them that, if he'd known.

'Months rather than weeks, as I said. Possibly longer than that, but I don't think so. I'll have a better idea once I have the technology of the lab and what's left of her on the table. The entomologist can tell us all kinds of things from the development of the maggots, though I'm not sure how much the altitude and the cold would affect that and what's happened since.'

There was the sound of a four-wheel-drive vehicle in the still air outside, coming closer, picking its way cautiously across the snow-covered fields, until the sound of its engine seemed to vibrate within the damp stone walls of the place where they stood. Jack Chadwick went to the low doorway and looked out. 'It's the meat wagon,' he said. Unnecessarily, for all of them had realized what it was. With no paved roads to the derelict farmhouse, no other vehicle would have been allowed to come so close. The SOCA team would look for tyre marks on the unpaved track, when the snow melted. It was unlikely they would find anything significant, after such a time had elapsed, but not impossible, in an isolated place like this.

The experienced crew of the long-base Land Rover were charged with the collection of the corpse, with the careful stowing of whatever remained into the plastic zipper case of the body bag, with the lifting of that into the 'shell', the fibre-glass coffin in which it would be transferred to Chorley for the post-mortem. Lucy Blake caught a whiff of diesel as the engine was switched off outside.

And with that sudden silence, the people inside the stone room, who had been frozen into a tableau of their own thoughts by the arrival of the vehicle, sprang again into life.

There was a sudden, blinding flash as the photographer snatched a last view of the position of the corpse and the way it lay beneath its covering. Then they moved out of the building and stood bleakly in the cold, forming into two rough lines, moving a step or two in a silent cortège behind the corpse, as the men moved carefully between them and slid the shell and its grisly contents into the back of their improvised hearse.

No one moved as the Land Rover chugged slowly away across the frozen field, its wheels spinning a little as it rejoined the paved road and turned towards Clitheroe and civilization. It was a last, futile, scarcely conscious mark of respect to the woman who had long been dead. Then the scene-of-crime team went back into the ruin to complete their work, to search for whatever might be revealed on the ground now exposed to them, where the corpse had lain.

DCI Peach exchanged a few quiet words with Sergeant Jack Chadwick, who had years ago been his CID colleague, before having been shot and almost killed in a bank raid. Then Chadwick disappeared back to his work and Peach and Lucy Blake walked slowly back across the fields to the gate where they had left the police Mondeo.

It was fine but cloudy, with a biting north-east wind. Peach looked across towards the top of Pendle Hill, well above the tree-line, stark and white with its winter covering against the deep grey of the sky. From this angle there was not a single habitation visible. It was a scene that would have been exactly the same four centuries and more before, when the Pendle witches had been dabbling in the supernatural and paying for it with their lives.

They picked their way over the frozen ground in silence. They were two hundred yards from the ruined farm before Lucy Blake turned to look back at it and said, 'I'm glad to be out of there. I felt there was something evil in the air.'

Percy Peach knew that he should reassure her, should smile away such childish superstitions and remind her of their professional responsibilities. Instead, he repeated with terse conviction his first words when he had seen the body: 'It's not going to be easy, this one.'

Three

'They'll want to see us, you know.'
  'Who will?'
'The police.' Dermot Boyd was impatient with her denseness. 'They'll want to ask us questions about how we found the body, about whether we saw anything suspicious.'
'But we didn't.'
'Of course we didn't. But they'll want to know that. It's just routine. They're not very intelligent you know, the police. So they have their routines, so that they don't need to think. The average woodentop isn't much good at using his initiative, so they operate by the book all the time. The book tells them what to do, so they do it. Saves them from the painful business of thinking. It's a bit like women following fashion: it saves them from thinking.'
He'd managed to get a dig in at her, or her sex, at the end. That was characteristic. But it wasn't like him to say so much. It was almost as though he was nervous. Eleanor thought waspishly that she'd like to prolong this exchange, in that case. 'But it hadn't just happened, had it? We couldn't possibly have seen anything that was helpful.'
'Of course we couldn't. And the sooner they've finished with us, the better. But that's what I mean: they put their procedures into practice, whether they're appropriate or not. They do what the book tells them to do. Some PC Plod will be round to see us, you mark my words.'
'I expect you're right.'
He wondered why it annoyed him so much when she said that. Perhaps it was not the words but the way she turned away from him, signifying that the argument was at an end, or perhaps that she didn't think it worth her while to argue with him. He could remember when they had loved to argue

14

with each other, to pursue a point for its own sake, stretching their minds, knowing that it would end in a happy resolution, whatever the subject. That seemed a long time ago, nowadays. He said stubbornly, 'It's no big deal. I just thought we should agree what we're going to say, that's all.'

She looked back at him from the books she was putting into her briefcase. 'Why on earth should we do that?'

He sighed. 'Because we don't want to look silly, that's why. They'd be delighted if we said different things, even if they were only slightly different. They'd get a kick out of making us contradict each other. It's their job to do that. And they hate schoolteachers, the plods.'

Eleanor hadn't heard that before. She would have thought that police and teachers were both authority figures in a world which had less and less respect for authority – that they might have had a fellow feeling about the excrescences of the worst of modern youth. But she had neither the time nor the inclination for more argument. 'All right. If they do come to speak to us, there's nothing to say anyway, is there?'

He turned ostentatiously away from her, watching her movements in the mirror over the mantelpiece. 'Not much, I suppose. But we should say that it was completely by chance that we went to that old farmhouse at all. That we'd no intention of going there when we set out.'

'Of course we should say that. For the very good reason that it's the truth. We'd never have gone near the place if the lace on my boot hadn't broken, would we? And that body would still have been lying there now.'

He nodded, with what she thought was an odd eagerness. 'That's what we need to say, then. I just think it's important that we both say exactly the same thing – don't get our wires crossed.'

He'd have picked her up on it if she'd used a cliché like that. Eleanor rather enjoyed saying, 'You sound almost as though you were nervous about it, Dermot. You haven't got a criminal record you've carefully concealed from me for twenty years, have you? I hope you're not the phantom rapist of old Brunton town!' She laughed at the ridiculous thought as she walked to the hall cupboard and took out her car coat.

'It's not a subject for hilarity, as far as I'm concerned.

This is almost certainly a suspicious death, you know. And in any case, you've no good reason to think that that poor girl was raped.'

She turned to face him in the dimness of the hall, giving him her full attention for the first time. 'You must have looked at that thing up there far more carefully than I did. I didn't even know that it was female, let alone whether it was young or old.' But he hadn't, she thought, with a little frisson of horror. He'd hardly looked at the thing in the corner at all, as far as she could remember.

He stood very still in the shadows for a moment. Then he came forward with a false, unchanging smile and held her shoulders. 'You're right. Of course you are! I don't know why I said that. I suppose I just assumed it was a girl because so many of the bodies found nowadays are young women. I'd no real reason to say that, as you so rightly point out.'

She couldn't help glancing sideways at his right hand as it grasped her shoulder. He didn't often touch her nowadays, apart from their routine couplings in bed. It was as though he was trying to convince her of something. She said ungenerously, 'It's good to know that I can be right about something, after all!' and glanced at her watch.

He gave her that forced smile again, then said, 'That just underlines what I was saying, though, doesn't it? We need to be careful what we say to the police. The kind of slip I made then might give them totally the wrong impression. It might start them off on a wild-goose chase – one that would be entirely profitless for them and embarrassing for us.'

'I suppose you may be right. I'm going to be late if I don't go now.' She slipped free of the grasp he still had on her shoulders and went through the kitchen to the utility room.

Her hand was on the door that led into the garage when he said, 'That's agreed, then. We'll both tell them that we were set on climbing Pendle Hill, that we'd no intention of going to that farmhouse until your bootlace snapped and the miniature blizzard caught us. That it was only because of those things that we were glad of any shelter in an emergency, even of that derelict place we'd never have even glanced at otherwise.'

'All right. Must go, I'm afraid. See you tonight.'

'Have a good day then, old girl!' It was an expression he hadn't used for years, one of the phrases he had teased her with when they were first married, because her father had used it to her mother and he knew it annoyed her. He reached for her as she turned away from him and kissed her lightly on the forehead.

Dermot never did that.

Eleanor Boyd drove through the morning rush hour towards the comprehensive school where she was head of the history department. Dermot shouldn't have gone on about the police like that, whatever his anxiety. It had made her think back to those minutes in the blizzard, when she had been limping along, looking desperately for any kind of shelter.

It had made her remember what she would otherwise surely have forgotten: that he had not wanted her to go into that ruined farmhouse at all.

An hour later on that Monday morning, Chief Detective Inspector Percy Peach climbed the stairs to the top floor of Brunton police station with a heavy heart. He glanced through the wide windows of this new building at the view of the old cotton town, stretching away towards the moors and the clear winter sky above them. But his mood was nothing to do with the grim industrial landscape outside.

It was a depression that normally settled upon him at the prospect of a meeting with his CID chief.

Chief Superintendent Thomas Bulstrode Tucker looked every inch a senior policeman, as far as most of the public he was paid to serve could see. He was in his fifties now, but held himself erect at just under six feet. He was running just a little to fat, but not so much that you would notice it in the well-cut uniform he favoured for his public appearances. He still carried an excellent head of well-groomed hair, greying a little at the temples; his regular features were lined a little now, his brow habitually furrowed with the responsibilities he carried, but that only added to the air of gravitas he carried so impressively into his media pronouncements.

His grey-blue eyes invariably looked straight into the television camera, his well-modulated voice enunciated his carefully chosen phrases perfectly into the radio microphone. He was the perfect figure to carry the police viewpoint into the world at large, the perfect man for the public relations which were now so important to the modern police image.

He was also, in the view of Percy Peach and almost everyone who worked for him, a complete prat.

That was one of the more moderate phrases Peach used to describe the man he invariably referred to as Tommy Bloody Tucker. His dislike of his chief was returned with interest by Tucker. But the senior man was shrewd enough to know that his image and reputation depended upon the odious Peach. Indeed, when Tucker had reluctantly engineered Peach's promotion to Chief Inspector and put him back in uniform for a year, the clear-up rates in CID had dropped dramatically with his absence. Tucker himself had even been forced occasionally to return to the crime-face and try his hand at real detection rather than public relations, and the results had been disastrous. He had been glad to see Peach return to CID.

Tucker depended heavily upon the younger man's successes, and both of them knew it. It meant that Tucker had to preserve the appearances of politeness towards his execrable chief inspector whilst checking the worst of his insolence. And it meant that Percy Peach, who knew his own worth but had no aspirations towards further promotion, baited his superior mercilessly whenever the opportunity arose. A little innocent wordplay was, Peach maintained, the only thing that made life with Tommy Bloody Tucker bearable.

He knocked on the door and watched the three panels which said 'Engaged', 'Wait' and 'Come In' light up in quick succession. Then he walked in and stood at attention before his chief's desk, his eyes fastened rigidly upon the wall behind the man's well-coiffured head. 'Routine report on the weekend crime in the metropolis of Brunton and surrounding areas, sir,' he said stiffly.

'All right, Peach, I've a busy morning ahead of me, even if you haven't. Cut the bullshit and talk normally, please,' said Tucker irritably.

Percy made a show of relaxing the tautness of his shoulders, then looked at the almost empty surface of his boss's desk. 'Golf go well at the weekend, sir?'

Tucker frowned his most formidable frown at his chief inspector. He hadn't meant him to take such liberties when he told him to cut out the bullshit; and he'd lost more than he cared to admit to whilst playing cards in the clubhouse of Brunton Golf Club on the previous afternoon. 'There was no golf this weekend in view of the snow, as you well know,' he said sternly. 'I spent most of the weekend catching up on paperwork and preparing myself for the North-West Conference on Serious Crime.' He rolled out the title as sonorously as he could in his mellow baritone.

'Very necessary, I'm sure, sir.' Percy nodded sagely, yet somehow managed to convey the message that he didn't believe a word of it.

Tucker peered at him suspiciously. 'We've got to match the thinking of criminals, Peach. Some of them are quite intellectual, these days. We need to meet intelligence with intelligence. There is a need for original thinking and fine minds in the upper echelons of CID.'

Indeed there is, thought Percy. And what do we get? Blockheads like Tommy Bloody Tucker. 'I'm sure those contemplating serious crime will have second thoughts when they hear about your conference, sir.'

'Fraud, Peach.'

Percy raised his eyebrows and said nothing. This surely couldn't be a confession from his chief: Tucker had never been a man for self-knowledge, and still less for self-criticism.

'That's the crime that's on the increase, Peach. Millions are being embezzled at this very moment.' Tucker stopped, impressed by his own sense of immediacy.

Percy brightened. 'Yes, sir. Fraud features largely in my dissertation on crime in this area – the one which reveals that Freemasons are four times more likely to commit a serious crime in this part of Lancashire than ordinary citizens.' He beamed his enthusiasm at Tucker. The statistic was based on the fact that a local accountant who happened to be a Mason had been convicted on seven different fraud charges; but Tucker was too lazy or too dense to have rumbled that one, so Percy kept quoting the statistic.

19

Tommy Tucker's mouth set in the thin, petulant line of a frustrated child, a sight that warmed Percy Peach's heart. 'I've had quite enough of that favourite fact of yours, Peach. I'm quite sure that there is no one in my own lodge who would ever be accused of serious crime. You cast a slur upon a fine body of people, who achieve a tremendous amount of—'

'Yes, sir. Can't change the facts, though. Much as I'd like to, of course.' Somehow he was back in his 'attention' position, bolt upright, straining upwards in every fibre of his five feet eight inches, his dark eyes fixed again on a line three inches above Tucker's head.

Tucker looked with distaste at the man who stood so stiffly before him: he had a striking bald head above a very black fringe of hair and eyes that were almost as dark as the eyebrows above them and the neat moustache beneath his small nose. He scarcely looked like a thief-taker, but both of them knew that Peach was the policeman the local villains feared more than any other. 'DCI Peach, you'd better give me your report and be off and do some work. Has anything else happened on our patch over the weekend which you think worthy of my attention?'

'Usual violent exchanges on Saturday night in the town centre, sir. Some of it racially based. Only to be expected, with the local elections coming up and British National Party candidates canvassing enthusiastically.'

Tucker sighed the sigh of a man who should not be troubled with such trifles. 'You accept these situations far too easily, Peach. I expect you and your team to solve problems of racially motivated crime, not just to accept them.'

'Yes, sir. Would you care to come and do a few interrogations yourself, sir? Show the lads and lasses who have to deal with these thugs exactly what they should be doing? Show the new uniformed girl who has seven stitches over her eye how she should have dealt with the knife that was pulled on her when she lay in the gutter? I'm sure the staff would be most receptive to your guidance.' He kept his eyes upon the wall behind Tucker, aware that he had allowed passion to creep into his last phrases, a thing he normally eschewed with Tommy Bloody Tucker.

Tucker was alarmed as usual by the suggestion that he should dirty his hands with the work of his section. 'I would love to give a lead, as you well know, Peach. But I have to concern myself with the overview of crime in this area, not get involved with the detail, as I've told you often enough. I have to maintain a certain detachment from the everyday business of the station.'

'Yes, sir. And you detach yourself very efficiently. It's often been remarked upon.'

Tucker glared at him but could not catch his eye. It was difficult to express distaste to a man who did not seem to be looking at you. 'Is there anything else of note to report?'

Peach pursed his lips, as if trying to determine what was worthy of this lofty overview. Then he became suddenly voluble. 'Bishop urinating in the fountain on the Boulevard last night, sir. Mooned at the statue of Queen Victoria, then whipped up his robes and had a copious and prolonged pee, apparently. Then made certain advances to a woman dressed as Christine Keeler.'

'Christine Keeler?'

'You remember her, sir? Upper-class tart in the sixties, apparently. Helped to bring down a government. Harold Macmillan's government, I think it was. Wasn't he the bloke who said we'd never had it so good? Do you think he was perhaps thinking of Christine Keeler at the time? Long before my time, sir, but just about the beginning of your era, I should think. I bet as a young PC you wouldn't have minded giving that Miss Keeler a right good—'

'Peach!' Tucker had paled as Peach knew he would at the mention of a bishop. Race and religion were areas of high danger for anyone concerned with police public relations. 'I hope you've handled this matter sensitively, Peach. You know my views on matters connected with—'

'Wasn't there myself at the time, sir, more's the pity. I'm noted for my sensitivity, as you know. But the lads seemed to have dealt with the bishop quite diplomatically. He was banged up in the cells for the night. He's been charged with being drunk and disorderly and indecent exposure, sir.'

'But – but . . .' Tucker was so aghast that he was lost for words.

21

Percy thought that a most welcome development. 'Church of England bishop, sir. Just as well, that. With all this happy-clappy stuff going on, they're allowed a lot more licence than the papists, I should think, but then in these ecumenical and liberated times—'

'You say the man's been charged. That it's too late to prevent—'

'In court this morning, sir.' Percy looked at his watch and brightened visibly. 'Should be getting his comeuppance at this very minute, sir, if my calculations are accurate. You all right, sir?'

Tucker was gripping the edge of his big desk and looking very pale. 'Have you any idea what this could do to our relationship with the Church in Brunton? Have you any notion—'

'Oh, he wasn't a real bishop, sir.' Peach allowed himself a small chortle at such a ridiculous idea. His chortle was a rare and unnerving sound.

'Not a real clergyman?' Tucker spoke like one who did not fully comprehend the idea.

'Didn't I mention that, sir? Apparently he's a drag artist from our local gay club. He'd been to a vicars-and-tarts party. Fancied the purple dress and the gaiters, he said. Apparently the woman dressed as Christine Keeler was quite disappointed in him. Said she'd have him under the trades descriptions act for waving a thing like that at her without malicious intent. The man couldn't roger a woman bent over a barrel, according to her.'

'I don't want to know that, Peach!'

Percy thought he had never seen a man's face transformed from parchment-white to puce in so few seconds. It was a most pleasing effect. 'Thought you might like a few of the juicier details, sir. Thought it might help to relieve the monotony of having to maintain a general overview of crime in the area.'

'Is there anything of real moment, Peach?'

Tucker's tone was dangerously controlled. Percy's expertise told him that this was a man near the edge. It was time to move on to the real reason why he had come up to Tucker's penthouse office. He said, 'A corpse was discovered on

22

Saturday afternoon, sir. On the slopes of Pendle Hill. In a derelict farmhouse.' Peach could be as concise as anyone, when he chose to be.

'A woman?'

'Yes, sir.'

Tucker nodded sagely, congratulating himself on this penetrating insight, trying to recover the equilibrium he had lost. 'A youngish woman?'

'It appears so, sir.' Peach was intrigued to see where Tucker's percipience would lead him.

'Be a prostitute, I should think.' Tucker nodded again with increasing confidence. 'You mark my words, Peach, a prostitute. I'm right, aren't I?'

'Couldn't say, sir.'

'Couldn't say, Peach? Surely you've visited the scene of the crime?' Tucker found himself hoping heartily that the man hadn't.

'Yes, sir. Went out and talked to the SOCA team and the Home Office pathologist yesterday. When you couldn't play golf because of the snow, sir.'

'So who was she?'

'Don't know yet, sir. Waiting for more details from the forensic laboratory at Chorley, sir.'

'Surely you could be getting on with something, Peach.' Tucker waved his hands palm-uppermost in the air above his desk. 'Instituting house-to-house enquiries, asking around the pubs and the knocking-shops, looking for—'

'Be easier when we know when and how she died, sir. We've not even established that this wasn't a suicide, yet. We need a detailed PM report to indicate where we should start.'

'She didn't die this weekend?'

By Jove he's got it, thought Percy. 'Several months ago, we think, sir. That's minimum: it could be longer ago than that.'

Tucker breathed deeply, forcing himself to remain calm. 'Then why didn't you tell me this at the outset?'

'Was about to, sir, when you came in with one of your penetrating insights.'

'Insights?' Tucker now had the look of a sorely perplexed goldfish.

'Said she was a prostitute, sir. When you were maintaining that detachment you said was so necessary for a chief superintendent. Told me to mark your words. So I did, sir.'

Tucker stared down at his desk, wishing he hadn't committed himself so early. Then he glared at Peach and asked the question he should have framed at the outset: 'Is that the sum total of your knowledge at this stage?' He was pleased to hear that he had managed to make such ignorance sound like a deficiency in his DCI.

'Yes, sir. Until I get some more gen from Chorley, sir. Probably later this morning, I'm told.'

'Get on with it, then. Make it a priority.'

Suspicious deaths were always a priority. Percy reflected that Tommy Bloody Tucker hadn't lost his talent for the blindin' bleedin' obvious. He said, 'There's nothing you'd care to volunteer at this stage, sir. In confidence, of course.'

The goldfish looked even more lost. 'Volunteer?' Tucker didn't like that word at all.

'We're both men of the world, sir. Both long enough in the tooth to be shocked by nothing.'

'What on earth are you talking about, Peach?'

'Your view that this woman was a prostitute, sir. You seemed very certain about that.'

'It was merely that I considered it a possibility that—'

'Probability, I'd say, sir. You seemed pretty certain of it at the time.' He leaned forwards confidentially, looked full into Tucker's apprehensive face for the first time in minutes. 'If you've been patronizing the ladies of the night, sir, if you have some special knowledge about this case, it would be far better to have it out in the open now. We all have our needs, and if it turns out that you've got yourself involved in a sordid murder case, it would be far better to place the facts in my understanding hands at this stage than to—'

'PEACH! You misunderstand me wilfully! And completely. For your information, I do not patronize and have never patronized the prostitutes of Brunton!'

'Yes, sir. Far better to keep it off your own doorstep, I agree, if you're going to indulge your little male weaknesses and—'

'Nor the prostitutes of anywhere else! Now get out and get on with your work.'

'Yes, sir. If you have any more of your insights, I'm sure you'll—'

'GET OUT!'

'Yes, sir. Right away, sir.'

Percy Peach's contrite expression did not change until he had shut the door behind him. He went back down the stairs feeling much more joyful than when he had climbed them.

Four

Eleanor Boyd was fully occupied with her work for the first hour and a half of Monday morning. The two different classes of lively fourteen-year-olds with which she began her teaching week were yet to be convinced of the central place that history should occupy in their lives and thoughts. Eleanor strove to acquaint them with the facts of life in Tudor England.

It was not until she was stirring her coffee at break that her attention was recalled to the events of the weekend. It was Tracey, the bright, pneumatic, blonde girl, who taught media studies and was no doubt the subject of nightly pubescent fantasies, who said, 'Someone found a body at the weekend. Out Clitheroe way, I think. It was on Radio Lancashire this morning.'

'On Pendle Hill?' The words were out before Ellie could check them.

'Yes, that's right. An unidentified female. In some derelict building, I think they said.'

'That was me.'

'You?' The round blue eyes stared blankly at her.

Ellie smiled. 'Not the corpse. I meant that it was me who found it. Well, Dermot and me.'

'I.'

She looked interrogatively at the lean, balding, older man behind her. Graham Smith looked embarrassed and said, '"It was I," not "It was me." And "Dermot and I." Sorry. It comes automatically to an English teacher. Now that they've decided we're going all out for correct grammar again.' Smith was already wishing that he hadn't spoken to a colleague like that.

'Never mind that!' The blonde girl looked round the

26

crowded staff room. 'Hey, everyone, Ellie Boyd found a stiff at the weekend. And that means a body, not what you smutty PE boys think it is!'

There were a few giggles, but also a stirring of excitement which was much more pronounced. Ellie was suddenly the centre of attention, with requests from several quarters to tell them more about it. She said as calmly as she could, 'There isn't much to tell really. Dermot wanted to climb Pendle Hill in the snow – well, we both did, really. When we were about halfway up, there was a blizzard. Didn't last long, but you couldn't see more than fifty or a hundred yards for a little while. And just in the worst of it, the lace broke on my boot. We went into this broken-down building to try to get a bit of shelter and do emergency repairs.' She realized suddenly that she was rehearsing what she would tell the police. Dermot had made her nervous about it, with his silly caution.

'And you found a body there?' Ellie had paused for a moment to organize her thoughts, but Tracey could not stand the tension of even this momentary break.

'Yes. There's not much more to say, really. It was against the wall of a room, stowed away in a corner.' Ellie felt herself shudder at the recollection. She was trying to be careful with her words, but she realized that even that word 'stowed' implied that someone had put the thing there. It showed how careful you had to be in saying things to the police: perhaps Dermot was right to be cautious, after all.

'Was it young or old?'

'I don't know. It must have been there for months, perhaps even years. It was – well, rather horrible. Not at all exciting. That's really all there is to it.' She was back again with that awful vision of stretched black skin which had disturbed her last two troubled nights.

Most of them saw that she was upset and left it at that. Tracey threw her a couple more questions and then went away. The bell rang and the staff filtered out of the room and away to their classes. Ellie Boyd gulped down her coffee and went with them.

There was one woman who did not go. She had asked not a single question during Ellie's sensational revelation, but she had listened to every syllable of what the history teacher had said. Jo Barrett had a free period now, but she did not turn immediately to marking or preparation. She sat alone in the deserted staff room, her elbows on the table, her dark eyes staring into space.

She was a tall, slim woman of thirty-four, with slender but muscular hands and a long, oval, strikingly pale face, beneath straight hair which was such a stark black that it probably owed something to a bottle. She was always to be seen in dark clothes and black footwear, and in school at least she wore no make-up. She seemed to paint herself deliberately in black and white, so that the smile which frequently lit up her face came somehow as a surprise. She made no secret of the fact that she was gay, though she was at present without a partner.

Jo Barrett was a valued member of the school staff, a conscientious teacher of general science and chemistry, who stood no nonsense but was both respected and liked by her pupils.

She sat unmoving for minutes on end, her mind churning with rapid thoughts, her heart thumping with a sick excitement. She told herself that nothing was certain as yet, that there was nothing to be gained by jumping to conclusions. After a quarter of an hour, she made a series of swift, sudden moves, shut her case with a snap, dragged a pile of exercise books resolutely towards her and began determinedly to mark the work.

She marked only two of the books before she threw down her red ballpoint pen and abandoned the task. She looked swiftly round the empty room, then took a mobile phone from the black handbag beside her. 'Kath? . . . I'm fine, thank you. Look, a body's been found, out on Pendle Hill . . . No, I hadn't heard, either, not until break time. Look, it's one of our staff who found it . . . No, a woman called Ellie Boyd . . . that's right, Dermot's wife . . . I know we shouldn't. I think all that's been released officially is that it's the body of an unidentified female . . . Of course that's true, yes . . . But from what Ellie Boyd says, I'm sure this is going to be the body of Annie Clark.'

* * *

28

Peach drove the few miles out to the Home Office forensic laboratory at Chorley to see the pathologist who had done the post-mortem examination on the remains found in the high stone ruin on Pendle Hill.

The pathologist was a man more at home with corpses than living humanity, a man of few words in most social contexts. But he knew Peach from previous investigations, and on his own ground and his own subject he was much more forthcoming. 'Could be a tough one for you, this,' he said as he waved an invitation to a chair.

'They nearly always are when they're not found immediately.'

'You've got yourself a bonny lass for your sergeant. She never looked like fainting during my dismemberment of that corpse this morning.' That was obviously a major plus mark, from Colin Steel. The pathologist was from the north-east, though he had needed to confess to being a Sunderland supporter before Peach had pinned down his accent to Wearside.

'DS Blake said it was a young woman. She's checking our missing-person computer files at this moment, but I didn't ask her anything else, as I'd already arranged to see you.'

'A young woman who was probably in excellent health at the time of her death.'

'Which was when?'

'Several months ago. The maggots have long since been and gone. Very informative chaps, maggots. You can often date a death pretty exactly from their state of development, when they're still making hay with a corpse.'

'How many months?' Peach sensed that the man wanted to enlarge upon the chemistry of human decay: probably he didn't get many opportunities to display his expertise.

Steel steepled his fingers and pursed his lips. Though he was scarcely conscious of the fact, he was quite enjoying this. He regarded Peach as that most welcome of audiences, a professional man from a different field, who needed to be enlightened. 'Very difficult to say just how many months. Certainly more than two. Certainly less than seven.'

Peach gave him his encouraging smile. 'Colin, you're not in court now. I won't cross-examine you; I won't even come screaming to you if you happen to be wrong. Let's have an opinion.'

Steel gave him an answering grin, and for an instant looked disconcertingly like a mischievous schoolboy. 'All right. I'd say she died some time at the end of the summer. It's very difficult to assess the rate of degeneration of human flesh when it's happened at an altitude like that and in a place like that; I think it must have been below freezing on about forty of the last sixty nights up there. I wouldn't say this in court, so that you'll find my official report will state "between two and seven months", but I'd say this girl died around four months ago. That's an informed guess, mind, no more.'

It was now the twenty-fourth of January. So this unknown girl had died in September or October, according to expert opinion. He'd ring Lucy Blake as soon as he got outside and help her to pinpoint the search. 'A young woman, you said.' His mind went back to that thing in the corner of the derelict building on the hillside which could have been male or female, a teenager or a pensioner. Death robbed you so quickly of everything which had distinguished you as a vibrant, individual, living thing. 'How young, do you think?'

'I can be a little more definite for you there. I'd say early twenties. Perhaps twenty-three or twenty-four. Her teeth were healthy, and there'd been minimal dental work: just two fillings, I think. We can get a chart to you by tomorrow, if you should need it.'

'How did she die?'

A pause from this man who liked to deal in certainties, who had found pathology more attractive than the diagnosis of living bodies, because you could cut up the dead and be certain. 'Almost certainly manual strangulation. What flesh is left around the throat is too far gone for us to be absolutely certain that some form of rope or scarf wasn't used, so I'd have to say ninety per cent sure in court. There's no possibility whatever that she hanged herself. Privately, I'd be confident from other corpses I've seen that this woman was strangled by hand.'

'So probably a man.'

Steel smiled thinly, aware that he was being led. 'Afraid not. The throat is too far gone to say that she wasn't taken

30

from behind. If she was surprised, no great strength would have been needed. Sorry about that.'

Peach answered the man's smile with a rueful one of his own. They knew now how this girl had died and when. Both of the answers were less vague than he had feared when he'd seen the state of the corpse in its icy resting place, but less precise than he would have hoped for if luck had been on their side. Time to establish the third of the big details of a suspicious death. 'Can you give us any idea of where this young woman died?'

'Afraid not. She could well have been killed at the spot where you found her, but there's no certainty of that.' There was silence for a few seconds, as both of these men, who were hardened to the facts of death, pictured this girl being lured to her doom in that lonely place by person or persons unknown.

Then the pathologist went on: 'But she could easily have been killed elsewhere and taken up there in a vehicle. I imagine that would be easy enough if you chose the right time of day. Normally there'd be hypostasis, with the blood settling to show us if she'd been left lying in a different position for any length of time, but there isn't enough of her left for that. She's partly mummified. I've taken DNA samples, of course. I think you might find that the most reliable as well as the kindest method of identification for the relatives will be by DNA.'

'The SOCA team went through her pockets, as well as they could, and found nothing. There was no handbag. Have you come up with any rings or personal possession that might help to place her?'

'Her clothes have been bagged for your forensic crime experts. I doubt whether they'll find much. And I haven't found any birthmarks on what little skin is intact. I think that someone removed a ring from the third finger of her left hand. She could have taken it off herself, but it seems much more likely that it was the person who killed her. But that's your field, not mine.'

'Yes. It looks to me as though someone has been over the body after she was killed and removed anything he or she thought might be useful to us. And she could have been killed almost anywhere in the north of England and dumped in that place on Pendle.' Percy Peach stared thoughtfully, almost resentfully, at the lined face of Colin Steel.

'Except that whoever chose to put her in that building didn't do so at random. I should think they selected it as a place where she wasn't likely to be discovered for some time. That implies a degree of local knowledge, surely?'

'You're right. You should have been a detective!' said Peach dryly. 'Is there any other information you can offer which might be of interest to us?'

Steel smiled. He had planned to throw his one dramatic finding in casually at the end of his verbal report, where it might make the greatest impact. 'There is one thing which will certainly be of interest. This girl was pregnant. About three months gone, I'd say.'

Five

Thousands of people go missing every year in Great Britain. Their absence is noted and their details are filed, but unless they are children, or criminals fleeing from justice, or divorced men disappearing to avoid paying maintenance, or there is some reason to suspect foul play, not much effort is made to locate them. The law does not favour it, and police resources are spread too thinly across the burgeoning industry which is British crime for missing adults to receive much attention.

But a murder victim is an immediate priority. An urgent follow-up of all women between twenty and twenty-five who had been reported missing in September and October of the previous year was instituted in Brunton, Burnley and all the Ribble Valley towns and villages which adjoined the Pendle area. Other towns in Lancashire were also asked to co-operate, wherever the computer threw up the names of women in the right age-bracket who had disappeared in their areas.

The first thirty-six hours produced nothing, and Percy Peach offered the gloomy opinion to his team and to Tommy Bloody Tucker that their victim might be a Mancunian or a Liverpudlian, bringing into the equation the vast numbers of women disappearing in the conurbations of south and west Lancashire. He was fond of the statistic that more people lived within thirty miles of central Manchester than central London, feeling vaguely that that was one up to the north-west of England in the north–south divide.

DCI Peach's hunch was wrong, as hunches tend to be, despite the respect accorded to them by the writers of crime fiction.

It was on the outskirts of Preston that the painstaking routine of checking produced results. An alert, fresh-faced, uniformed constable came up with something that seemed promising.

'You've won the lottery, if you're right,' his grizzled station sergeant told him. 'It won't do your career any harm to be noticed by the bleeding aristocrats of CID at this stage. If you're right, they'll take over. Only appear when things get interesting, those buggers.' The sergeant's cynicism didn't make him forget to claim the credit for this. He reported to the super that he'd spotted 23 Church Terrace as a promising possibility and had sent his best young constable round to check.

Ten miles away in Brunton, Percy Peach nodded his head over the e-mail and decided this was promising enough for him to send Lucy Blake and DC Brendan Murphy round to investigate.

Twenty-three Church Terrace was what the agents called a 'superior town house'. It was in fact an unremarkable place, high and narrow within its terrace of eighteen houses, faced with the smooth red Accrington brick which seventy years earlier had been used to announce that the frontages of these residences at least had a touch of quality about them.

The woman who opened the door to their ring was around fifty, with a worn face and tired, defeated-looking grey eyes. She wore an apron on which she wiped her hands as they introduced themselves and showed their warrant cards. Perhaps she had expected to be invited to shake hands with them. Instead, Lucy Blake smiled at her and said, 'I think it would be best if we came inside, Mrs Clark. You don't want the neighbours to see you with police officers on your step!'

There was no answering smile from Mary Clark. 'I can't see why you've come, you know. I said everything I had to say to that young man in uniform this morning.'

Brendan Murphy said, 'It's the way the system works, Mrs Clark. It takes time, but it gets results, and it doesn't usually miss things. In circumstances like this, we try to follow up all the possibilities with a blanket coverage. The constable who came to see you was part of that coverage. When something seems more likely, we follow it up in detail.'

That meant that a mother should have read something sinister, some possibility at least of bad news, into this second

34

visit. But Mary Clark showed no sign of distress. 'You should be Irish, with a name like that.' She took in his fresh face, his dark curly hair, his large brown eyes. He looked younger than his twenty-five years, and unversed in the seamier ways of life. But Percy Peach had spotted when he recruited him that an appearance of innocence, even naïvety, could be a valuable asset in a CID man.

'Indeed I should be Irish, Mrs Clark. My mother's as Irish as they come, so I suppose you could say it's in the blood. But I have to tell you that I've spent all my life in Lancashire.'

Mrs Clark looked a little disappointed at that. She said, 'You'll be of the Faith, though, I expect,' as if that were a second prize, and looked at him with her head a little on one side. She had the trace of a brogue herself, though it was overlaid with a generous helping of Scouse.

'Indeed I am!' said Brendan Murphy. He wouldn't tell her that he was entertaining serious doubts about his Roman Catholicism, that he was now an irregular attender at Sunday mass. This woman might need every small comfort she could get, if she proved to be the mother of what had been found on Pendle.

DS Blake was patient with their small talk, because she understood what was going on. She said, 'Has Annie got a father around, Mrs Clark?'

A wry smile. 'No. He left here fifteen years ago. I've no idea where he is.'

Lucy Blake nodded. 'When exactly did Annie go missing?' She knew from the file when she had been officially recorded as missing, but that was not always the same thing.

Mary Clark looked appreciatively at this pretty, polite girl with dark-red hair and such an air of competence. She was a little older than Annie, but this is how she had hoped her daughter would turn out, if . . . For the first time, she met head-on the thought which she had thrust to the back of her mind until now, and the tears started to her eyes.

But they did not fall. Not yet. She steadied herself, though her voice broke a little as she spoke. 'She left home in April last year.' She held up her hand as Lucy threatened another question, recovered herself as she said, 'Annie wasn't reported as missing then, because she wasn't. She kept in touch for a while, even came to see me, once. And she phoned. Once a week at first, then less often.' On that last phrase, the tears burst out at last, and she cried silently into the big man's handkerchief she snatched from her sleeve.

Lucy Blake waited until she had controlled her tears, then put a hand on top of the older hands that had dropped back into Mary Clark's lap. She wanted to say that all might yet be well, that this corpse might not be Annie's at all, that the daughter might be back in this room next week, laughing and apologetic, clasping her mother and mouthing the platitudes of reconciliation. But false reassurance was worse than false hope. She said nothing for several seconds, then said quietly into the stricken woman's ear, 'Before we go, we'll need to know any phone numbers that you know Annie was ringing, Mrs Clark.'

Mary Clark nodded, went on snuffling for a few seconds, blew her nose resolutely and said abruptly, 'What's in there?'

She was pointing at the plastic bag that Brendan Murphy had carried into the room and set down awkwardly beside his feet. He glanced at DS Blake, then opened the bag. 'There's nothing conclusive about this, Mrs Clark, and we don't want you jumping to hasty conclusions. But we wondered whether you might recognize this shoe?'

He took a small white trainer with green trimming from the bag and held it a yard in front of Mary Clark's anguished face. If they expected something dramatic, some heart-rending cry of grief, they were wrong. She took the trainer into her hands, turned it over, looked with wide eyes at its sole. Then she said dully, 'This is nearly new.'

Lucy Blake said hastily, 'Yes. If it belonged to Annie, she probably bought it after she'd left home. We just thought it was worth showing it to you.'

'I don't recognize it. She didn't have these shoes when she was here.' She turned it over again. 'Was this – was this shoe worn by the girl that you . . .'

'By the girl whose death we're investigating? Yes, it was. But the shoes were quite new. We didn't really expect you to recognize them.'

'They're – they're quite nice, I suppose. They're the kind of things Annie would have bought. She wore trainers quite a lot, you know. And they're size five. That's her size; she always had quite dainty feet.'

'Yes.' Lucy thought of that thing she had seen in that bleak, derelict building, when these shoes had been the only item that looked as if they had a connection with a living girl. She thought of the careful, scientific dismemberment of that thing, half-skeleton, half-mummy, which she had witnessed at the PM examination. She could almost smell again the appalling assortment of odours that she had tried so vigorously to rinse from her nostrils in the hours which followed.

She said, 'I must emphasize that we're still not sure that this girl is your daughter, Mrs Clark.' Yet she was conscious that all three of them in that warm and dingy room felt that she was mouthing a formal phrase rather than a real consolation.

Mary Clark looked at her steadily, her tired grey eyes clear now after the tears. 'Don't you have to identify her? Doesn't someone in the family need to . . .?'

'Yes. Usually that's a formality, though a distressing one for the people involved. When a corpse is only discovered after it's been dead for several months, it's rather more difficult.'

The grey eyes widened with horror over the damp cheeks. 'You mean that she wouldn't be recognizable, don't you? You mean that—'

'Mrs Clark, it would be useful if you could provide us with a DNA sample. Do you know what that is?'

'Yes.'

'It doesn't have to be now. We could—'

'I'd rather it was now. I'd rather have it done with. I'd rather know if this is Annie.'

'If you could come to the station with us, it could be done right away. Someone will run you back here afterwards.'

They helped her into her best blue coat and went out to the car with her, watching her closely for any sign of distress. But she walked erect, looking neither right nor left, moving with a stiff, steady dignity towards the horror which would come with certainty.

They told her again in the car that other people were being checked out, that there was no real certainty yet that this woman was her daughter. Yet in the subsequent silence, each person in that slowly moving vehicle was sure that the police had now established a victim in this case.

A twenty-three-year-old girl who had once been Annie Clark.

Six

'I need to speak to you. Just routine. At least I trust it will be.'

Dermot Boyd didn't like that last bit. And the man on the phone had seemed to enjoy saying it. But perhaps he was becoming paranoid about this, as Ellie had seemed to think he was. You surely couldn't be threatened by any detective called Peach.

Dermot was wrong about that, as he was to be wrong about many things in the days that followed.

DCI Peach bounced into his office like a rubber ball, exuding energy. He was followed in by a man who was as tall and lean and still as Peach was short and stocky and mobile. He was six feet three tall and very black indeed, his darkness emphasized by the white squares on the chequered policeman's hat he carried and the trimmings on his constable's uniform. He might, indeed, have been designed as a contrast to the chief inspector. His very smart navy uniform set off the neat grey suit of Percy Peach; his plentiful crop of short-cut black hair accentuated the shining white baldness of Peach above his black fringe and moustache. Only his eyes, a dark brown against the glittering black of Peach's watchful orbs, were lighter than those of the older man.

'This is Police Constable Northcott,' said Peach with an affable smile.

He didn't tell Boyd that this was a man he had recruited to the police after coming across him as a suspect in a murder case a year or two earlier. Clyde Northcott had been keeping bad company then, dabbling with drugs and dicing with danger, but Percy had recognized potential in him. 'You can't go wrong as a black man in the modern police service,' Peach had told him, when Northcott had expressed his doubts about joining the force. 'If you could just change sex and become a lesbian, you'd probably become a chief constable, but you'd need to be a real career fiend to do that.'

Peach had a good eye for potential, and Northcott was doing well. Percy had his eye on him as a recruit for his CID team in due course – hence his presence here beside his mentor – but it was early days yet. Percy nodded towards his protégé. 'Constable Northcott's here to learn. Not that there's much for him to pick up here. This should be quite straightforward.'

Dermot Boyd thought the man gave a slight emphasis to that 'should', which he didn't care for, but he wasn't sure. He said, 'I made a statement and signed it as I was asked to. I can't think I've anything else to offer you.'

'You never know. We might be able to prise out the odd interesting fact that you didn't even realize you possessed. These things happen, sometimes. Of course, the person who finds the body is often a suspect, but when it's after all this time, that's hardly likely, is it?'

He chuckled on the thought, and Dermot said, 'I should certainly hope not, Chief Inspector!' He tried a little answering chuckle of his own, which did not quite come off.

Clyde Northcott did not join in this strange hilarity, which would have sat uneasily on his smooth ebony features. Instead, he flicked open his notebook, looked hard at Dermot Boyd and said, 'So you don't expect to be a suspect, sir. You didn't know the deceased, then?'

'Of course I didn't!' Dermot's answer came almost before the question was completed.

'Strange that you should be so certain,' mused Peach quietly. 'I went up there on the day after you'd found the remains, and I'd have said the corpse's own mother would have been pushed to recognize what was left.'

'Of course she would. That's what I meant, really. As a matter of fact, I scarcely glanced at what was in the corner of that room. I was more interested in protecting my wife from the sight, in getting her out of there as quickly as I could.' Dermot was glad he'd thought of that aspect of the incident; he thought he'd managed to deliver his concern for Ellie with a fair measure of sincerity.

'Who was it that saw the body first, sir?' This was Clyde Northcott again, with Peach silently applauding his sense of timing.

'I don't know. Ellie, I think. Yes, I'm sure it was my wife who saw the thing first. She gave a little scream, if I remember right.'

Peach allowed himself the dazzling smile that anyone in Brunton CID would have told Dermot Boyd was highly dangerous. 'Oh, I hope you do, sir – remember things right, I mean. It's so important that we get these things correct from the start, you see. In the interests of which, it seems that you can't be certain that you didn't know the victim, first because the remains you found in that isolated place were unrecognizable, and second because on your own admission you "scarcely glanced at what was in the corner of that room".'

'Well, yes, that's—'

'So we've gained something already by coming to see you in person, haven't we? It's possible that you might have known the victim, even though you stated categorically to our uniformed officers making the original enquiry that this was not so. And PC Northcott has been able to make a note to that effect.'

Clyde Northcott came in right on cue with a broad smile of confirmation, displaying his large, regular and very white teeth to Dermot Boyd for the first time.

Promising boy, this, thought Percy Peach approvingly: I knew he would be. And he carries an air of menace with him that will be useful when we're dealing with harder men than this marshmallow.

Boyd tried to muster his diminishing resources. 'I really don't see that it makes much difference, Chief Inspector. What we're all agreed on is that the girl was unrecognizable. That—'

'Girl, sir? I don't remember saying anything about the sex of this body, let alone its age.' The black eyebrows lurched disconcertingly, impossibly high beneath the shining bald pate.

'Didn't you? I'm sure I . . .' Dermot floundered for a moment, then felt relief rushing into his voice. 'Yes, I heard it on the radio. They said on Radio Lancashire that a girl had been found on Pendle—'

'Female, they said, Mr Boyd. The remains of a human female. We're always careful about these initial releases. There was no indication given about the age of this lady at the time of her death.'

'Well, I suppose I just assumed it was a young woman. Most females who are murdered are young, aren't they? It seems that way to me, anyway.' As he heard how unconvincing he was, Dermot faltered to a halt. Then he thought of something. 'She was wearing trainers, wasn't she? It's usually young girls who wear trainers, isn't it? That must have been what gave me the idea that she was young.'

'Indeed she was, sir. You seem to have taken careful note of that footwear, even though your only concern was to shield your wife from the sight and get her out of the place.'

'Yes. The trainers must have registered with me without my recognizing it.'

'I suppose they must, sir. Well, you're right, of course: this was a young woman. We are now pretty sure of her identity, as a matter of fact. So you can tell us if you did know her, can't you?'

'Yes. I want to give you all the help I can. But it's surely most unlikely that—'

'Anne Marie Clark. Probably known as Annie. Lived locally, sir. In Brunton, during the months before she died. Name mean anything to you, sir?'

This time Dermot made himself pause and weigh matters before he spoke. But he still made a mistake. He said slowly, 'No, I can't say that it does, Chief Inspector Peach. As I've thought all along, I didn't know your victim.'

The young man tried hard to wait patiently. He hunched himself within the short leather jacket and thrust his hands more deeply into its pockets. But he couldn't keep still. He'd been in police stations before, and they made him nervous.

The station sergeant had mastered the art of keeping a careful eye on people without appearing to be watching them at all. He assessed this one as jumpy. Like as not, he'd lose his nerve and bolt for the door if he was kept waiting too long – shoot off like a nervous trout and be lost for good. The sergeant made a note of the address and telephone number of the lost dog that had just been reported, showed the drunk who had been kept in the cells overnight where to sign the form to acknowledge that the contents of his pockets had been returned to him. Then, with the reception area quiet, he judged that this youth had been left alone for long enough. He nodded over his counter at the figure with carefully tousled hair and the healing scar on his young, unlined forehead.

The young man came forward, understanding the ways of authority without the need for any command.

The sergeant said, 'If you can give me a better idea of what it is you want, I might be able to put you in touch with someone who could help you.'

'It's – it's about this body that's been found. The one on Pendle Hill.' He took a big, painful breath. He'd come out with it; there was no turning back now. 'I think I might know who it is.'

'Should have said that to start with, you know. Murder's a priority. Murder opens doors that might otherwise remain shut to lads like you.' The sergeant was taking care to cover himself against the charge of delaying things. The wrath of Percy Peach had the status of legend in Brunton nick.

'Murder?' The young, revealing face stared owlishly across the counter.

The station sergeant shuddered at the thought of what Percy Peach might do to such a weak reed. 'You want the man in charge of the case. Always go to the top, when it's murder.' Strictly speaking, that would be Tommy Bloody Tucker, but no one thought of him as taking charge of any actual case. The sergeant dialled a number on the internal phone, announced that he had a Matthew Hogan at the front desk, who might have information to reveal, then looked a little disappointed. 'You're in luck, lad. DCI Peach is out. Means you might get the delicious Detective Sergeant Blake. It really is your day!'

The young man understood none of this. It was the kind of thing which happened to you when you ventured into a place where everyone knew the workings of the system except you. People talked over your head, made you feel stupid. But a little of it became clear two minutes later when he was ushered into an interview room. Detective Sergeant Blake really was delicious, as that balding veteran on the front desk had told him.

She said who she was and told him that the lanky, pale-faced young man who sat beside and slightly behind her was Detective Constable Pickering. The man was quite tall, but Matt Hogan had hardly noticed him in the shadow of this spectacular beauty with the splendid figure and the striking chestnut hair.

Lucy Blake was not unconscious of the effect she had on impressionable young men. She gave this one a quick smile and said, 'I believe you think you might have known the dead woman whose body was discovered at the weekend. What makes you think that?'

Matt Hogan's mind was racing. He shut his eyes for an instant, then blurted out, 'Was her name Annie Clark?'

Lucy Blake knew better than to show her excitement. 'We think it may have been, yes. You knew her, obviously.'

'She was my girlfriend.' It was the first time in months that he had said it, and he realized that he was proud of it. 'We were going out together. Then she disappeared, without telling me she was going.'

'I see. How long had you been in this relationship?'

He was cast down by the question, and he looked suddenly much younger – sixteen or seventeen rather than his actual twenty-three years. 'Not very long, actually.'

DC Pickering said, 'How long? We need to know: you must see that.'

He hadn't. He should have done, he supposed. He said stupidly, 'You say Annie was murdered?'

'We haven't any doubt of that, now. You didn't kill her, did you, Matthew? Be far better to tell us now and get it over with, if that's why you've come in here.' Gordon Pickering said it as quietly and casually as if he had been talking about a parking fine, and gave his contemporary an encouraging smile across the small, square table.

'No! I wouldn't be here talking about it, if I had, would I?'

44

Lucy Blake swept her most dazzling smile over the appalled, vulnerable face. 'You might, if you had any sense. Coming forward with the truth and asking for mercy is often the best tactic, if killers only understood it. We usually get them in the end, you see.'

'I didn't kill Annie.'

'I see. Well, we'd better have some details from you. How long had she been your girlfriend when she disappeared?'

Matt reddened. He should have anticipated they'd ask him this. That didn't make the answer any less embarrassing. 'About a week.'

Lucy tried hard not to smile. 'That's not very long, is it? Are you sure you're entitled to say she was your girlfriend?'

'Yes. I'd known her longer than that, used to see her with other people, but it was only—'

'And how long would this period be? – the time when you saw her as part of a group, but she wasn't your girlfriend.' This was Gordon Pickering, pen poised over his notepad.

'Three months.' Very prompt, very precise.

'And in the last week, your relationship changed. In your view, at any rate.'

'In both our views. Annie agreed to go out with me. Agreed to become my girlfriend. I'd asked her before but it was only in the last week that we became an item.'

Lucy smiled at his earnest use of that word. It was the one she used to her mother to explain her relationship with Percy Peach. Committed, not engaged, she insisted firmly, to a woman who longed for wedding bells and grandchildren. 'And did Annie Clark feel the same way that you did about this relationship?'

'Yes. I told you: we were an item.'

'Had you slept together?'

For a few seconds, he stared hard at the table without answering. Lucy said, 'It's not idle curiosity, Matthew. We need to know these things, when we're pursuing a murder enquiry.'

'It's Matt. Everyone calls me Matt.'

'All right, Matt. So you and Annie were an item. Were you sleeping together?'

45

'Yes.'

'How long?'

'Not until we were going out together. Not until she became my girlfriend. Only in that last week.'

So he wasn't the father of the foetus that had died with the girl. If he was telling the truth, that is.

'Where was Annie Clark living at this time?'

He gave them an address in the town, not more than a mile from where they sat. He gave them his own address, four streets away from where he said the girl had lived. He gave them his age and hers: both twenty-three. He watched Gordon Pickering note all of these things down. Then the DC looked up at him, studying him hard as he said quietly, 'How did she die, Matt?'

'I don't know. You can tell me that.'

'Not for release at the moment. You're still maintaining that you didn't kill her, Mr Hogan?'

'Yes! I've told you I didn't.' Matt felt his old fear of the police rising at the back of his throat with the use of his surname. They'd frame him for this, if they could. They needed to arrest someone, anyone, for the sake of their clear-up figures. This tall bloke he'd thought might be sympathetic was doing the hard-cop routine on him now. He said desperately, 'I wouldn't have come in here to tell you about her, would I, if I'd killed her?'

They let his question hang in the air of that quiet room for a moment before they responded: you couldn't work alongside Percy Peach without becoming schooled in the techniques of pressure. Then Pickering said, 'In your favour, that is, I grant you. But it could be a bluff, of course. And certain other questions occur to suspicious people like police officers. Such as why it took you so long to come forward. If she was your girlfriend, why didn't you report her as a missing person when she disappeared?'

'I kept thinking she'd turn up.'

But he wasn't looking at them: he was holding something back here. Matthew Hogan's lips set in the line of a sullen child, who is going to say nothing more because he knows that words will only make matters worse. They couldn't force him to speak: he was here of his own free will, helping

46

police with their enquiries, as people were encouraged to do. He wasn't under arrest or caution, wasn't even being taped.

Pickering went for the sudden switch of subject, which was another of Peach's techniques for unnerving suspects. 'Nasty cut you've got on your forehead, Mr Hogan. How did you come by that?'

Matt's hand flew up automatically to the wound he had fingered so often over the last few days. 'Cupboard door. I walked into it.'

Pickering shook his head slowly, offered a grin that was almost conspiratorial. 'Not a cupboard door, whatever it was, Matt. We see quite a lot of facial injuries. My guess would be that you got that in a fight.'

'All right, I did. But it was something and nothing. Just some bloke in a pub – argument that got a bit heated. Ended in a punch-up.'

Pickering shook his head sadly. 'It wasn't a punch that did that, Matt. Quite deep. Bled a lot, I should think: wounds do that, when there isn't a lot of flesh around them. How many stitches?'

'Five.' The word was out before Matt Hogan could stop it, almost as if he was proud of the fact.

'Knife wound, I should think. I'm right, aren't I?'

This time Matt stayed silent. His tongue seemed to be leading him into trouble.

'You need to watch the company you keep, Matt. You got away with it this time. It could have been much worse. You could have lost an eye, or even your life. Best avoided, knives, believe me. We see too much of what they can do.'

It was so nearly what the doctor had said to him as he stitched him up in Accident and Emergency that Matt found it very disconcerting. He said stubbornly, 'This had nothing to do with Annie.'

'No, I shouldn't think it did, Matt. Going to tell us why you didn't report her missing, are you?'

'I told you: I thought she'd just gone away for a few days. At first I did, anyway. And then I was a bit – well, a bit scared.'

Lucy Blake, who had been studying him in silence for five minutes, said, 'Scared, Mr Hogan? Now when a strong

47

young man like you has been scared, that's got to be of interest to us – especially when a missing girl turns up as a corpse. So who was it that scared you?'

'They didn't threaten me. Not me personally. But I didn't like what they were doing to Annie. I didn't like her being involved with them at all. I was trying to persuade her to give it all up. And then she disappeared.'

Trying to persuade her to give up what, Matt?'

He stared at them with widening eyes, defying them to mock him. 'Witchcraft. Annie was into witchcraft.'

Seven

'I need to be able to report progress, Peach.' Chief Superintendent Thomas Bulstrode Tucker drummed his fingers upon the surface of his large, empty desk and presented himself at his most masterful.

'Yes, sir.'

'I'm seeing the Chief Constable later today and I wish to give him the most positive possible report on our CID section. And the thing he will be aware of is this body that was found at the weekend on Pendle Hill.'

'Yes, sir. And you've released the information to radio and television first of all that this was a youngish woman and secondly that this was a murder. So now *everyone* is very aware of it.' Percy let out a little of his resentment. 'And chief constables are only human, after all. Or so people tell me.'

'There is no need to be flippant, Peach. I want to know whether you are anywhere near to an arrest.'

'No, sir.' Even with his years of experience of the man, Percy was still sometimes taken aback by his effrontery.

'That's honest, at least. But it's not good enough, you know.'

'Perhaps you'd like to come downstairs and take personal charge of the case yourself, sir. Go for a more "hands-on" approach, as they say. I believe that's the correct expression, sir.'

Tucker was so appalled at this suggestion that for a moment he let it show. Then he resorted to bluster. 'You know that that is not my approach, Peach. And you should be aware that I have far more important things to concern me.'

'More important than murder, sir?' Peach's mobile eyebrows reared towards his shining bald pate.

'No, of course not more important than murder. Must you pick me up on everything I say?'

'Sorry, sir. I was just trying to respond to your queries. Fill you in, as you might say. I'm afraid I don't have the overview of things which is so necessary in your job, sir. I tend to get bogged down with crime. Especially when the crime is murder.'

Tommy Bloody Tucker looked at him sourly. He suspected irony, but that wasn't a thing he was very knowledgeable about. You didn't meet a lot of irony in the police service. 'I merely meant that I have a mass of paperwork to comprehend and organize. I have to balance our budget, find all the money that you fritter away so prodigally on overtime, present our work in the most favourable possible light to the public . . .'

Tucker stopped. He was wallowing willy-nilly in the welter of his own waffle, thought Percy Peach. He'd better remember that phrase, for Lucy Blake: he liked it when she giggled in bed. 'All these things are part of maintaining that masterly panoramic view which is your greatest contribution to our CID section, I'm sure, sir. Your splendid detachment. A rare quality, sir, if I may say so. And one even our respected Chief Constable appears to lack.'

'Appears to lack, Peach?' Tucker, always sensitive to any criticism of a superior, took on that baffled look of a low-IQ fish on a marble slab which always lit up his Chief Inspector's day. 'I have to warn you that any insult you offer to the CC will be taken as—'

'Sorry, sir. I was just referring to your opening remarks – when you indicated that the CC would be very concerned to have the latest details on our progress in a murder investigation. Not much of a panoramic view about that, sir. Not much of the detachment which enables you to—'

'Yes, the murder. Please desist from your scurrilous criticisms of our leader and give me an account of your investigation.'

'Well, first of all, sir, it definitely is murder. We had to establish that. Method, sir: strangulation. Almost certainly manual strangulation, the pathologist says. By man, woman or child, sir, he says.'

'Man, woman or child?' Tucker was back on the fish slab.

'Sorry about that, but he says at this distance of time it's impossible to be certain. She could have been surprised from behind, you see, or—'

'All right, Peach, you needn't spell out everything! I'm not a simpleton, you know.'

Oh, if only I did know that, thought Percy. 'She had been dead for approximately four months, sir, though the pathologist says he'd have to give a much wider approximation than that in court.'

'And where did she die? Do I have to prise everything out of you with a jemmy?'

'Oh, very droll, sir. The idea of a law-abiding man like you with a jemmy, I mean. Quite amusing!'

'PEACH!'

'Sorry, sir. It's just that you said you didn't need the obvious things spelling out for you. Makes it confusing for me, that. Well, sir, the pathologist couldn't give us an informed opinion on where she was killed. Or rather he could, but his informed opinion wasn't much help. He said she could have been dispatched at the place where she was found or killed somewhere else and taken there by car.'

'Sometimes I wonder what we pay these people for.' Tucker's frown was fearful to behold, a rare attempt to include Peach with him in a condemnation of a malignant outside world.

'Yes, sir. He said the corpse had degenerated too far for him to learn anything from hypostasis. The body had been lying up there for four months or thereabouts, sir.'

'They give you any specious excuse, these people. You're too easily taken in sometimes, Peach.'

'Yes, sir. I don't have your panoramic view, sir.'

Tucker glared at him suspiciously but as usual failed to catch his eye. 'This corpse was discovered on Saturday afternoon last and it's now Thursday morning. And you haven't even established the identity of the victim yet. It's not good enough, Peach. I give you free rein and you—'

'Victim's name is Anne Marie Clark, sir.'

'Eh?'

'Probably known as Annie, sir. Resident on Raikes Road, Brunton, at the time of her death.'

'Peach, why wasn't I informed of this? I stand back and give you your head, on condition that you keep me fully informed and—'

'Identification confirmed only ten minutes ago, sir. Phone call gave me the results of the mother's DNA test, which was the only reliable means of identification. Came straight up here to keep you fully informed, sir.' Peach bit the inside of his lip firmly to prevent the smile that threatened to disrupt his impeccably noncommittal face.

'A young woman?'

'Yes, sir. Twenty-three years old at the time of her death, according to information given to DS Blake by her mother.'

Tucker brightened a little, seeing a possibility of re-establishing himself. 'I expect she was a local prostitute. I suggested that to you on Monday, I believe.'

'I believe you did, sir, yes. There is no evidence as yet that she was selling her favours around this or any other town. She has certainly no convictions for soliciting, sir.'

'No criminal record of any kind?' Tucker did not attempt to conceal his disappointment.

'No, sir. We know very little about Annie Clark, as yet. As I said, her identity has only just been confirmed. No doubt the Chief Constable will be pleased to hear that we know who the victim is now.'

'Yes.' For a moment, Tucker's visage brightened as he thought of how he would reveal the efficiency of his section to the CC with a becoming modesty. Then he resumed his frown and his drive. 'Well, you'd better be about your business then. Don't be sanguine, just because you have an identification.'

Peach's thoughts were sanguinary rather than sanguine. That was Tommy Bloody Tucker all over. Never a word of praise, always trying to crack his highly ineffective whip. Peach half-turned to go, then stopped. 'There's one more fact you should know, sir – to complete your overview of the situation as it stands at present, that is.'

'Well, what is it?' Tucker snapped out the question as if he had several other murders requiring his immediate attention.

This is Brunton, not Scotland bleeding Yard, you prat, thought Peach. 'The girl was pregnant, sir.'

'Pregnant?' Tucker looked baffled anew by this latest development.

'With child, sir.' Peach was a model of patience. 'About three months gone at the time of her death, the pathologist thought.'

Tucker leaned forward, raising a thick finger into the air. Peach inclined his barrel of a torso towards him eagerly. 'One of your insights, sir?'

'You should get the boyfriend in. Give him a real grilling. I'm not definitely saying you should charge him at this moment, of course, but you mark my—'

'He's been in, sir. Lad called Matthew Hogan. Came into the nick of his own free will, as a matter of fact. Helped us to establish the time of the death and the final address of the dead girl, sir.'

'And what does he say about the . . . the . . .' The finger which had so recently been commanding waved ineffectively in the air.

Peach watched its movements for a moment before he said, 'The foetus, sir? Not his, sir. Only slept with her in the week before she disappeared, he says.'

'And you believe him?'

'No reason not to, at the moment. We shall check it out in due course, sir. Along with a lot of other things.'

'Anything else?'

Peach pursed his lips. 'Not sure this is anything to do with her death, sir. Might be a complete red herring, you know.'

'I'll be the judge of that, Peach. What is it?'

'Well, it seems possible that Annie Clark might have been a witch, sir.'

DCI Peach carried the image of his chief as a saucer-eyed cod happily back down the stairs with him.

'You're nervous about this, aren't you? I'll stay with you, if you like. They can't stop me doing that.'

'No, it's all right. I'm not nervous about it. Not really.' Heather Shields wished that her flatmate would just shut up and go. That was what they'd agreed. So why did she have to start arguing about it, at the last minute, like this?

'I'll only be providing you with moral support. I won't

say anything. They surely can't object to you having a friend with you.'

If only she'd just shut up and go – leave Heather with time to compose herself for this: suddenly she was certain that she needed that time. 'It's all right, Carol – honestly it is. You can't have anything useful to tell them. You didn't even know Annie.'

'Of course I didn't. But if you're all on edge like this, they surely can't object to a friend giving you a little—'

'I'll be all right!' She realized she had shouted, and tried to moderate her tone. 'It's not that I don't appreciate your help, Carol. But they'll think I'm wet, won't they, if I need a nursemaid with me to talk to them?'

'All right, I was only trying to help. I'll just go, if that's how you feel about it!'

She strode into the bedroom and came out with her coat on a minute later. 'I'll be back in a couple of hours. When the VIP visitors who are causing you so much alarm are long gone!'

Heather didn't trust herself to speak again, merely nodding gratefully as Carol flounced out of the door. She listened to her footsteps on the stairs, to the slam of the outside door as she left the house, and breathed a long sigh of relief. She went into the bedroom and stood in front of the mirror, making adjustments to her hair which it did not need, trying hard to make use of these few minutes that were left to her to collect her thoughts.

It seemed to her only seconds before the bell rang shrilly in the corner of the room. She pressed the button beneath it and a harsh, distorted voice told her that Detective Chief Inspector Peach and Detective Sergeant Blake were here to see Miss Heather Shields, as previously arranged. She put her face to the mouthpiece and said, 'Come up, please. It's the first door on the left on the first floor,' and was pleased to hear how calm her voice sounded.

He was shorter than she had expected, a dapper, bald man in an immaculate grey suit. And it turned out that this Detective Sergeant Blake was a woman. Not much older than she was, Heather thought.

They accepted the seats she had planned for them, on the

other side of the dining table in the big living room, with their backs to the kitchen door she had carefully closed ten minutes ago. 'Nice flats, these,' the squat man said. He was not unfriendly, but he watched her carefully; he had not taken his eyes off her since they had appeared at the door, and Heather was already finding his scrutiny disconcerting.

'It's not usually as tidy as this in here. Good thing you told me you were coming!' Both of them were smiling at her, but her little giggle rang unnaturally loud in the high room.

'Well, this shouldn't take long. But we're hoping you will be able to give us useful information.'

'Oh, I'm afraid I won't be able to tell you very much. I didn't know a lot about Annie, really.'

'You know a great deal more than we do, at this moment, Miss Shields. We have to build up a picture of a dead girl that we didn't know at all, through people like you, who knew her when she was alive.'

'Yes, I suppose so.' Heather revolved the thought in her mind, then found herself saying abruptly, 'Was she murdered?'

'She was, yes. Did you expect that?'

What a strange, disturbing question – one she'd invited, by her own query, but one that she hadn't anticipated, when she had tried to plan her responses for this meeting. 'Yes. Well, I suppose when I heard that she'd been found up there, I sort of feared the worst.'

'Only feared, though. You didn't actually *know* anything that made you think she'd been murdered?'

'No. That's right.'

'By person or persons unknown. With malice afore-thought.' Peach rolled out the sonorous legal phrases appreciatively, as he continued to study her in that distracting way. He saw a round, open face in a frame of thick, dark hair that was curled in a curiously old-fashioned style, as if she had tried to straighten it and nature had refused to cooperate.

'And I suppose when I heard that I was to be visited by a chief inspector and a detective sergeant I realized it must be important.' Heather giggled again, trying to dissipate the tension she felt building around her. And again it failed, her voice ringing tinny and artificial in her ears.

55

Lucy Blake produced a small black notebook and took the top off a gold ballpoint pen. 'How long did Annie Clark share this flat with you, Miss Shields?'

'It's Heather.' She looked for encouragement at the green-eyed woman with the rich chestnut hair, and received a small answering smile and a nod. 'We were together here for three or four months. No longer than that.' She wished she hadn't added that last phrase. It sounded negative, almost as though she had something to hide from them.

Lucy nodded, making a careful, unhurried note. 'And did you know her before that?'

'No. She was from Preston, not from Brunton.' That sounded silly, too – sounded Victorian, as if she couldn't have known anyone from ten miles away. 'I advertised for someone to share the rent of this place. They're good flats, these; it's a nice conversion of the big old house. But the rent is too much for one, unless you have a very good job.' She resisted the temptation to go on further, to enlarge in an area she knew was safe.

'And when did you last see Annie Clark?'

'On the twenty-first of September.' That was too prompt, too precise. She said apologetically, 'I've been thinking about it, you see, since you said you were coming to see me about Annie.'

DS Blake made a note of the date, nodding slowly. It was Peach who said to her, 'That's commendably precise, Miss Shields. A Saturday, I think. Have you any reason to remember it so vividly and exactly?' His dark eyes opened wide and his eyebrows arched above them; he looked to Heather, who had studied *Dr Faustus* at school, like a modern Mephistopheles.

'No. I just remember her going out on that Saturday night. The picture has come back to me quite vividly over these last few days. Since I heard about her body being found up on Pendle.'

'Understandable, that. Very upsetting, these things, for those who were closely involved with the deceased.'

He looked at her with his head a little on one side, like a curious but dangerous bird. She resisted the impulse to say again that she had not really known the dead girl very well at all. Peach said, 'What time would this be on that Saturday?'

'When I last saw her? About half past six in the evening, I suppose. Maybe a little later. She was – she was going out for the night.' Her voice had faltered, almost broken. But they couldn't read anything into that: they'd surely take it as emotion natural in one having to recall her last sight of a dead friend.

'And where was she going?'

'I'm not sure.' She was looking at the table, her brown eyes staring fixedly at the two oranges in the bowl in the middle of it.

'Was she going to meet her boyfriend, do you think? It was Saturday night.'

'She might have been, I suppose. I really can't remember.' She could feel the silence stretching, but she did not lift her eyes from the fruit.

After seconds that seemed to her like minutes, it was DS Blake's softer voice which said quite gently, 'You're sure of that, Heather? It could be important, you see. It's quite possible that you were the last person to have seen her alive, apart from her murderer.'

She roused herself, made herself lift her eyes to look at them, and said earnestly, 'I realize that. But I can't remember where she was going, or even if she told me that. She might have been meeting Matt Hogan, I suppose.'

She switched her eyes from Lucy Blake's lightly freckled face to the paler one beside her, and found DCI Peach studying her as intently as ever.

Eventually he said, 'Would you describe your own relationship with the deceased for us, please, Miss Shields?'

'We were friends. You have to be, when you share a flat together.'

'Good friends?'

'I'd say good friends, yes.' But she had given the faintest shrug of her shoulders before she answered.

'So tell us about her lifestyle. Tell us about the people you both knew during those months you spent together.'

'There isn't really a lot to tell. We both worked in offices, but they were at opposite ends of the town. I work in the packing department at a mail-order firm. I do most of the processing of orders.' It sounded almost like a boast. She hadn't intended that: she'd simply been looking for a way to seem helpful without offering them too much about her and Annie.

'And what did Annie Clark do?'

'She worked in a travel agent's. She was doing very well there, I think. She was a bright girl, you know.'

'No, we didn't. We're going to find out all about her, though, in the next few days.'

He made that sound like a threat, she thought. But perhaps that was her overactive imagination. Heather said, 'We got on well enough in the flat. I don't think we ever had a serious argument. But we didn't have the same friends. We didn't go out together much at all.'

'What about her boyfriend, Matthew Hogan?'

'I knew Matt. He and Annie were friends whilst she was here, but they weren't – well, they weren't an item, until quite near the end.'

The very phrase the lad had used himself. But there was nothing significant in that, perhaps. Peach said, 'Quite near the end? You speak as if you know exactly when she died.'

She looked into his dark, relentless eyes in panic. 'No I don't! I meant the end of the time when I knew her, I suppose. I was just – well, I was just assuming that she died soon after she left here on that Saturday night.'

Peach relaxed into a broad smile, showed her a perfect set of very white teeth. 'And you may very well be right, Miss Shields. But until we know exactly when she was killed, we can't make assumptions like that, you see. It could have been a week or a fortnight or even a month after she left here that she was killed. The pathologist couldn't be more precise than that about the time of death, you see, from what was left of her.'

Heather shuddered. 'I see what you mean. Well, I never heard another word from her after that Saturday night.'

'I see. And why didn't you report her as a missing person?'

It was said so quietly that she didn't realize at first how hostile it was. 'I – I just didn't think of it. I told you, we got on well enough, but we weren't all that close. She'd paid her rent until the end of September, so at first I suppose I

58

expected her back.' She looked desperately at Lucy Blake for some sort of relief, but found that the woman sergeant was now watching her as curiously as Peach. 'It's difficult to recall exactly what I was feeling all these months later. And she had a mother, you know. Her mother only lives in Preston. I think perhaps I assumed she'd gone home, and that if there was anything wrong it would be her mother who reported her missing, not me.'

She had seized eagerly on the sudden thought of Mrs Clark – too eagerly, perhaps. Peach studied her for another moment before he nodded slowly. 'Who do you think killed her, Miss Shields?'

Another bit of dynamite which he had slipped in almost casually. Heather felt her mind racing as she said, 'I don't know. I've really no idea.'

'No idea at all? What about the people she worked with? What about the people she saw in the evenings? The chances are that she was killed by someone who knew her quite well.'

'I suppose so. But as far as I know, she was a girl without enemies.'

'I see. So she didn't mention that she'd had a serious disagreement with anyone in the days before she disappeared?'

'No. But she might have done, without telling me. I told you: we got on well enough, but we weren't intimate friends.' That was a summary she'd planned to use before they came, but it had taken her a long time to get the phrases in.

'What about the boyfriend? Anything there?'

'Not as far as I know.' She faltered a little, staring again at the oranges between them. 'They'd only begun a serious relationship a few days before she disappeared. I think one reason why I didn't report her missing was that I thought they might have shacked up together somewhere.'

'But she'd have told you, wouldn't she? – if she'd been planning that. She wouldn't have simply disappeared to set up house with Matt Hogan without telling you about it?'

'No, I don't suppose she would have done that. She'd have told me about it, I expect, as you say.' Heather Shields was curiously listless.

They took the address of the travel agent's where Annie

Clark had worked and then stood up. Heather tried not to show her relief as they prepared to leave, her eagerness to have them out of her flat and to breathe a long sigh of relief. She never drank on her own, but she might even allow herself the luxury of a beer, if there was a can in the fridge.

Peach slid his arms into his car coat, prepared to face the cold of the night outside. For the first time since he had set foot over the threshold, he was not looking at her as he said conversationally, 'You've been able to let the flat again, have you? You said you needed someone to share.'

'Yes. I parcelled up Heather's things and took them to her mother, after we spoke on the phone. It's a fully furnished flat, so there wasn't a lot of stuff.'

'Yes. Our people have taken that stuff to forensic, just in case it tells us anything significant about Annie. Her mother hadn't opened the plastic bag, she said.'

'I see.' She wanted to say something about the pathetically small things that were left behind from a life. Instead, she found herself wondering whether there was anything in that black dustbin bag of clothes and trivia that could undermine what she had said to these two today.

'Been with you long, your new flatmate, has she?'

'Carol? Two or three months, yes. She was a friend before she came here. She was looking for accommodation and I needed someone, so it just seemed right. I didn't even need to advertise. There was hardly any time when I had to pay the rent on my own. And it's really worked out very well. We get on well together, without living in each other's pockets.'

She wondered if she was talking too much, in her relief to be finished with the questions about Annie Clark; but Peach said nothing, and Lucy Blake gave her a farewell smile as they left.

They were half a mile away from the place and the heater was putting some warmth back into the police Mondeo before Peach said, 'She moved in a replacement flatmate very quickly, then. She says vaguely that it was about two or three months ago, but I expect it was earlier than that. About the beginning of October, I'd guess, from what she said. She must have been sure very quickly that Annie Clark wasn't coming back.'

Eight

In Brunton, January is always the longest month.

It is the deepest month of winter, and people in the north-west of England take it for granted that their winters will be hard. It is especially so in this northern corner of Lancashire, where the snow winds sweep in from the Irish Sea and the Pennines raise their heights to the east. Of course, the days when the clogs of workers hurrying to the mills clattered loud on the frozen cobbles of the old cotton town are now long gone. Central heating and a succession of milder winters have made some of the younger residents careless of the dangers of cold. Frozen pipes are no longer the constant fear in every house, and chilblains are a thing of the past for Brunton's noisy children.

But to the older people of the town, at least, the days of January still seem to stretch interminably. It is now the night of the twenty-seventh of the month, and the daylight is beginning to stretch a little. It has been a clear, bright day today, and light enough to see the hills around the town until five o'clock. In two months, people will be slipping their clocks an hour forward and thinking of spring.

But by seven o'clock on this evening, the stars have disappeared, clouds have crept in, and winter is reminding Bruntonians that it has plenty to throw at them yet. The whiteness that only fell upon the flanks of Pendle Hill in the previous week, picking out the greater heights of Ingleborough and Pen y Ghent forty miles to the north, is beginning to descend into the towns of the area. The first flakes of snow are tiny ones, drifting almost tentatively between the long rows of terraced house and into the narrow streets. They drop through the still, cold air as a gentle warning of what is to come. But within fifteen minutes, the flakes have grown larger and their fall steadier, as if some unseen presence above has tried its hand and gathered confidence.

The old cotton town of Brunton acquires a strange, unreal, deceptive beauty as the snow becomes first a film and then a thin carpet of white. The tall new buildings in the centre of the town look from a distance like a Manhattan skyline as the curtain of falling snow alters proportions. The steep slate roofs of the cramped terraces that were built to house mill workers at the end of the nineteenth century lose their meanness under the sparkling white mantle, acquiring a Disneyesque charm that has no relation to their normal appearance.

It is eight o'clock now on this bitter evening, and the few vehicles that are using the wider thoroughfares of the town are hastening home, their drivers anxious to be safely indoors before winter asserts its full grip. There are no cars in the smaller streets, which seem wider as the thickening snow obliterates the lines of their footpaths and the snow swirls silently across street lamps, yellowing and softening the light that falls from them.

There are few pedestrians abroad, as the temperature drops and the snow continues its steady accumulation upon the town. There is one, however, making whatever haste she can in the treacherous conditions, looking neither right nor left as she hurries with head down and eyes assessing the treacherous footing of the snow-covered stone flags.

Fifty years ago, a woman abroad on such a night would have been hunched in the then ubiquitous shawl. She would probably have been hurrying the short distance to the off-licence with her jug beneath the wool – it was inconceivable then that any 'respectable' woman would venture alone into a public house. Those days have long gone, though some of the old streets and roads remain. Tonight's walker is a taller, fitter woman, with a longer stride and a perspective that stretches far beyond the end of the street where she lives.

This woman is, in fact, Jo Barrett – educated, independent, lesbian and defiant; the same Jo Barrett who was so animated in the school staff room three days earlier by Ellie Boyd's account of the discovery of a decaying body.

She knows exactly where she is going, for she has trodden the route often enough before. But never in conditions like these: everything seems different under the snow. The absence of cars on the streets and of walkers along the pavements brings a feeling of emptiness to normally busy streets. But it is the silence that the snow brings, softening and muffling every movement, which lends an eerie quality to her progress.

She stamps her high black leather boots hard as she reaches a corner, as much to hear the sound of the heels on the stone as to clear them of snow. She looks back down the street she has left and forward along the one she is now to tread, but there is no other human presence visible. Both streets look much longer than usual under their white covering, and she cannot quite see the end of either of them through the veil of thin, stinging flakes. She is suddenly glad of the lights from the windows of the houses, reminding her that the area is not after all deserted.

And Jo Barrett is not, as she fancies, the only person abroad on this picturesque but bitter night. An aerial view of the town would reveal another figure, invisible to her because it is moving from a different area altogether towards the same point. The figure has come the first part of its journey by car and it is male. But the man does not drive to the house he plans to visit.

He parks and locks his car three streets and a quarter of a mile away, looks carefully and automatically to his right and to his left, and then sets off alone towards the house.

It is an Edwardian house, a high, detached villa that was erected in the heyday of King Cotton, shortly before the First World War. With the obliteration of normal landmarks under the white blanket, the house is not as distinctive as usual, and he checks the number to make sure he is right before he turns into the drive.

He is standing looking up at the high elevations of the house, watching the snow swirling against its eaves in the light of the street lamp behind him, when Jo Barrett, arriving from the opposite end of the road, turns into the drive behind him. Each of them endures a brief moment of alarm, then the relief of recognition.

They exchange brittle greetings, which sound unnaturally

loud in the pervading silence. Then both of them stamp their feet clean of snow on the broad stone steps beneath the wide door, and Dermot Boyd follows Jo Barrett into the dark interior of the house.

By eleven o'clock on this bitter night the snow had ceased to fall; but it lay two inches thick in the streets of Brunton, and there was the sparkle on its surface which denoted frost. There would be treacherous skid-pads on untreated roads by the time the citizens of the town rose to the challenges of a new January day.

Percy Peach did not have double glazing in his nineteen-fifties house, and the central-heating system was due for a new boiler. Lucy Blake parted the curtains, scratched a small peephole in the ice that had accumulated on the inside of the window, peered out into the night, and said, 'It's stopped snowing. But it's freezing hard now.'

'It's winter out there, then. High time respectable folks were in bed and saving on heating.'

'You're already doing that. It's cold in here.' Lucy slid her hands within the arms of her thick red sweater and hugged herself in her armchair. She thought of her own cosy modern flat, with its efficient central heating and its double-glazed windows, and wished it hadn't been her turn to come here.

'Have to do my bit for the environment, you know,' said Percy cheerfully. 'The world has a finite supply of fossil fuels, and I'm doing my bit to preserve them. And it's high time we got to bed and generated our own warmth. It will be nice to feel we're helping the environment.' He gave her his most benign beam and switched off the television.

Lucy shivered anew when she reached his icy bedroom. 'Can't sleep if it's too hot, you see,' Percy explained. 'I'll nip into bed and warm the sheets for you, whilst I watch you undress. I'm the soul of consideration, aren't I? Don't feel you have to hurry. I can be patient, too, when the need arises – especially when there's a show like this.' He slid his tie expertly over his shining bald pate. And seconds later, he was somehow out of his clothes and into the bed, whilst she was still summoning her nerve to the ordeal of disrobing in this environment.

'This place is like a morgue. It's too bloody cold for me! I'm going to have a hot shower to warm me up.' She grabbed her sports bag and slipped into the bathroom, ignoring Percy Peach's wild shout of deprivation, drowning the continuing litany of complaint from the bedroom across the landing by turning on the shower. 'It's time you had an en suite!' she shouted through the door by way of defiance.

The bathroom wasn't much warmer than the rest of the upper storey of this rather neglected semi-detached house. But at least she could strip swiftly here, without the selection of erotic growls and moans with which her lover invariably accompanied the process. And the water in the shower was mercifully hot. She luxuriated in it for a few minutes, then stepped reluctantly from the warmth of the little cubicle and dried herself quickly in the sudden cold outside it.

'Hurry up in there! I'm getting terribly lonely in here,' said a plaintive voice from the bedroom.

Lucy Blake grinned to herself and slid her curves into the garments she had taken from her sports bag. Then she spread her towel carefully on the radiator for the morning, took a deep breath, and tripped lightly back across the landing into Percy's bedroom.

The sound that greeted her went some way towards repaying her considerable outlay on her new nightwear. It was a gradually rising whine of pure animal pleasure, beginning low and moving through several octaves to a triumphant howl. She had never really appreciated lust before; now she decided that lust in the one you lusted after was a wholly admirable quality.

'Bloody 'ell, Norah,' said Percy Peach. It was his highest term of approbation and delight, the most welcome piece of the code they had developed between them on these occasions. As if to emphasize that, he repeated the phrase at a higher volume: 'BLOODY 'ELL, NORAH!'

The object of his attention was a pair of light-blue silk pyjamas, now filled to their optimum capacity by the buxom figure of Lucy Blake. He reached his hands imploringly towards her as she remained just out of his reach: it was a skill she had quickly learned was necessary with Percy. 'Must have cost you a bomb, those!' he said, 'and worth every damned penny!' He growled again, his voice rising from a throaty rattle to a yelp of pure pleasure.

'The neighbours will hear you,' said Lucy, affecting to be unconscious of him, studying her new outfit approvingly in the mirror. The pyjamas were worth the money. And on the whole, she was glad she had chosen the smaller size: it was comfortable enough, and just about adequate.

'Bugger the neighbours! They can't see what I can see. Come to bed, or I shan't be responsible for my actions.'

Lucy allowed herself a coquettish twirl in front of the wardrobe's full-length mirror, turning her head to see how the silk clung to her splendid posterior. 'I got them in the sale,' she told Percy. A Lancashire woman couldn't have her man thinking he'd taken on an extravagant partner. 'They're pure silk, you know. They weren't cheap, but they're excellent quality.'

'Worth every damned penny, whatever they cost,' Percy assured her again. He watched her adjust the elastic of the waistband and gave a ritual groan of anticipated pleasure. 'But it's the model that sells things. It's like a box of chocolates: it's what's inside that really matters, in the end.' And with a superhuman effort of will, his powerful arms became telescopic, his strong fingers seized Lucy's hips and drew her inexorably towards his bed.

She subsided with a becoming little yelp of female appreciation. Percy had warmed the sheets as he had promised, and he now ran what seemed to be at least two pairs of hands repeatedly over the treasure that had come into his lair. Lucy giggled gratefully; she was always surprised anew by his combination of energy and approbation. Then she caught his manhood almost by accident in her hand, and gasped some appropriate nonsense into his ear.

'Pure silk,' he said in muffled tones, 'pure silk!' Whether he was referring to her new garments or to something else entirely, neither of them was quite clear.

'I wasn't sure whether to buy these or not,' she said, when next a pause presented itself. 'Pyjama trousers aren't the most practical wear, when one is spending the night with Percy Peach.'

'Be fun taking them off!' he said stoutly. Then, suiting the action to the words, he removed them, quite unhurriedly, and with many pleasurable diversions along the way. It took him some time, and then he said softly that he didn't think he had the inclination or the energy to remove the top as well.

'Just treat it as if it were a very short nightie,' said Lucy softly, almost drowsily.

So Percy Peach did. And it worked. And he thought he was the luckiest man in the world. And Lucy Blake assured him that he probably was. And certainly the most vigorous.

When he returned from a pee at three o'clock in the morning, Percy was surprised to find that the pyjama trousers had returned to base – a very desirable base, to be sure, but they were back in position. The skills of womankind are varied and manifold.

So Percy Peach removed the silk pyjama trousers again – more quickly and skilfully this time.

Practice makes perfect.

Nine

'Thank you for agreeing to see us about this.'

Ellie Boyd said, 'It wasn't a problem. I have a free period first thing this morning.' She wondered if they would explain why they had wanted to see her alone, why they had made sure that Dermot would have gone to work before they agreed to come to her house at this time. She had been expecting this meeting for thirty-six hours now, ever since Dermot had come home on Wednesday night and told her that they had been to see him at the office.

DCI Peach said, 'This shouldn't take very long.'

Ellie glanced at her watch as she led them into the sitting room. She had spent several hours in here on the previous evening, but at this time in the morning the room felt cold and unfamiliar, as if it had not been occupied for months. It was almost ten to nine. She said, 'I'll have to be out of here by twenty past nine, at the latest. The roads will be bad with this snow.'

'Then we'd better get down to business, hadn't we?' said Peach. He sat down on the sofa beside the woman he had introduced as Detective Sergeant Blake, who produced a small notebook and a neat gold ballpoint pen, and who looked at her with a smile which Ellie supposed was meant to be reassuring.

She had expected one of them to tell her that this was just routine stuff, but neither of them had.

They took her through the preliminaries of her aborted attempt to climb Pendle Hill in the snow six days earlier, listening carefully to the account she had gone over so often in her mind. She told them of the blizzard, of the lace in her boot breaking, of the need for shelter to conduct emergency repairs. Then Peach said, 'When did you decide to go into that old farmhouse?'

68

'As soon as we saw it.'

'And when was that?'

A curious question; she hadn't expected it. 'Well, it might have been visible earlier in the day, from a distance. If it was, I don't remember it. When the blizzard came, you could only see about a hundred yards. I just caught the low shape of some sort of building, below us and to our right. With it snowing as hard as it was and my lace going like that, I was glad to spot any sort of shelter.'

'So it was you who decided to use the place?'

'It was both of us. As I say, we were glad of anything that would offer us respite from that blizzard!' But she knew now that it was she that had been determined to make for the place, that Dermot, even in that harsh environment, even in the midst of her distress, had tried to persuade her against it. She wondered if she would have remembered that, if her husband had not been so insistent that they should both tell the same story to these people. His story.

She watched the woman making a careful note of what she had said. Wonderful hair, Ellie thought with irrelevant envy, as her head bent over the notebook.

Then DS Blake looked up at her and said, 'And it was then that you discovered the remains which we now know were those of a twenty-three-year-old woman named Anne Marie Clark – in the room at the end of that derelict farmhouse. Who went into that outbuilding first?'

'I can't remember.'

'Try, please. We need the fullest possible picture.'

'Why? Why is this important?'

As soon as the question was out, she wished she hadn't asked it. Peach looked at her steadily for a moment, then said quietly, 'We don't even know that it is. The probability, indeed, is that it isn't, as you imply. But we have to gather every detail we can when there is a suspicious death. What is important and what isn't only emerges much later on.'

'I suppose so. It's just that I can't see—'

'So if you can just cast your mind back and remember who decided to go into that particular room, we'd be obliged to you.'

'I think I did. Yes, I remember; I was particularly anxious

to get some shelter, to do something with my lace, so I went into the first place that offered itself.' She remembered Dermot trying to dissuade her from entering the outbuilding now. She wished she had gone through what Dermot had said to this man with him now. All he had said, in his scathing, dismissive way, was that Peach had taken a forbidding black constable with him, and that they had been a formidable pair. She wondered if she was going to contradict anything he had said, despite her best efforts to present the united front Dermot had been so insistent upon.

'And who was it that first saw the body?'

'It was me.' That surely couldn't do him any harm. She remembered that first appalling moment, when she had seen the thing in the corner, the brief instant when she had wondered what on earth it could be, before she realized that it was a body. Or what was left of a body. Dermot had not even been inside the place then. He had responded to her cry. She remembered him stooping low, coming unwillingly through the crumbling entrance after her scream of anguish. Even then, he had scarcely entered the place.

'So Mr Boyd didn't go very near to the remains.'

'No, I don't think so. He was anxious to protect me from the sight, I think. It wasn't a thing either of us wanted to linger over.'

'I agree with you there. DS Blake and I saw the body the next day. We had to look closely, of course, for professional reasons. You get used to that. But you still don't enjoy it. And what was left in that farmhouse was a particularly harrowing sight.'

'Yes. Neither of us looked at it very closely. We got out as quickly as we could.'

'Indeed. And that's the normal human reaction which I would expect. And yet when we spoke to him on Wednesday, your husband seemed very certain that these remains were not only female but those of a young girl.'

'But you've just said they were. You've just told me the girl's name.'

'Yes. The identity of the victim will be in this evening's papers and on radio and television newscasts. The fact that it was a young woman was released by my chief superintendent

on Wednesday night – not until some time after I had interviewed your husband about your discovery of the remains.'

Ellie felt her head reel as she sat and endured this, under
the scrutiny of the two very different but equally watchful
faces opposite her. She remembered now that Dermot had
spoken of the body as being that of a young woman when
he had talked to her about this, when he had been emphasizing the necessity for them to present a united front. He'd
said there was no reason to suppose that the poor girl had
been raped, and she'd picked him up on it at the time. Was
this why it had been so necessary for them to be careful?
Had he known all along who that victim was? Was that why
he had not wanted her to go near that abandoned building?

She said as firmly as she could, 'I'm sure Dermot didn't
actually know that. I'm sure he merely assumed that it was
going to be a young girl. Most murder victims are, aren't
they?'

Peach smiled glumly, 'A great many of them are, certainly,
Mrs Boyd.'

'And I think the body had trainers on. Yes, I'm almost
sure it did. White, or mainly white. And you'd be able to
tell from them that it was female. Even if it didn't register
at the time, those small feet would stay in your mind, wouldn't
they?' But she sounded desperate, too anxious to convince
them that it must be so.

Peach said, 'Yes. I suppose that's how it must have been.
I'm glad you've been able to clear that up for us, Mrs Boyd.
Thank you for your help.'

Alan Hurst inspected himself carefully in the mirror above
the tiny washbasin: hair carefully coiffured, its hint of grey
arrested at what he considered the right level; maturity with
virility – that was the image he wished to convey. And the
face was still handsome; the small lines developing around
the clear grey eyes suggested experience rather than decline.
The nose was still good: regular and definite, without being
too prominent – women didn't like a big hooter, whatever
the more racy myths said about what went with it. Well, he'd
never had any complaints from the women in that department. He grinned a roguish grin at himself in the mirror. For

most of the time, Alan Hurst had a very good opinion of himself.

He went out for a moment to the counter at the front. 'I have to go out for a couple of hours, as I told you last night.' He dropped his hand on to the back of the girl's chair, felt the warmth from her back against his thumb. Next week, if all went well, he'd let his fingers run around the lace at the back of her blouse: one of the first erogenous zones, a woman's neck. And when they were twenty-two and impressionable, doubly so.

But he wouldn't push it. He didn't want her shying away like a nervous kitten and claiming sexual harassment. You couldn't be too careful, these days. Much better to be sure before you made your move. But Alan was confident enough: power was still the great aphrodisiac. And he did own the place, even if the business was modest. He'd made sure that she hadn't got a regular boyfriend when he'd interviewed her a month ago. This girl would still be flattered when she found her handsome, masterful boss taking an interest in her. But don't push it; there was plenty of time.

Anna Fenton kept her eyes on the computer screen, watching the latest holiday offers from the big firms flashing up for those who could get away this weekend. She quite enjoyed it when he left her in charge. She said, 'I'll be OK. I know my way around the place now.' She nodded at the screen. 'There's a great offer just come up here for a fortnight in a four-star hotel in Tenerife – ideal for those who can just drop everything.'

He almost took up the sexual-innuendo possibilities in the phrase, then decided that it was probably too early for that. No need to risk frightening her away; you wanted her to see you as an interesting mature man, not a dirty old one. You had to maintain the illusion of a sort of innocence, however ludicrous that might seem to you. He looked at the screen over her shoulder. 'They're filling up places at the last minute. But not many people can go off at the drop of a hat. They think they can, but when it comes to it, they usually have commitments.'

As he had. He thought of patient, uncomplaining Judith, at home with her multiple sclerosis, watching herself grow weaker and more helpless, as the drugs began to have less effect and she felt her limbs losing their strength. The succession of girls who worked in the shop didn't know and would never see that other life he led. It was a private world, that one where his wife and he watched each other tenderly and waited for her to die.

'That girl they've found – the one up on the moors: she used to work here, didn't she?' Anna Fenton was still looking at the screen as she spoke, staring fixedly at it, as if further details would come to her there, not from the man behind her left shoulder.

'She did, yes.'

'Why didn't you mention it?'

'I was going to. I only found out yesterday that it was Annie Clark. It was a hell of a shock to me, as you can imagine.'

'It must have been.' Anna felt that she couldn't ask the bold questions she wanted to ask if she turned to look at the boss. She tapped out an instruction on her PC, watched the screen flash up a new file. 'She had a first name almost the same as mine. What was she like?'

Like you, he thought – far too much like you. The same age. The same combination of prettiness and naïvety which I have always found it impossible to resist. Very nearly the same first name. He said, 'Annie Clark was quite different from you, Anna. She was blonde. A little shorter than you. Probably not quite as good a figure. And her eyes were a different colour, I think. I don't remember her all that well. She wasn't here that long.' He felt a sudden, searing shaft of conscience at his treachery. But what else could he do?

'How long?'

'How long was she here? I'm not quite sure. About three months, as far as I can remember.' It was four, but his instinct was to play it down, to make it as brief and as trivial an episode as he could.

'Your employment records would tell you.'

'Yes. Perhaps I'd better check them – get it exactly right. The police want to speak to me about her, you see. Just routine, they said. I expect they'll want to know if I can think of anyone who might have killed her. But I can't, of course. It was as big a shock to me as to anyone when I heard what had happened to the poor girl.'

There was a little pause. He watched a couple outside looking at the list of special offers in the window. He willed them to come in, to finish this exchange he didn't like but didn't know how to end. The middle-aged pair spoke to each other, pointed to different cards with their blazing red letters. But they didn't come into the shop. The slim girl at her desk said stubbornly, 'You should have told me, Mr Hurst. Apart from anything else, we might have customers coming in here talking about it. I'd look a fool if I didn't know, wouldn't I?'

'But you do know, don't you? You're on the ball, as usual! How did you find out, anyway?'

'My sister told me last night. We were out together, with three other girls. The name of the dead girl had just been announced on Radio Lancashire, apparently. And one of the girls had known her.'

Alan Hurst had a glimpse of that other life she lived, the one he would never see. For the first time in the day he felt the burden of his age. He wondered where he would be, what kind of life he would be living, in ten years' time; but the picture was blank. He resisted the impulse to put his hands on her shoulders. He wanted the touch of warm, human flesh beneath his fingers, but he knew that this wasn't the moment for that.

Anna Fenton said quietly, 'What kind of girl was she?'

'Annie Clark? Oh, she was efficient enough, I suppose. Well, better than that, really. She'd made a very promising start here, as a matter of fact.' He owed her that much at least, poor dead Annie.

'Then why did she leave?' Anna Fenton was bold and persistent; he had probably been the same, at her age.

'She didn't. She just didn't come in one morning. It was a fairly quiet period, so I managed without her for a week or two. Then we began to get the bookings in for winter sun and short breaks, and I had to get help of some kind. I made do with a temp for six or eight weeks, until I was sure she wasn't coming back.' He told himself that it was useful that this girl was curious, that the police would want to know all this, so that it was a useful rehearsal for him. 'And then you came along and filled the vacancy. My lucky day, that was!'

'And mine as well!' She turned round at last and looked at him with a smile, and it was only with a supreme effort of will that he resisted the instinct to reach out and pull her towards him. He was surprised how talking of Annie Clark had made him randy – made him want this other girl with a first name that was almost the same.

Fortunately, the shop door opened at that point and the couple who had been studying the information in the window came in. He gave them his bright, professional smile, confirmed to them that the Canary Islands were an excellent holiday bargain at the moment, and said, 'I'll leave you in the capable hands of Miss Fenton here.'

He heard her talking to them in her brisk, cheerful way as he shut the door of his office at the back of the show-room. He took out the key from his pocket and unlocked the bottom drawer of the filing cabinet. He drew out the video tapes, slipped them into his briefcase, went out through the rear door of the building and moved quickly to his car.

It was a maroon Vauxhall Vectra, with all the extras. He had got it only three months ago, and he was pleased with it. You didn't want anything too flashy, anything that would make people ask questions about how you could make that sort of money in a small local travel agent's shop. The short answer was that you couldn't, of course – not with all the competition from the big boys and more and more and more people using the Internet. If it wasn't for this lucrative little sideline, the business would be in real trouble.

He was surprised how quickly his market had grown, how the word passed round that he could supply these things. He was making two or three deliveries a week now. It was amazing how many people there were who had a taste for this sort of thing. Perverts, he supposed, though he didn't care to think of them like that: they were increasingly his bread and butter, weren't they?

He drove twenty-eight miles in all, delivering video tapes to seven very different residences. All of them knew he was coming; all of the buyers took his packages carefully into their own hands. The only exception was the last call. He left the tapes in their plain white box in the shed beside the garage as he had been instructed to do. The circuit judge was somewhere else in the county, meting out the justice of the land to those arraigned before him. Alan Hurst had never seen him, and he felt now that he never would. It was re-assuring to him to know that men like that had such tastes, such secrets. It made his own double life seem relatively innocent.

He called in at home, made Judith a sandwich for her lunch, gave her thirty minutes of his time and his love. She seemed to him a little paler, a little more frail, with each passing month. She was resolutely cheerful, pathetically grateful for every little consideration that he afforded her. She insisted on coming to the door in her wheelchair to see him off. He bent and kissed her on the forehead; it was one of the little rituals of affection they had kept up over the years of her decline.

'I won't be late.'

Not tonight, he wouldn't. And he wouldn't be going out again in the evening, wouldn't be needing to feed her one of the range of ingenious excuses he used when he had a mistress in tow. He despised himself, sometimes – more and more often, nowadays. But a man had needs. You didn't sign up for a life of celibacy with a crippled wife, even when you went through all that rubbish that everyone mouthed about it being for better or for worse.

He was more ashamed of this other stuff really: the tapes. But it paid well – paid for the home care and the little treats that he wanted to give Judith as life closed in on her and she got worse. What he was doing was against the law, true, but if it wasn't, it wouldn't bring in the easy money he was making from it. There had to be a certain element of risk attached, if you were to make big money as easily as he was doing.

He prepared himself for a big effort when he had parked the car in the little yard at the back of the shop. Energy always went down well with these girls in their early twen-ties. God knows, they had enough of it themselves – that was one of the attractions. And most of them hadn't got the inhibitions about sex that they'd had even a generation ago, he thought. Or perhaps he was just getting a little more experienced, a little better at handling the many-faceted creatures that made up this fascinating gender.

He allowed himself a small smile at that thought. Then he went breezily into the shop and asked her how she'd been getting on.

Anna Fenton was pleased with herself. She'd sold a package in Prague to eight lads on a stag weekend and a *QEII* cruise to two couples who wanted to travel together.

'Excellent! I'll make us a pot of tea to celebrate,' said Alan Hurst. He went into the little cramped kitchen and put the china cups and saucers on the tray beside the silver-plated teapot, spread the chocolate digestives round the plate. No beakers this afternoon: make it a special occasion. He felt confidence growing within him as he made the simple moves. They'd have a little intimate snack together and get a little closer to each other.

Young girls liked it when you did the domestic thing for them.

Modern witches do not seek publicity, any more than did their ancient counterparts. There are reputed to be up to forty thousand of them in Great Britain, and many more in North America, but they do not boast about their numbers. Secrecy is part of their code, for a variety of reasons. The most important one of these is self-protection.

The Wiccan order of West Brunton was only one of several groups in the town and the Ribble Valley to the north of it, that area from which, four centuries earlier, witches had been hauled off to Lancaster, tried and executed. These modern witches included men as well as women. They practised white magic, invoked the Mother Goddess and her consort, the male Horned God, and believed that there was a mysterious strength in their numbers which individually they would not have been able to muster.

There was a muted air about the group as they met on this last Friday night in January. The snow had melted during an afternoon of wintry sunshine, but it was freezing again now. The wet roads were turning treacherous, with that thin film of black ice which is the most dangerous surface of all.

They had never been a large group, and tonight there were only three of them present. They bowed their heads to the deities and prayed for guidance and help. They asked for help from the Life Force, that pillar of the witches' world which united rocks and trees, deserts and streams, mountains and valleys, the humblest living forms from amoebae to human beings. Their leader reminded them that all of the earth is a living, breathing organism, a manifestation of the Goddess and the God. All was sacred, all was to be cared for and revered.

And through such harmony would come strength. The witches, by subsuming themselves in this whole, by understanding the wholeness of the natural world and their place in it, could learn how to live, could bring power into their lives which they would not have alone.

Normally it was easy to subsume themselves into the personality of the leader, to follow her incantations and make them their own. But tonight each of them knew that one of their number had passed on. Each of them knew that their youngest member had in fact been violently dispatched from this world, which they were seeking so earnestly to harmonize. Each of them knew that it was even possible, though none of them dared to voice the thought even in this intimate company of fellow Wiccans, that one of the people in this room had played a part in their sister's removal from the world.

Their service was muted tonight, not because the words and the thoughts they used were very different from their normal ones, but because they could not submerge themselves as normally into the depths of their worship and their celebration. Each mind in the room reserved a part of itself not for what they were doing and saying but for what they knew was to come.

It was almost a relief to them when the bell shrilled in the distant hall. Their leader did not look at them. Katherine Howard moved with a stately dignity from her position facing them at the front of the room, divesting herself of the voice she used for the higher world which they had been seeking to enter. By the time she passed through the door, she was back in that more tawdry world all of them inhabited by day. It was her house, and she strode out to answer the ring of the bell and meet the challenge which all of them had known was coming.

The man whom she brought into the room behind her did not at first sight look very formidable. He had a neat grey suit and wore no topcoat, even on a freezing night like this. He was small and bald, with a fringe of very dark hair beneath his white head and a moustache and eyebrows that were equally black. But the darkest things of all were his eyes, which flashed round each of the faces in turn as they blinked in the full light which their leader had switched on as she ushered him in. The centres of the eyes sparkled like small pieces of bright coal as they assessed the two women and the man in the room.

He said evenly, 'My name is Peach and I am a senior policeman. I shall need to speak to all of you individually in due course.'

Ten

Eleanor Boyd had a strange Saturday morning. Her husband brought her breakfast in bed.

It wasn't her birthday. It wasn't their wedding anniversary; they hadn't made much fuss about that in the last three or four years. It must be the old male thing of guilt. He must be trying to cover something up, or to make amends for something he had done. Dermot Boyd was much more conventional than he liked to think he was.

She watched him come into the room diffidently, as if she was not his wife but some guest to whom they were giving this special treat. He held the tray awkwardly in front of him; it had on it her cereals and one of the silver-plated dessert spoons they kept for dinner parties. Then, when he had broken the ice and seen that she was going to accept his gesture, he bustled back more confidently five minutes later with a boiled egg, toast, marmalade and her mother's little china teapot, with a woollen cosy on top of it. 'Time you were pampered for a change,' he said firmly. 'I feel I've been neglecting you, lately.'

Ellie resisted the temptation to ask him bluntly what all this was in aid of. He'd tell her soon enough, and a churlish voice at the back of the brain told her not to make it easier for him by asking the right questions. She beheaded her boiled egg expertly and found to her surprise that it was just as she liked it: runny but not half-raw. She cut her toast with slim, expert fingers, dipped a soldier into the yolk, and said, 'I could get used to this.'

Dermot smiled at her, then went into the bathroom and shaved. He came back into the room fully dressed. If this did not go well, he might need to be out of the house and away from his wife. He watched her pour a thin amber stream

80

of tea into the china cup, then said, 'I'm sorry we didn't have children. It leaves life a bit empty for us sometimes, doesn't it?'

She said, 'It's old ground, that. Perhaps we should have tried harder to get an adoption, when we were still young enough.' They were only forty-one now, but both of them knew that the time for a family had gone. 'And we both have interesting jobs to keep us busy.'

'Oh, yes. Our jobs.' He looked at her bitterly in the dressing-table mirror. 'Yours seems rewarding enough, even if you have to work harder at it than I think you should. But I shouldn't have been an accountant. I'm a square peg in a round hole, most of the time.'

This was more old ground. She tried to laugh him out of it. 'You read books, you mean? You can quote the odd line of poetry – well, more than the odd line, if I'm honest. It might make you unusual, but I don't think there's an actual ban on accountants being literate.'

'Literary.' The correction was out before he could stop himself. 'Anyway, it's perhaps boredom in the job that has made me look for – for outlets.' He had hesitated over the last word, trying to find something she wouldn't think too controversial.

'Outlets.' She weighed the word, nodding over it, watching his fingers twining in the fringe of the blanket at the edge of the bed. 'Is this what breakfast in bed is all about – outlets?'

Dermot wasn't looking at her as he said, 'We get on well enough with each other, don't we? It may not be as passionate as it was at first, but we get on well enough.'

She wondered what he was going to tell her. Had he got another woman? Was he going to say he'd fallen in love, that he wanted a divorce? And what would she feel if he did? She'd be shocked – of course she would. But would there also be a sort of relief, a comfort in being able to acknowledge at last that they were failing with each other, that their marriage had dried up? She said, 'Dermot, don't you think you'd better tell me whatever it is that you want to tell me?'

He gave her a quick smile of gratitude that she had brought it to a head, then looked down at the hand fiddling with the

81

fringe of the blanket, watching it as if it were someone else's hand altogether. 'These nights when I've been going off to the Freemasons.'

'Yes. You're going to tell me you haven't been going there at all.'

'Yes. How did you know?'

He looked both startled and discomfited. Men were dense creatures, at times – and this one most of the time. 'You weren't cut out to deceive, Dermot. You'd never have made a spy.'

'I hope that's a compliment.'

'I've no idea whether it is or not. I wondered why there was none of the usual regalia, no aprons or anything of that kind. And Masonry didn't seem quite your thing, really. I think *that* might just be a compliment, but never mind. Tell me what you've really been up to.' She wondered if the woman would be much younger than her, the way they usually were, whether she was about to be what her colleagues at school called 'traded in for a newer model'.

'You'll think it's weird. You'll think it's much odder than Masonry. People always do, until they know more about it.'

'It's not a woman?'

'What? No, of course it's not a woman.' His old irritation with her surfaced for a moment. How could Ellie be so far off the ball? 'I wouldn't want another woman when I've got you, old girl, would I?' He reached out a hand and put it on hers on the edge of the tray for a moment, trying to win back one of those moments of intimacy they had neglected until they were perhaps lost for ever. 'It's just another interest – something I'd have told you about earlier, if I hadn't thought you'd laugh in my face.'

He'd never been able to stand ridicule. Ellie felt a sudden shaft of sympathy for him and his deficiencies. She squeezed the hand which lay still on top of hers and said, 'You'd better tell me all about it. At least I won't have to face Ladies' Night at the Masons, will I?'

'It's witchcraft.'

'What?' For the first time in years, he had genuinely surprised her.

'Modern witchcraft. Not all that dancing round the cauldron

in *Macbeth*. It's a sort of lay religion. We try to do good in the world. We're Wiccans. I can tell you all about it, if you want me to.'

She knew that she mustn't laugh, but that very knowledge had her biting the inside of her lip and staring hard at her mother's china teapot. Some seconds passed before she could trust herself to say, 'Not now. Later, perhaps, when I've had time to get used to the idea.'

Then he said something that suddenly shredded her hilarity. 'You need to know, because the police are interested in us.'

Her leg twitched beneath the blankets, almost upsetting her neglected tea. 'Why? What have you done?' This was getting more bizarre by the minute.

'Nothing, really. But it's to do with that girl we found up in that farmhouse on Pendle last Saturday. Annie Clark, her name was. She was a Wiccan. She was one of our group.'

Katherine Howard said, 'We're a small group. We always have been. There were eight of us at one time, but two of them moved away, joined other covens. And one man and one woman have ceased to attend. Perhaps they no longer believe; we don't press people about that. And now poor Annie Clark is dead.'

Peach said stiffly, 'I should emphasize that Detective Sergeant Blake and I are interested in your activities only insofar as they concern a serious unsolved crime. We are here to investigate the position which Annie Clark had in your group and the relationship of the other members with her.'

Sitting upright beside Peach, Lucy Blake was aware that he was not at ease. Very few things threw Percy Peach, but investigating a coven of witches might just be one of them. The most surprising thing to Lucy was how very normal Katherine Howard looked. She was a tall woman of around fifty, carefully and discreetly made up, even at quarter past nine on a Saturday morning. She had fair hair, cut rather short around a broad face, which was handsome rather than pretty. She had long, athletic-looking legs, which were shown at their best in rather close-fitting black trousers. She had alert blue eyes and what seemed to be a habit of stroking the rings on her left hand. These looked like an engagement and wedding ring, but the CID officers had so far seen no sign of a man in the house.

She said, 'We don't publicize our activities, largely because what we do is much misunderstood.'

Peach said, 'Secret societies are always misunderstood. They bring it upon themselves.' Like Tommy Bloody Tucker's Masons, he thought: Percy made no claims to objectivity about the Masons.

'I wouldn't call us a secret society, Chief Inspector. There is plenty of information available, for those who wish to acquire it.'

'I read *The White Goddess*, a long time ago. I had a thing about Robert Graves, when I was a teenager. I think it all came from seeing *I, Claudius* on the telly when I was a kid.'

It was Mrs Howard's turn to be surprised: a senior policeman who read books! She said, 'At least Graves tried to get rid of the idea of witches as old crones with black cats, who fly about on broomsticks and cast evil spells. But things have moved on a lot since he wrote that book.'

'Perhaps you'd better fill us in on the modern picture, then. As briefly as possible, but bearing in mind that we're trying to find out all we can about Annie Clark. If this was important to her, we need to know about it.'

Katherine Howard looked at the man's round, alert face and the younger, lightly freckled one of his companion. They were watchful and experienced, these two. Whatever else she did, she would not make the mistake of underestimating them. 'First of all, we have no connections at all with ancient pagan cults or those poor local creatures who were dragged to Lancaster and hanged because vicious people alleged that they were witches. Wicca is creative, imaginative, and entirely an invention – or I should more correctly say a discovery – of the twentieth century.'

'And what do you believe?'

She smiled. 'It's sometimes easier to list the things we don't believe. Most Wiccans have examined one or more of the great world religions and found they are based on super-stition or the self-interest of their clergy. We rely on a recon-struction of pre-Christian religions. Most of us would call ourselves neo-pagans: we distrust the tyranny of the doctrines and demands of traditional religions and practise magic rather than religion.'

Percy Peach kept his face very straight. If this was going to be gibberish, it might be important gibberish, if it offered any clue to the death of Annie Clark. 'And what particular form does this magic take?'

Katherine smiled. 'If you're expecting black masses and Satanism, you won't get it from us. Our system is based on the supremacy of natural phenomena. We believe that nature both instructs and guides us, if we will only listen.'

Lucy Blake said, 'I seem to remember learning that Wordsworth believed in something very like that.'

It was Katherine Howard's second surprise in three minutes. A bright girl, this woman she had thought might be just here for the ride with her superior officer. Katherine wondered for a second if things might have turned out differently for poor Anne Marie Clark if she'd had the extra brightness and experience of this girl with the earnest face in its frame of chestnut hair. 'Wordsworth is interesting. Perhaps he might have become a Wiccan, if he'd been born a hundred and fifty years later. We take it further than fluttering and dancing with the daffodils, mind you. We take in all natural phenomena. Celestial objects such as the sun and the moon and terrestrial forces such as water and fire are all part of a whole.'

'And how does this manifest itself? How does it affect what you actually *do*? How did joining your group affect the life of Annie Clark?' Peach let a little of his impatience come out in the series of quickly spoken questions.

'I can't tell you that. You'd need to ask *her*! – which of course you cannot do.' Katherine nodded grimly as she was forced to acknowledge their problem. 'It's not easy for me to put myself into the thoughts of someone nearly thirty years my junior, but I'll do my best. I think people tend to come to Wicca from two broad but very different areas. There are those who have weighed the conventional religions and found them wanting, and yet feel there is something beyond the everyday world we see around us. That is how I became interested.'

She glanced at them, looking for a reaction, but they were too well versed in their techniques to give her one. 'And then there are those who have never had any strong religious belief at all, and thus feel a need for something supernatural, some belief which suggests a better world than the sordid one around us. Most of this group are younger people, and I'd say that this was the need that drove Annie Clark towards Wicca.'

'And would you say that she was an impressionable young girl?'

'Yes. Twenty-three years old, but young for her age.'

This at least was pleasingly definite. 'How well did you know her?'

'Not at all, until she came here; but quite well, by the time of her death. That may seem strange to you, Chief Inspector, but belief cuts through a lot of flummery. Annie had originally thought of witchcraft as the work of crones who met secretly at night, indulged in cannibalism and orgiastic rites with the Devil, and performed ceremonies of black magic. As I disabused her of such notions, we became quite close.'

'Have you any children of your own, Mrs Howard?'

'Why do you need to know that?' She was immediately prickly.

'Because this is a murder enquiry. We need to know all about the lives of the people nearest to the victim at the time of her death. You have just indicated that you were one of them.' He managed to deliver it without clichés, without any air of boredom, though he had had to put these arguments many times over the years, to a vast range of people.

She looked at him hard, then gave him an unexpectedly friendly smile. 'All right. I'm a widow. I run my late husband's business, which involves the provision of temporary staff in all sorts of office and cleaning situations. We had one child, a son. He's now in America and I don't see very much of him. And yes, it is possible that Annie Clark saw something of an elder and a guide in me. That was perhaps inevitable.'

A quick, intelligent woman this, who would miss very little in those around her, and would only give them what she chose to give. Peach said, 'Thank you for your frankness and understanding.' But he was already thinking of what she might be concealing beneath that calm and competent exterior: that was what being a detective did to you. He said, 'You mentioned worship of the Goddess. What does that involve?'

'The actual details of our prayers and incantations must remain secret. I couldn't reveal them without the consent of other members of the group.'

'So you operate under a cloak of secrecy?' Like the bloody Masons, thought Percy Peach.

'Not at all. You are welcome to come and join in any of our meetings, to witness and take part in our prayers to the Mother, or Triple Goddess, and the Horned God who is her male counterpart. Provided only that your interest is genuine. We have to guard against mischief-makers, as you can perhaps imagine.'

Indeed I can, thought Percy. I can just imagine some of our Brunton thugs muscling in on impressionable young witches. Finding it difficult to reconcile this seemingly very practical middle-aged woman with horned gods and triple goddesses, he said abruptly, 'Who do you think killed Annie Clark?'

'I've no idea. I should point out, of course, that there is no reason to think it was one of our coven.'

'But you can't rule it out.'

'Of course I can't. You know that. But Annie had a life in the world outside this house. It is my belief that you will find your murderer in that wider world.'

'Didn't you think it odd when Annie Clark suddenly stopped attending your meetings?'

'I did – very odd indeed, in view of the fact that she had established a close relationship with us.'

'And with you in particular.'

'Perhaps. If you're asking me if I was hurt, then yes, I was. But I haven't lived to the age of fifty-one without receiving greater hurts than that in my life.'

Lucy Blake thought of her own mother and how she would react if her daughter suddenly vanished. This woman was not the girl's mother, but she had already confessed to establishing some sort of intimacy with her. Lucy said, 'Did you not think of reporting Annie's disappearance to the authorities?'

Katherine Howard looked for a moment as if she were about to take offence. Then she controlled her anger and said, 'To the police, you mean. I wasn't her next of kin, you know. Annie Clark had a mother – and a boyfriend, recently acquired, to whom she seemed very attached. I thought that the most probable reason for her sudden absence from our meetings was that she'd gone off somewhere to begin a new life with him.'

'Wouldn't it have been hurtful if she'd done that without even a word to you about what she planned?'

'I've already indicated that it was painful. And of course I wish with the benefit of hindsight that I'd reported the poor girl missing at the end of September. But I thought she might have gained a new set of beliefs, perhaps subscribed to one of the major religions after all. She was still very young in many respects, as I told you. Her mind was still at what you might call a formative stage, I think, as far as things like philosophy and serious beliefs were concerned. I thought she might not have wanted to confront me and argue with me about deserting Wicca. And if I'd reported her as a missing person, would you have done any more than make a note of it and send me away?'

Peach looked hard into the strong, determined face for a moment, as if he was going to argue with her. Instead, he said, 'Probably not, no. Unless you could have given us any reason to suppose that her safety was at stake.'

'Which I couldn't have done.'

'What about the other members of your group? Did Annie Clark form close relationships with them?'

'With the coven, you mean? We're not ashamed of the term, Chief Inspector. Yes, she did. We were a much larger group at one time, as I said. But at the time when Annie disappeared, there were only four of us, including her. So we all got to know each other quite well. But it's not just a matter of numbers. When you have common beliefs, when you worship the Triple Goddess and the Horned God together, when you pray together and hope together and work for a better world, you become very close.'

'As you know, we took all your names and addresses last night, and we shall be interviewing your fellow Wiccans in the near future. You've already accepted that we have to include them as suspects. Now I'm asking you again: do you think one of them killed Annie Clark?'

It was like a slap in the face, and she recoiled as if she had been hit. 'No. Of course I don't. I just told you that.'

'Someone killed her, Mrs Howard. And statistically, the odds are twenty to one against this being a random killing. The odds are overwhelmingly that Annie knew her attacker, and very heavily that it was someone with whom she had quite a close relationship.'

'I don't think it was anyone I know. I refuse even to speculate about it.' She was flushed a little with her emotion, staring hard at the carpet between them.

Peach ended the meeting as stiffly as he had begun it. 'If anything occurs to you which may have a bearing upon this death, it is your duty to get in touch with us immediately.'

She said, 'That would be not only my duty but my inclination. I want you to put away whoever killed poor Annie for a long time, Chief Inspector Peach.'

Peach decided as they drove away that he liked Katherine Howard. He wondered if it denoted some deficiency in his own personality that he liked feisty middle-aged ladies. This one had a lot of the qualities he admired. But those same qualities would equip her very adequately to be a murderer.

Eleven

Chief Superintendent Thomas Bulstrode Tucker was not a very good golfer. That, indeed, is a charitable understatement. Chief Inspector Peach would have said that he was a dreadful hacker. And this particular Saturday at the end of January, when the ground was frozen and a biting wind swept over the course from the north-east, would have taxed the skills of far more competent sportsmen than Tucker. His lack of ability was complemented rather than ameliorated by his choice of clothing. A golfer conscious of his frailties would have chosen something grey and self-effacing, and tried to pass unnoticed across the crowded landscape of human suffering.

Tommy Bloody Tucker had opted to clothe his lower limbs in bright-red tartan plus twos above salmon knee-length socks. The leaf-green sweater and bobble hat above these were relatively muted, but they clashed sonorously with what moved beneath them. This was a figure that needed to play good golf to redeem itself and quell unseemly hilarity.

Tommy Bloody Tucker was quite incapable of good golf.

Percy Peach, watching from the edge of the course, confirmed that to himself before advancing upon his chief and conveying upon him the broadest and most benign of his many smiles. 'Good morning, sir,' he called affably, as Tucker stooped beneath a frosted hawthorn to retrieve his ball.

'What the hell are you doing here?' Tucker shouted at him from beneath his emerald arm. After eight holes of torture on a frozen golf course, he had been thinking that things could not get any worse. Now the arrival of his chief inspector announced to him that he had not yet supped full of horrors. 'Can't I even get away from you on the golf course?'

90

It was a savage welcome, but more or less what Percy had expected. He looked suitably hurt and said, 'You said you wanted to be briefed, sir – indicated to me that you might come into the station on a Saturday, if you remember, sir.' Peach stressed by his inflection what an unusual departure from custom that would be, as he noted that Tucker's two curious companions were now within earshot. 'As you didn't turn up, I thought, when it got towards midday, that the mountain should come to Mahomet.'

'I forgot,' said Tucker, with the hue of his face turning towards the colours of his lower limbs. 'I have a lot to think about, you know!'

'Yes, sir, I can see that. Perhaps you should try lowering your right shoulder a little more at address.' Peach's smile was gone now, his face serious as a praying nun's, despite the muted titters from Tucker's playing partners. 'There have been *developments*, sir.' He gave full weight to every syllable of the word, then studied the leafless birches thirty yards to their left as if they might conceal hidden eavesdroppers.

'This is neither the time nor the place for a briefing,' said Tucker. Having retrieved his ball with some difficulty, he now topped it savagely along the ground and into the frozen ditch sixty yards ahead of them. 'Now look what you've made me do!'

'Bit of a lurch, that one, sir. Try to keep your head still as you take the club back.' Peach nodded sagely, ignoring the threat of apoplexy in his chief and the suppressed hilarity in their tiny audience. 'Won't take long, sir. I'll do it as you go along, if you like: I wouldn't want to interrupt your enjoyment.'

Tucker should have told him that all enjoyment had ceased with his arrival and that he was certainly not going to prolong his sporting ordeal in front of his junior officer. But, being a golfer, he was an incurable optimist. Despite a wealth of evidence to the contrary, he continued to believe that his next shot would begin a dramatic improvement in his play. Peach, who played much less than he did, was an eight handicap man, against Tucker's shameful twenty-four, but the chief superintendent could never bring himself to acknowledge their relative status in the game, especially in front of

91

witnesses. So he accepted Mephistopheles' suggestion that he should be briefed whilst he played on. It was a grave error.

The ice broke beneath him in the ditch as he retrieved his ball, so that one of his salmon stockings was now covered to the calf in an icy blackness. The green was within range, but he sliced his short iron wildly to the right and snarled, 'I can't score on this hole now. I'll pick it up!' He strode in peacock fury after the offending missile.

'We've now managed to compile a list of those people in the dead girl's intimate circle,' said Peach, pursuing his man relentlessly over the icy ground.

'About time too,' said Tucker automatically, ignoring the fact that things had really moved rather quickly in the circumstances.

'We have six people to follow up: an employer, a boyfriend, a flatmate, and a group of people with whom she spent important sections of her leisure time,' said Peach mysteriously.

'Leisure time. Why can't you come straight out and say what she did. Is there some sort of mystery about this?' Tucker examined his scarred ball, then took a new one reluctantly from the packet in his golf bag.

'They were quite a secretive group, sir. I did think at first we might have a Masonic element – which, as you know, would have given a high statistical probability that our killer would be found—'

'I don't want you repeating this tiresome theory of yours about Masons being more likely to commit serious crime,' said Tucker firmly, looking a little nervously towards where his companions were putting out.

'No, sir. Well, so far as I know, none of the people we are investigating is a Mason. Disappointing, I know, but—'

'Get on with it, and then get out of here!' said Tucker grimly.

'Expressed with your usual economy, sir. Well, the group I'm talking about are Wiccans.'

'Wiccans? What on earth are Wiccans?' Tucker stared suspiciously at his *bête noire* as his companions prepared to strike off from the ninth tee.

'Witches, sir.' Peach nodded as if instructing a backward child. The two long-suffering golfers, having now driven, showed renewed interest in the exchanges behind them.

'You mean you've interrupted my game of golf to tell me some nonsense about old women flying about on broomsticks and casting spells?' Tucker shook his head disbelievingly and teed his ball.

'Popular misconception, that, sir. This lot do believe in magic, though, they tell me. Gosh, you could do with a bit of magic, at the moment, sir, couldn't you?' This last was occasioned by Tucker's wild attempt at a drive, which disappeared irretrievably into a dense clump of brambles on their right. 'Bit of a waste of a brand-new ball, that one, sir.'

Tucker's long drawn 'Aaaaaargh!' of agony would have been identifiable only to fellow golfers. He turned to Peach and said with ominous control, 'And you think that one of these wild women might have killed this Clark girl?'

'Not all women, modern witches, sir. They include men among their number.'

Tucker looked at his two golfing companions as they waited patiently and had a sudden inspiration. 'Warlocks.'

'If you say so, sir. I was only trying to be helpful.' Peach's brow furrowed with hurt.

'Male witches. They're called warlocks. As I've no doubt you know very well.' Tucker hastily teed another ball and dispatched it along the ground with a galvanic heave. He glared at Peach and said, 'So what do you expect me to do about this?'

Peach studied him for a moment with his head on one side. 'You could try taking your right foot back a little at address and swinging more slowly,' he said thoughtfully.

Alan Hurst lived in a 1930s detached house which had once been on the very outskirts of the town. Suburbia had surrounded it now, but it was still the last house before the paved road ended and the route became a wide, stony track, which carried only dog-walkers and farm vehicles. The house's mature bricks stood out starkly and dramatically against the snow and the darkening blue of the winter sky when the CID visited Hurst in the twilight of January's last Saturday.

Peach and Blake parked their car and walked the forty yards up the drive, their breaths forming long funnels of white vapour in the still, freezing air. Hurst opened the door without their needing to ring the bell. The heat from within the house hit them like a wall of warmth, so that they both accepted his invitation to remove their coats as he led them into a sitting room at the front of the house.

Hurst was in shirt sleeves himself, and when Lucy Blake commented upon the welcoming warmth of the house, he said, 'We like to keep the temperature well up. My wife's an invalid, you see.'

It was a natural enough explanation to volunteer to them, but Alan felt immediately that he was playing Judith's illness as a card in the game, a ploy to give him some sort of psychological defence, as these two police officers and he played their respective hands. He knew he was being too sensitive: he could have taken them into the even more stifling room on the other side of the wall, and displayed the visual evidence of his wife's handicap, if he had really wanted to use her like that. But then she might have heard things that he didn't want her to hear: he didn't know how this meeting was going to go yet.

They said they were sorry to hear that, mouthed the conventional things that well-meaning people always offered. They didn't ask him what was wrong with her, and he found himself stumbling into an account of the progress of Judith's multiple sclerosis which he need never have given to them.

Then, signifying that the preliminaries were over, Peach said briskly, 'Well, you know why we're here, Mr Hurst. You were one of the last people to see Anne Marie Clark alive.'

Alan smiled, taking his time as he had told himself he would, feeling surprisingly confident. 'That seems a very dramatic way of putting it.'

Peach arched his eyebrows in the little gesture of surprise which any copper at Brunton nick could have told Hurst was dangerous. 'If you can tell us that lots of other people saw her later than you, that would be exactly the kind of information we want to collect, wouldn't it, DS Blake?'

'Indeed it would be – especially if Mr Hurst could furnish us with a few names.' She produced her tiny gold ballpoint

94

pen, deftly removed its top, and poised it expectantly over her small notebook.

'I'm afraid I can't be helpful in that way. I was just surprised when you said that I was one of the last people to see poor Annie Clark alive.'

Peach weighed this for a moment before he said, 'When did you last see her, Mr Hurst?'

'On Saturday the twenty-third of September. You said you would want to know that, so I checked my records at work. She worked on that Saturday for me. She used to do alternate Saturdays.'

'In your travel-agency shop.'

'Yes.'

'Did she give you any reason to think that she was proposing to leave that employment?'

'On the contrary, she seemed very happy. I was certainly happy with her work. She was doing very well. She'd made herself very well informed about the business and tourism generally. She was a bright girl.'

'Too bright not to be ambitious, perhaps?'

It was a chance to distance himself from her, this – a chance to show that he was a considerate employer, who saw things objectively. He felt a little spurt of excitement as he realized how coolly his mind was working: that must be the adrenaline which improved the performance of sportsmen under pressure.

He nodded a little and took his time as he said, 'I know what you're getting at, Chief Inspector. Would a bright girl be content to stay in a small shop for ever? My answer to that is probably not. But she'd only been with me for three months or so, and she was learning all about the business. And she said she enjoyed working for a small firm rather than the large and faceless corporation she had been with before she came to me. Of course, it's possible that after a year or two she might have wanted to spread her wings in a bigger company, to go for the career and promotions which would only have been possible there. But I like to think that I wouldn't have stood in her way if it had come to that, that I might even have been encouraging her to move on, if I'd felt that was the best thing for her.'

For Percy Peach's taste, it was a little too oily, however deprecating the smiles with which the man accompanied it. But it might be perfectly genuine, in character. He didn't know yet whether this man was genuinely a moralizing windbag, or whether that was a front he was adopting for his own purposes. He said, 'Our information is that Annie Clark died around the end of September.'

'So she probably lived for a week or so after I had last seen her.'

'No, Mr Hurst, we certainly can't say that – not as yet.' He looked at the wedding photograph on top of the display cabinet beside them, saw a young and innocent-looking version of the man opposite them with a pretty, willowy girl in white, who was as tall as he was. 'Do you know what happens to a corpse when it is left undiscovered for four months?'

'No. And I hope you aren't about to tell me.'

Peach considered the matter. 'It deteriorates. Grubs move in, develop, and move out, unless some predator comes to claim them. Birds remove the eyes from the body. Then the rats move in, usually.' He studied his man's face with every phrase. 'After four months, what's left is mostly black and you can hardly tell whether it was male or female.'

'You have the advantage of me, Chief Inspector. I've never seen a corpse, except after it's been subjected to the embalmer's arts. But I really can't see the point of your—'

'Impossible for even the best pathologists and the best forensic-science people in the country to say exactly when a four-month-old corpse was dispatched from this life, you see, Mr Hurst. So the young woman you described as "poor Annie Clark" could have died anything up to a month after you last saw her. Or she could have died on that very day: Saturday the twenty-third of September.'

'Yes. I realize that I was naïve in my assumption that she died a week after I'd last seen her. But you really can't expect me to—'

'What was your relationship with the deceased, Mr Hurst?'

He was shaken now. He could feel his heart thumping. He had expected neither this aggressive line of questioning nor this abrupt introduction to the most important area of all. 'I think I've already indicated that. I found her a good worker. She was both intelligent and diligent. In my opinion, she had the prospect of an excellent future in the travel industry, if she wanted it.'

'And if someone hadn't strangled her and hidden her body in that ruin up on the side of Pendle Hill.'

It was brutal, and it was clear that this policeman was being deliberately so, in an attempt to ruffle him. Alan decided it was time for a protest about these tactics. 'I hope you're not suggesting that I killed Annie and took her body up there, because I should have to—'

'Your suggestion, Mr Hurst, not mine. You're telling us that Annie Clark was killed somewhere else – in Brunton, perhaps – and then transported to that deserted farm in a vehicle of some kind.'

'Well, wasn't she?'

'Don't know, Mr Hurst. From what was left up there, it was impossible to tell whether she was killed on the spot or whether the corpse had been brought there from somewhere else entirely. It's interesting that you should be so sure that the latter is what happened. Why are you so certain of that?'

'I'm not. I just assumed it must have happened like that.'

'You weren't certain of it?'

'No, of course I wasn't.' Alan told himself that it was just a trick – that this man who seemed so certain was only trying things on. Perhaps he did that with everyone. Yes, that was it: he must be the hard cop, and this pretty girl would come in with the soft-cop routine, when it suited them. Well, he'd be ready for that. He said to Peach, 'I'm an innocent citizen, doing my best to help the police. You really mustn't treat me like a hardened criminal.'

Peach gave him a smile which held no hint of embarrassment. 'I'm sorry about that, Mr Hurst. But do bear in mind that one of the many people we shall be speaking to over the next week or so will almost certainly be a person guilty of the worst of all crimes.'

'I appreciate that. It can't be easy for you, when a murder isn't discovered until four months after it's happened.'

'Thank you. I don't think you answered my question about your relationship with the deceased girl. You told me something about her abilities and her prospects, but not about your own relationship with her.'

'Professional.' Alan hoped he didn't sound too satisfied as he delivered the word he had decided upon before they came. 'I had a high estimation of the potential of Miss Clark, as I've already indicated. And I trust that she in turn found me an understanding and considerate employer.'

Peach nodded slowly, listening to the phrases as if he hoped to detect some subtext beneath them. 'But you worked very closely together: Annie Clark was your only full-time employee.'

How could they know that? Had they researched him before they came here? Or was it merely a reasonable deduction for a small business? He forced a smile, as lightly as he could. 'That is correct, yes. We have to be open every Saturday, and I employ part-time assistance to cover all the hours we need, but Annie and I were the only ones who worked a full week in the shop.'

'And as you've already indicated, you have a difficult domestic situation.'

'Yes. What has that to do with anything?' It was the first time he had really lost his composure. He heard his voice rising on the question.

'I've no idea. I was hoping you would tell me that, Mr Hurst. I would imagine that you must surely have put a great deal of trust in Miss Clark, once you had discovered how competent she was – that you must have come to rely upon her quite a lot.'

'Yes. I found that I could trust her to work on her own when I needed her to.' They surely couldn't know anything about the lucrative sideline he had developed, which took him increasingly out of the office. He added rather lamely, 'Annie was very helpful, whenever my domestic situation needed my time.'

'You sound as if you had grown very close to her? Would you say that your relationship went beyond the merely professional?'

He had taken up Alan's word and delivered it back to him with what sounded to his sensitive ears something like a sneer. He forced himself to take his time as he delivered the necessary clichés. 'No, of course it didn't. I'm a happily married man, Chief Inspector.'

Peach studied his face for two or three seconds, then nodded curtly. It was Lucy Blake who looked up from her notes and said quietly, 'Did you know that Annie Clark was pregnant, Mr Hurst?'

'No.' He didn't trust himself to say anything more as he concentrated upon his look of surprise. They seemed to expect something else from him, so he said eventually, 'She had a boyfriend, you know.'

'We do, yes. As a matter of fact, it was left to him to come forward on Wednesday and tell us that she had gone missing. He was instrumental in establishing her identity for us.'

'Well then, isn't it probable that he was the father?'

'He says he wasn't, Mr Hurst. Have you any idea who else might have been the father?'

'No.'

'You obviously got to know Miss Clark very well – professionally, at least. Would you say she was the kind of girl who slept around?'

He felt an overwhelming urge to tell this girl with the striking ultramarine eyes that Annie had been that sort of girl, to broaden the field of suspicion, to leave them floundering among the testosterone of Brunton's youth culture. But they would be talking to others, as well as to him – they'd already reminded him of that. He would only draw attention to himself if he said things out of line with what others were going to say. And despite all his instincts to distance himself from Annie, there was a small part of him that wanted to do its best to make sure she was well remembered. 'No. Annie Clark wasn't that sort at all. I'm very surprised to hear that she was pregnant.'

They left him then, with the usual injunctions to get in touch with them if anything significant occurred to him.

Alan Hurst spent five long minutes analysing their exchanges in that stifling front room before he felt calm enough to go back to Judith. It had been tougher than he'd anticipated, but he couldn't see that he'd given anything vital away.

Twelve

Jo Barrett loved her Saturday afternoons.

The best ones were when the Rovers were at home to a big team in the Premiership and much of her neighbourhood of Brunton was deserted. She could run to her heart's content then – exhaust herself, if she wanted to. It was unlikely that she would be spotted by the children whom she taught at the comprehensive during the week. Those who weren't at the match would probably be shopping in the town centre.

Jo left her outing until the edge of dark, when she was confident that she would have the roads to herself on this icy evening. Within a hundred yards of parking her car, she was on the grass, feeling the ground hard beneath her feet, dropping into the rhythm that she dreamed of in moments of stress at school, the steady pattern of physical movement that calmed her mind and assisted the processes of thought.

Jo Barrett was thirty-four now. She had given up all competitive running three years ago, and found to her surprise that she did not miss it. She had been a miler and a fifteen-hundred-metres specialist, and some said she had been unlucky not to go to the Olympics in both 1996 and 2000. She would have liked to go to Atlanta or Sydney, not just for the trip, but because it would have been, for her, the ultimate recognition of her prowess.

Like most middle-distance athletes, she found that she could have stretched out towards the longer races as she moved past thirty; she could almost certainly have had a real go at the five thousand and perhaps even the ten thousand metres, if she'd chosen to do it. But you had to be a full-time athlete nowadays to go right to the top, and nothing but the top really interested Jo Barrett. And you had to be single-minded, almost paranoid, about training and times and success, which was easier when you were eighteen than when you were past thirty.

Jo wore the black vest and shorts she had always chosen for her running, the garb which had made her a distinctive figure at athletics meetings and on television during her peak years. And today, as a concession to the rigours of January, she had put on black leg-warmers as well. As day dropped into evening and the first stars appeared in a clear sky, she was a distinctive, swiftly moving figure, dark against the horizon for any who might be abroad to observe her.

Jo Barrett enjoyed the tempo of her running. She knew she could outdistance all of the women and most of the men who chose to exercise like this, but she relished the very fact that this was not competitive, that she was here solely for her own satisfaction and enjoyment. She grinned to herself in the near-darkness: not many people would call this enjoyment, this pushing yourself to the limit as a freezing day moved into an even colder night. But she had always been exhilarated by it, always enjoyed pushing herself hard. Years ago it had been against the clock. Nowadays it was just against herself, against the elements, and sometimes, she felt, against a hostile world.

She hit the tempo she wanted, held it for two miles and more, felt the exultation of her fitness, as her heartbeat rose and the blood pulsed through her racing limbs. She was breathing hard but easily; in the days of her track racing, she would have had resources left for a sprint finish. And on that thought, she raised the rate of her steps, keeping the long stride-length which had always been her strength, not cheating to give herself the illusion of a faster pace.

She pushed herself harder than she had done for months over her last three hundred metres, feeling the beat of the blood in her head, calling on that masochistic streak which all athletes must have to push her towards her limits. She was flying now, flying fast over the ground her eyes could scarcely see, leaving her imaginary pursuers toiling hopelessly behind her. She was almost through the pain barrier; she felt her control of her limbs and her stride failing at the last, as she drove herself over the final thirty yards to the stile which was her finishing post.

And then she was leaning in a state of near-collapse on the gate, her breath coming in huge, gasping wrenches, her shoulders twitching uncontrollably. As her breathing eventually slowed, she wondered for a moment what the strange, uneven sound around her head was. Then she realized that it was her own wild laughter, her own exultation in this strange and private achievement.

She moved back on to the metalled road, walked unevenly for a moment in her exhaustion, then forced her body back into some sort of rhythm and trotted the short distance to her car. You had to wind down, especially on a night like this, if you were to avoid the risk of pulling muscles. She still had it in her, Jo Barrett; she could still be up there with the best in Britain, if she chose.

Jo was still giggling a little to herself with the excitement of her run when she turned the Audi into the drive; and, as usual, exercise had clarified her mind. She knew now what she must do, as clearly as if it had been outlined for her in a book of instructions.

She took the photographs and the letters from the little drawer in her bedroom and went through to where the wood-burning stove glowed softly in the lounge. The glow flickered into flames as she opened the door of the stove. She put the letters in first, watching them swiftly disappear into the flames. She paused only for a second before she slid the photographs on top of the red heat.

Jo Barrett watched the smiling face of Annie Clark curl swiftly at the edges, then disappear for ever in a tiny twitch of smoke.

Matt Hogan considered that he was quite an authority on policemen. The boyfriend of the late Annie Clark had lived rough in his time, which meant inevitably that he had met a lot of policemen.

He had never met one like Detective Chief Inspector Peach.

Matt lived in the first block of flats that had been built to replace the slums cleared in the nineteen-sixties. It had been a symbol of hope at the time, a solid token of the brave new Brunton world which was to come. It had not remained so for long. Architects had discovered too late that creating a bold new skyline was not enough, that people did not like living in aseptic rabbit warrens.

Forty years later, the flats were even more undesirable and considerably less hygienic. People lived as tightly together in them as in the old terraced houses they had replaced, but did not support each other in the way they had in the hard days of the cotton mills.

In the first decade of the new century, you kept yourself to yourself in Wilson Square. You didn't look for help from your neighbours, and you didn't enquire too closely into what they were doing, if you knew what was healthy for you. 'Streetwise' was a word that might have been invented for the area. Matt Hogan prided himself on being streetwise, and in most respects he was.

That didn't make him in any sense a match for Percy Peach.

The chief inspector bounced into the flat like a solid-rubber ball, glanced with distaste at the flickering gas fire and inspected the healing scar on Matt Hogan's forehead closely but without comment. He said, as though it were an accusation of indecency, 'You've already met DS Blake.'

'Yes. And a Detective Constable Pickering.' Matt was glad he'd remembered the name of that lanky sod. Show them he was on the ball, that would.

Peach nodded, considering his man as if he was something he'd just scraped off his shoe. 'Nice chap, Gordon Pickering. Bit *too* nice, for my taste, but there it is.' He wouldn't reveal the fact that Pickering, like all of his team, had been carefully selected by Peach himself. 'We need to talk to you again, Mr Hogan. Now that we know a lot more about our murder victim. Now that certain discrepancies in the evidence are beginning to emerge.'

Matt found his fingers straying nervously to the scar on his forehead, which had reached the itchy stage of healing. 'Perhaps I should remind you that I came into the police station of my own free will.' The words were so starchy, so different from his normal speech, that they sounded odd. But that wouldn't matter, if it was the right way to deal with this cocky bugger.

Peach smiled at him, said nothing for so long that Matt

103

wanted to say something, just to fill the silence. He glanced at pretty Detective Sergeant Blake, sitting silently and watchfully beside Peach on his battered sofa. That delicious woman had done most of the questioning when he had gone into the station, and he had somehow expected that it would be so at this second meeting. He licked his dry lips and said, 'I came in to tell you about Annie. To tell you that the body you had found might be her.'

'Of course you did, Mr Hogan. And we're very grateful – of course we are. We'd be even more grateful if you told us that you'd killed her, of course.'

'Of course I didn't kill her! It's a bloody liberty that you should even suggest that! I've got rights, you know.' He was suddenly quite near to tears. It went oddly with his hard man's appearance. He'd had his hair cut very short since he had been into the station on Wednesday. His head was almost shaved, so that its thin covering of black hair was scarcely longer than the stubble on his unshaven face, and the scar on his forehead stood out even more lividly.

'Of course you've got rights. And of course we shall respect those rights. Make life very difficult for policemen, rights do. We like clear-ups, you see. We make a career out of clear-up rates, in CID, so if you'd been prepared to confess to a murder, it would have made our day.' He smiled wistfully at that thought, then studied his man for a moment, drumming his fingers upon his knee as if he needed some outlet for the violence simmering within him. 'So you didn't kill Annie Clark. But you were her boyfriend, it seems. Boyfriends are always suspects, when a young woman is murdered. I expect you realize that.'

'I suppose so.' Matt wondered why he was agreeing with the man.

'Serious, was it?'

Matt nodded earnestly. 'We were an item.'

'Ah, an item. And how long had you been an "item"?' Peach pronounced the word as if it represented a strange new semantic discovery for him.

'About a week.' The pale face reddened right up into the scalp, too visible beneath its scanty covering.

Peach paused to relish this reddening, then said with deep

disappointment, 'It's not long, is it? Are you sure that the lady would have agreed that you were an "item"?'

'Yes. We were serious.'

'Because our problem is that the lady isn't here to deliver her own opinions, and people say all sorts of things about what dead people thought. Some of them quite contradictory.'

Matt wondered, as Peach had known he would, exactly what it was that other people had been saying about his dead girlfriend. He repeated sullenly, 'It was me who came forward. Me who told you that it was Annie Clark.'

'Indeed it was. Took you rather a long time to come forward, though, didn't it? Four months or thereabouts.'

'I didn't know where she'd gone, did I? And I wasn't next of kin.' He couldn't say that where he came from you told the police nothing, that you didn't volunteer things until they were dragged out of you; that it had been quite an effort for him to set foot inside the Brunton nick.

'You see, policemen – and even nice policewomen like DS Blake – tend to be suspicious devils, Mr Hogan. A police officer might think it possible that you didn't report Annie Clark missing until you knew that she had been found and the CID were about to descend upon you.'

'It wasn't like that.'

'Descend upon you as the murder victim's boyfriend – who we've already agreed is always a strong candidate for a murder charge.'

Matt Hogan wasn't sure whether he'd agreed to that or not. He ran his hand over his scalp, feeling the still unfamiliar sensation of the prickle of his coarse, close-cut hair against his fingers. He said desperately, 'It's those bloody witches you should be harassing, not me!'

'Had a lot of girlfriends, have you, Matt?'

This was the woman, using his first name as the squat bugger had not done, trying to trap him by different methods, with her sympathy and her soft voice and her green eyes and her smiling, perfect teeth. Well, he knew all about things like that. 'I've had a few. Most people have, when they're twenty-three.' He tried to make it sound immensely mature and experienced.

'And what about Annie?'

'I expect she'd had a few boyfriends.'

'But you don't know?'

'I told you: we'd only been an item for about a week when she disappeared.'

She made a note of something in her neat, small hand. He couldn't see what it was that she was writing. It was Peach who said harshly, 'Slept around, did she, Annie Clark?'

'I don't know what right you have to—'

'Right of officers investigating a murder, son. Makes its own rules, murder does. And lots of twenty-three-year-old girls have slept around a bit. Way of modern life, some of them would call it.'

'Annie wasn't like that.' His lips set in a tight line.

'Thought you didn't know, one way or another. Because you'd only been an "item" for a week.'

Matt wondered how that word which had seemed to him so innocent could have been transformed into a stick to beat him with. He'd expected that they would take him up on what he'd said about the witches, but they seemed much more interested in Annie's relationship with him. He said wretchedly, 'I don't think Annie Clark was a girl who slept around. I'd known her for quite a while before she became my girlfriend, and I don't think—'

'How long?'

'What?'

'How long had you known her before she became your girlfriend?'

'I'm not certain of that. Three, four months perhaps.'

'And to your knowledge, did she have any serious attachments in that time?'

He didn't like that formal phrasing. It sounded too much like a prosecuting counsel in a court of law. 'No. But I didn't know everything she was doing during those months.'

'You admired her from afar.'

'If you like, yes.' He wondered if the man was mocking him, wondered how much he really knew.

'Because Annie Clark was pregnant, wasn't she? Three months pregnant.'

Peach and Blake were both watching him keenly, waiting

106

to see the effects of this bombshell dropped into the exchanges. But neither of them was sure when they compared notes afterwards whether this had come as a surprise to him. His face registered surprise, but it was like one of those grotesque masks that display only a single emotion. His mouth dropped open a fraction, and remained so; his eyes widened, but stared at the grubby rug between them, not at his tormentors. 'I didn't know that.'

'You weren't the father?'

'No. I couldn't have been.'

'So who was?'

'I don't know. I've no idea. It's news to me, this. Annie hadn't told me.' He went on repeating the fact, as if by repetition he could convince them.

Peach spoke more gently than at any time since he had come into the fetid, low-ceilinged room. 'Think about it, Mr Hogan. If you can think of anyone who might possibly have been the father, we'd like to hear from you. In confidence, of course.'

Matt Hogan sat staring at the gas fire, listening to its tiny puttering, for a long time after they had gone. It had been much worse than he'd expected. They'd probably be back to see him again, in due course: they'd hinted at that. But he'd know what to expect, next time. He'd prepare himself for it.

But at least the pigs hadn't got the key things out of him.

Thirteen

Heather Shields wanted to be a writer. Lots of people from her sort of background had made it as writers. You had to keep on trying, refuse to be discouraged, show that you had the determination. Then eventually, if you tried hard enough and showed that you were good enough, you'd win through.

Heather Shields was still very young and inexperienced.

The girl who had been Annie Clark's flatmate went to a writers' circle, where they showed their work to each other and read it aloud. Most of them were older than her, but they seemed to think that her work was really quite good. 'Promising,' someone had said, and the others had rather seized on that word; they'd all nodded their heads and agreed. Well, it was true that one of the older men had said that it perhaps needed a bit more of a rough edge to it; Heather wasn't quite sure what he meant by that.

Probably the man didn't really understand what she was trying to do. Heather wanted to be a romantic novelist. She'd always read quite a lot of romantic fiction, so she felt quite experienced in it, for a woman of twenty-three. People said you should know your market, and she thought she did. And there was an awful lot of romantic fiction published, so that had to be a good thing: lots of opportunity for a new young writer to break in.

The other thing that everyone in the group kept emphasizing was that you should write about things you knew about, draw upon your own experience. That wasn't always easy, when you worked in the packing department of a mail-order firm, with five other women who led lives rather like yours, when you spent most of your day at a computer, fulfilling routine tasks and sending out standard letters to clients.

Then this great slice of real drama had fallen into her lap, or been dropped there deliberately by a fate which wanted her to be a writer. First of all, she'd had the trauma in her own life, with her boyfriend ditching her. It had been too painful to write about, at first. But Heather knew that that was the amateur's reaction to personal tragedy. The proper writer had a splinter of ice in her soul, a detachment, which would enable her to use an experience like that, to make it the material of successful, publishable writing.

She'd made several attempts already at writing up this passionate experience, at capturing the ecstasy that had gone before and the pain of rejection. She hadn't quite pinned it down yet – not to her own satisfaction. But being self-critical, being prepared to revise and rewrite until you had it perfect, was part of the writing process, everyone said.

Besides, this even greater shock, this even greater gift to a writer, had come so shortly after her rejection that she must be meant to use it. There were very few people in the world who had a flatmate disappear from the face of the earth because she'd been murdered. You could surely make something out of that, even if it was not at first sight the stuff of which romantic novels were made. You must observe everything that went on, store it away, make notes on what was happening and how you felt about it at the time. And you must put yourself in the place of the central character, Annie Clark. That way, you could come up with it fresh as paint when you chose to integrate it into your fiction in due course.

Heather Shields had taken a day off work on Thursday, so that she could watch the scene-of-crime team at work in her flat. She explained to them that they wouldn't find much, because she'd put Annie's things into a bin bag and taken them to her mother's house in Preston. She'd had to do that, to make the place ready for the new flatmate she had needed to share the rent. She'd told Chief Inspector Peach all about it. They'd nodded, said they'd already been told that, that even so they had to search the place, just in case something turned up. They'd given her the impression they were just going through the motions, the three civilians and the single police sergeant who was in charge.

Heather had watched them taking photographs and

fingerprints and fibres from the carpet beneath the bed in what had been Annie's room. She'd followed them into the bathroom and watched them go through the cabinet and put Annie Clark's nail varnish carefully into a plastic bag with a label.

And all the time Heather Shields had known that the thing which would really have interested them, that little red-backed diary of Annie's, was safely locked away in the bottom drawer of her desk at work.

A writer had to have her materials.

Jo Barrett lived in what had once been the entrance lodge for a great house, with an estate of forty acres. The mansion had long since gone, and housing estates sprawled over what had been the rolling acres of the estate, but the square, solid little stone cottage, which had once stood by the main entrance, had sturdily outlived the architectural splendours that had brought it into being.

Jo had emulsion-painted the walls in strong, dark colours when she had moved in, which gave a dramatic air to the interior of the place. The furniture was mostly antique and mostly mahogany. The pieces did not always match, but the prevailing dark-red sheen of the wood gave a harmony to the décor and reinforced the vivid effect of the strong colours on the walls behind the furniture.

At eleven o'clock on a bitterly cold Sunday morning, the black wood-burning stove made the surprisingly large sitting room pleasantly warm. Jo seated her visitors on the Victorian chaise longue which faced the fire and was exquisitely uncomfortable. She herself took the black leather recliner which was the only really comfortable chair in the room – 'My concession to the sybaritic lifestyle,' she assured them as she slid gracefully into it.

Percy Peach did not immediately sit down beside Lucy Blake. He walked across to the table beneath the window and looked at the pile of exercise books on the table. 'You teach at Brunton Comprehensive,' he said.

She knew it was a statement, not a query, so she added a little information of her own that he might not have. 'For the last eight years. Chemistry and general science. I used to do a little Latin as well, when I started there, but there isn't much demand for that nowadays.'

It was an unusual combination, but Jo Barrett was an unusual woman. She watched this short, powerfully built man without resentment as he walked across to examine the photograph on the wall above her sideboard. He said, 'Before your time, this.' Then he turned and smiled at her. 'Geordie, are you?'

'Yes. My dad framed that for me – said it would help me to keep the faith when I went to university and moved away from the area.' It was a large picture of the Newcastle United football side of the fifties: tough-looking, determined men in vertical black and white stripes. 'Won the Cup three times in five years, that team. We haven't won a lot since.'

'Joe Harvey and Jackie Milburn. Before my time, too, but my dad brought me up on tales of Tom Finney and Jackie Milburn.'

'Wor Jackie. His autograph's on the back of that print. My dad's first action every time he comes here is to check that picture's still hung straight. He's accepted I'm gay, now. But he'd cut me off without a word if I didn't sing "The Blaydon Races" and support the Toon.'

She was as black and white as her team's strip. She had a white polo-neck shirt above black trousers and black leather low-heeled shoes which emphasized the slim, muscular length of her legs. Her hair was short and very dark around an attractive, small-featured face. He smiled at her and said, 'You haven't got pictures of yourself breasting the tape.'

'Oh, but I have, Chief Inspector. I'm just not brazen enough to plaster them all over my living room, that's all. The second bedroom is full of them, and there are one or two in the loo.'

The places where your parents would see them and enjoy them, when they visited, he thought. He knew without any emphasis from her that the bonds of family were strong for this woman, though she might never have children of her own. He went and sat down next to his detective sergeant on the chaise longue, with his short, powerful legs splayed a little, so that he reminded Jo of one of the weightlifters at her athletics club. He said without any further preamble, 'How long had you known Annie Clark before she was killed?'

'Eight years.' She enjoyed surprising him – gave him a little smile before explaining herself. 'I taught her, Mr Peach. Took her through a GCSE in general science.'

'I thought she lived in Preston.'

'She did. But she'd started to attend Brunton Comprehensive before the family moved there, so she continued to attend. The Preston bus goes past the school.'

'Was she a good student?'

'Average ability, in my subject. Discovering herself at the same time as taking exams. It's a thing a lot of kids have to contend with. She was better at the arts subjects. But then a lot of girls have mental blockages about maths and science.'

'You seem to remember her very well.'

'I do. I have a special reason to. She had a pubescent infatuation with me. Fancied she was in love with me. That was in the year before her GCSEs. In case you should be in any doubt, I didn't respond to her or reciprocate her feelings. There was no scandal.'

'But it must have been awkward for you.'

She weighed the word for a moment. 'It was certainly embarrassing, yes. It's not at all unusual, as you're probably aware.' She glanced automatically at the woman with the striking red hair who was taking notes; the two gave each other cautious, reciprocal smiles. 'It's a very common feature of the later stages of pubescence. I was new to the school and it was my first experience of it here. And I had to be particularly careful, because of my own sexual preferences. I've never made a secret of them.'

'And do you think that your preference might have encouraged Annie Clark's fantasies?'

'I'm glad to hear you call them that – because that is exactly what they were at that time.'

He nodded slowly. 'How did you deal with it?'

'I spoke to the head. When Annie's mother came in for the parents' evening, we had a quiet word with her together. I think she was more upset by it than anyone else, including Annie. We assured her that these things were quite normal in adolescent girls.'

'And it didn't seriously affect Annie?'

She shrugged. 'Not as far as anyone could tell. Who can

really say what effect our adolescent experiences have on any of us? Annie Clark was dating boys not long afterwards. You'd need to ask her exactly how the episode fitted into her life as a whole; but of course, you can't do that.' For the first time since they had come into the house, she looked a little distressed.

'You kept in touch with her, after she left school?'

'No. I wasn't even aware that she was still in the area, until four months before she – well, disappeared.'

'And died.'

'So it now appears. I wasn't aware of that at the time.'

He wondered why she found it necessary to stress that. 'You'd better tell us how she came into your life again.'

Jo Barrett stretched out her long legs and crossed them at the ankles, studying her feet for a moment, as if she wished to emphasize how relaxed she felt. 'Unexpectedly. But then I should think she was even more surprised to see me than I was her. I met her at our Wiccans meeting when she joined the coven.'

'You didn't introduce her to the group?'

'No. That had nothing to do with me. She came along experimentally to her first meeting, as most people do. I've always presumed that it was Kath Howard who introduced her to the idea of being a witch. It was certainly Kath who told us who she was and introduced all of us to her when she came to that first meeting.'

'Which was when?'

'About the end of April, I think.'

'And you recognized her?'

'I don't think I did, no. People change a lot between sixteen and twenty-three. She recognized me as the woman who had once been her teacher – came up to me rather shyly when we'd finished our prayers and incantations.' Jo wondered if she was being almost too light-hearted and dismissive; they were here about a murder victim, after all. She realized that she might not be very good at dissimulation. She did not have to practise it very often, these days. Those dark days fifteen years ago when she'd concealed her sexual preferences and trusted no one seemed to belong to another world.

It was Lucy Blake who said quite suddenly, 'How seriously did Annie Clark take these Wiccan beliefs?'

Jo looked at the younger woman coolly. You almost said 'all this witches nonsense' then, you smug bitch, she thought. It's what you think, isn't it? It's what most of you think, underneath this polite correctness with which you now have to mask everything. You don't dare say you hate gays, nowadays. You don't even dare to say you think witchcraft is rubbish, but you nearly did then. Well, I can play your games, as deadpan as you, my girl. 'Annie took her beliefs very seriously – the way all of us do who are involved in modern witchcraft. There are thousands more of us each year, you know.'

'I accept that. But not everyone is convinced. Mrs Howard told us that two of your group left shortly after Annie arrived.'

It was a reminder that they had talked to Kath, would no doubt talk to others. Thank you for the *aide-memoire*, pretty girl. 'That had nothing to do with Annie. They scarcely met her.'

'So you don't think that either of them should occupy much of our time. You don't think either of them would be involved in Annie Clark's death.'

'No. They wouldn't even remember her name.'

She let her contempt for the question come out in her answer, so that Lucy Blake reminded her softly, 'Someone killed Annie. Probably someone who knew her well. Possibly someone involved in your coven.'

'It seems ridiculous to me to suggest that. I follow your argument and I suppose I have to accept it, but it's inconceivable to me that any of us would be involved. I know the coven, and I know how fondly we all thought of Annie Clark.'

'And how did Annie Clark think of you?'

Jo made herself pause, told herself that she must not let the irritation she felt with this woman colour her replies. Peach was watching her as closely as a predatory bird, whilst his junior went through the standard questions: that man wouldn't miss any mistakes she made. 'Annie found our beliefs and our worship a great relief and a great release – as I did myself, when I discovered the centrality of nature and other Wiccan beliefs four years ago.'

114

Lucy Blake refused to be diverted into the intriguing cul de sac of Jo Barrett's beliefs. 'Would you say that Annie Clark was showing the enthusiasm of the convert?'

It was so exactly how Annie had been that she might have known her. Jo told herself that even if she didn't like her, she mustn't underestimate this girl, with her dramatic chestnut hair and her dark-pink lipstick and her freckles and her air of surprise. 'Annie was enthusiastic, yes. It would be fair to say she felt the zeal of someone who had discovered a true and convincing religion. But of course that would seem natural enough to us, as fellow believers.' She couldn't prevent edging her last sentence with the scorn she felt, and was annoyed with herself immediately for this weakness.

Perhaps Peach felt the tension between the two. He came back in abruptly with the bluntest of questions, 'So who do you think killed Annie Clark, Miss Barrett?'

She switched her attention back to the round face beneath the bald head. She was glad the enquiry had come from him: if it had come from Blake, she might have been tempted into asking how the hell should she know. 'That's for you to find out, surely.'

'Which we do by talking to people like you, Miss Barrett. By exploring what people think about the murder victim; about each other; about life in general. Sometimes they have very conflicting views on these things, and that is usually helpful to us.'

She did not like the way his black eyes never left her, had been studying her face for minutes on end now. She said derisively, 'And would you say that you've discovered anything this morning? Or that you've been wasting your time?'

He watched her for what seemed to Jo a very long time, before the slightest of smiles eventually lightened the bottom part of his impassive face. 'I'd say that we've learned very little indeed from you today. That in itself may of course be of interest to us, in due course.'

Just when she wanted him to go on, to enlarge on what he meant by that, he stood up, with one of those sudden movements which seemed an outlet for the energy surging within him. 'Let us know if you think of anything that may help us to unmask a murderer, Miss Barrett. Immediately.'

Jo Barrett tried to keep her contempt for them going when they'd gone, to convince herself that they were as bumbling and as clueless as she'd almost believed in their presence. She got herself a brandy, though she never drank at this time of day – felt the warmth of it coursing through her upper body, without it bringing the comfort that she had hoped would come with it.

She had given nothing away; she was almost sure she hadn't. But she was more disturbed than she had ever expected to be.

Sunday evening. Bitter winter cold on the hills outside. A fire flaming merrily in the front parlour of the old cottage at the base of Longridge Fell, and Agnes Blake entertaining her daughter and the man she was determined would eventually be her son-in-law.

It was one of the more startling facts of life that Percy Peach got on like a house on fire with Agnes Blake. Lucy had concealed the existence of Peach in her life for some months before she introduced him to her mother. That was partly because Percy concealed his better qualities as if he was slightly ashamed of them. Lucy knew perfectly well that her man would never have confessed to his sympathy for the underdog, his care for his juniors, his passionate integrity when it came to matters of right and wrong. In addition, Percy was almost ten years older than her, bald, aggressive and divorced – scarcely the qualities to endear him to a mother who had but one child in the world.

Yet Percy and Agnes had hit it off from the start, so absolutely that Lucy sometimes felt a little secret jealousy of their relationship. Lucy had not been born until her mother was forty, and her father had died when she was eighteen. He had been a notable league cricketer, and his photograph in cricket gear, a shy, smiling man with a sweater over his shoulder and six wickets under his belt, had occupied the place of honour on the mantelpiece of the parlour for as long as Lucy could remember.

Agnes Blake had never lost her enthusiasm for the game.

She had known of Percy Peach, before he had come into her house, as a dashing amateur batsman in the Lancashire League, who took on the West Indian fast bowlers who came there as professionals and used his dancing feet to dispatch them to the boundaries. When she had found that this man's father had insisted on christening him Denis Charles Scott, her cup had run copiously over. Agnes's hero had always been the laughing cavalier of cricket in the years of rationing after Hitler's war, Denis Charles Scott Compton. Her father had taken his young daughter to a bomb-scarred Old Trafford in 1948 to see one of the man's great innings, and Agnes had never forgotten it.

When a man whose own father had insisted on giving him the great man's surnames had come into her life, it seemed to Agnes Blake that some divine providence must be guiding her daughter's destiny. If only her daughter, normally an intelligent young woman, would accept how clearly this match was ordained for her, all would surely be well, and Agnes could begin to anticipate the grandchildren she craved. Cricketers, they'd be, with a bit of luck and a pedigree like that.

Percy was as complimentary as ever about her baking, and he proved his sincerity by consuming great quantities of apple pie, scones and sponge cake. 'You realize I only eat the salad so that I'll be let loose on your home baking, don't you?' said Denis Charles Scott Peach.

'Go on with you!' said Agnes Blake. She'd been brought up in the days when the man was the breadwinner in the house, when you 'liked to see a man eat'. And that suited her daughter's man just fine.

He insisted on washing up when they had finished their expansive and leisurely meal. 'Let him do it, Mum, for God's sake,' said Lucy. 'It's time someone called his bluff.'

So Percy busied himself at the sink, with his shirtsleeves rolled up to the elbow and the plates accumulating steadily in the draining rack on his right. And after five minutes, Agnes Blake came hesitantly into her own kitchen, as he had somehow known she would.

She gave him the smile which lit up her small, ageing face, then watched him for a moment or two before picking

up a towel and beginning to wipe the crockery. 'You shoul
use your proper name, not Percy,' she said. 'It's a prou
name, not one to be ashamed of.'

'You and I know that, Mrs Blake. Not many others d
though. Denis Compton is a name from the past for the young
sters. A lot of them don't even like cricket.'

Agnes shook her head sadly over this latest evidence
the decadence of modern youth. 'You gave up cricket muc
too early.'

There were times when Percy thought she was right abo
that. 'I was thirty-six, Mrs Blake. The eyes were beginnin
to go a bit. You have to be ready to duck nowadays.'

'Great waste, stopping too early. I hope it was nowt to d
with our Lucy.'

'Nothing at all; I'd given cricket up before I ever kne
her.' Percy hastened to reassure her against the awful thoug
that her daughter might have made a man give up cricke
'And I've still got my golf, you know.'

'Golf!'

Percy would not have thought anyone could hav
compressed so much contempt into a single syllable. As
noted practitioner of such techniques himself, he had
admire it. He came back hastily to the subject of his for
name. 'I've always been Percy in the police service. The
like a bit of alliteration, policemen.'

But both of them knew she hadn't come in here to tal
about his name. 'Get on well with our Lucy, don't you?'

'Almost as well as I do with you, Mrs Blake. She can
make cakes like you, though.'

'She can do it when she wants. When she doesn't thin
it's beneath her to do such things; when she's not going c
about her career.'

Percy lifted a pudding dish from the water, watched th
steam rising from it, turned it this way and that to make su
that it was spotless before consigning it to the drainer. 'She'
have a great career, your Lucy. She's a good detective. She'
go as far as she wants to go, will Lucy.'

Agnes balanced his pause with one of her own, drying th
dish with elaborate care before setting it on a pile with i
fellows. It was if she were following his steps in som

elaborate, old-fashioned dance. 'And how far will that be, Percy Peach?'

'I don't know. I've never discussed it with her. I'll give her all the help I can.' Chief Inspector Peach, the most feared man in the criminal fraternity of Brunton, was suddenly struggling for words.

'I'm getting old, Percy. It won't be long before I'm seventy.'

'No age at all, nowadays, Mrs B.'

'Young people always say that. As if they'd know. It's old enough, Percy Peach. I'm not planning to pop my clogs, but I'd thought to see our Lucy settled by now.'

He knew what she meant, of course. 'Settled' meant married, to Agnes Blake's generation, preferably with two or three kids by now. He said gently, 'She could do much better than me, Mrs Blake.'

''Appen she could. And 'appen she couldn't, in my book. But she only wants you, Percy Peach.'

'That's very flattering, Mrs B., but I'm not sure that we should be in here making assumptions about what—'

'Time you were getting her to settle down, Percy. Time I was looking forward to grandchildren.'

Percy, whose own parents were both dead, suddenly wanted to turn and take her into his arms, to hug her and to hold her tight for a long time. He did no such thing, of course. He said rather stiffly, 'I haven't a lot to offer Lucy, you know. I'm almost ten years older than her, divorced, and no oil painting. I'm grateful that she wants to be with me at all. I can't get over it, a lot of the time, if you want the truth.'

'And I know my daughter, Percy Peach. She wants you, not some empty-headed young go-getter. She told me how you wouldn't go for promotion, wanted to stay where you were, catching villains. She's got a lot of respect for you.'

'It's different nowadays, Mrs B. – women's lib and all that. I don't really feel I can take the initiative, with someone as beautiful and talented as Lucy.' He felt woefully inadequate. It was a feeling that was quite alien to him and no doubt very good for him.

'I'm not quite out of the ark, you know. I understand about careers for women and so on. I understand about the difficult

119

choices that modern women like Lucy have to make. But it's my belief that Lucy wants to marry you.' There: it was out in the open at last. She wasn't anything like as sure as she said she was – not about marriage, and all the word entailed; but never mind that.

Percy was floundering. He said, 'I was hoping she'd ask me to marry her, last year. On February the twenty-ninth. Hoping she'd take advantage of the old custom which allows women to propose.'

'Oh, you make me want to slap you, sometimes, you lot!' Her exasperation took in a whole generation. 'You think you've got everything worked out and end up making a mess of everything! She's not as modern as you think, our Lucy. She'd never have done that. Never be certain that you wanted her to do it. She'll have to be asked. And she'll say yes.'

Now he did turn and smile at her; snatched her towel and dried his hands; took her into his powerful arms and held her surprisingly hard against his barrel chest for a full half-minute.

'Thanks, Mrs B. I'll bear that in mind.'

Fourteen

Dermot Boyd normally took Monday mornings in his stride. He never had a weekend hangover, and he resumed his work at the office as if he had enjoyed the refreshment of a long holiday rather than a mere two days away. His colleagues, prepared to ease themselves back into work with a weary resignation, often found Dermot quite tiresomely sprightly.

This Monday, the last day of an eventful January for the Boyds, was different. The office would not have to endure his cheerfulness until later in the morning. The investigating officers in a murder enquiry were coming to see him at home. And he had things to explain to them.

They had offered to see him at the office, but he said that he would prefer them to come to his house, because it would be less embarrassing for him. The female voice on the phone had said yes, that would probably be better, in the circumstances. Dermot didn't like that last phrase.

He was impatient with Ellie, who was obviously nervous on his behalf. 'Just answer their questions straightforwardly,' she said, 'and then there won't be any trouble. Well, there can't be, can there?'

She sounded as if she wanted reassurance, and he tried to offer it to her; but really he just wanted her out of the house and off to her school, so that he could have half an hour to himself to prepare for this meeting. He ushered her to the garage door as if she were a visitor who had outstayed her welcome, waved to her from the front door as she reversed out of the drive, forced himself into a small answering smile as she waved.

But he couldn't settle even when he had the house to himself, couldn't make his mind work in the cool, logical way which his work at the office demanded and which he usually regarded as his forte. He washed the breakfast pots tidied the kitchen, strode into the sitting room and positione the chairs exactly where he wanted them for this exchange But every action seemed not an aid to thought but an excuse not to think, not to contemplate what they would ask him and what he would reply. The doorbell rang long before he was ready for it.

It was the detective chief inspector again, as the phon call had warned him that it would be – that man Peach whom he hadn't liked from the first. But at least he didn' have that tall black Police Constable Northcott with him thi time. Dermot was relieved that he wouldn't have to conten with that ebony, unsmiling, inscrutable stare, alongsid Peach's more mobile face. Especially when he found tha Peach was accompanied by a good-looking and voluptuou woman, with a bright smile and striking chestnut hair. Plai clothes for her meant a dark-green sweater and maroo trousers, which made a nonsense of the term.

She said, 'I'm Detective Sergeant Blake. We spoke on th phone.'

He said, 'We'll talk in the sitting room. It's the first doc on the right,' and paused for a moment to look at the polic car in the drive and the empty road beyond it.

That was a mistake. Before he could organize thing Peach had planted himself in the upright chair he had planne for himself, with its back to the morning light streaming i through the window. 'Need to clear up a few things, M Boyd,' he said without preamble. 'Hopefully we'll be abl to do it here and now. I say hopefully, but of course profes sionally DS Blake and I would be delighted if you burst int a confession.'

Dermot tried a little laugh, found there was no answerin mirth, and realized that what they said must be quite tru So he tried to talk it away. 'I appreciate that the public c Brunton are appalled that a young girl should have bee killed like this, but really—'

'Like what, Mr Boyd?'

'Well, I . . .'

'Details of the method of this death have not been mad

122

public. The press and the other media have been informed that the victim was young and female and that foul play is suspected. There has not as yet been an inquest.'

Dermot was not sure whether this was true or whether this squat little man was trying to rile him. He said, 'Figure of speech, Chief Inspector. I suppose I was still preoccupied with the preposterous idea that I might have killed this girl.'

'Preposterous, eh, sir? Well, I have to say, not so preposterous, from our point of view. Wouldn't you agree, DS Blake?'

The pretty girl pursed her lips, appeared to give the matter serious thought. 'I'd have to agree, sir. Not so preposterous, in the light of what we've learned over the last few days.' She looked hard at Dermot Boyd before she added, 'I'm speaking quite dispassionately, sir, you understand – looking at things from a purely police point of view.'

'Difficult for me to do that, of course. From where I stand, I can't see any reason why I should even be a suspect.'

'Really, sir?' Peach's black eyebrows arched impossibly high. 'I should have thought that the fact that you lied to us at our last meeting would have given you a clue about that. Never a good thing to do, lie to the CID. Makes us suspicious. Most murderers try to lie to us, you know.'

'Yes, I can see that. I'm sorry.'

'Sorry about which particular lie, Mr Boyd? Or is the apology supposed to embrace all of them?' Peach crossed his legs at the ankles and examined his gleaming black toecaps with approval while he waited for a reply. He was enjoying this, and saw no reason to disguise the fact.

Dermot forced a smile. 'You really must enlighten me about what particular felonies I have committed. I don't like games of cat and mouse.'

Peach, who enjoyed them thoroughly when he was the cat, nodded a couple of times, then rapped, 'You claimed you did not know Annie Clark, when in fact you knew her very well.'

'I wouldn't say—'

'Quite how well is one of the things we hope to establish this morning – along with other facts about you.'

'Look, Mr Peach, let me say that I'm sorry that I misled

123

you. It was very foolish of me. I see that now. Annie Clark was a member of our coven and had been for some time before she disappeared.'

'Which we discovered by our own methods, Mr Boyd. It's my belief you would not be confessing it so frankly now if there was any alternative for you.'

Dermot Boyd licked lips which had suddenly gone very dry. The man was right. And he didn't like his use of that word 'confessed'. 'I can only say again that I was very foolish. I can see that now, but when you're close to something, you don't see it so clearly.'

Peach nodded several times, as if preoccupied with his own thoughts rather than his victim's flounderings. 'When people lie to us, the interesting thing is often not so much the lie itself as the reason why they chose to lie. What would that be in your case, Mr Boyd?'

'The reason why I pretended to you that I hadn't known Annie Clark? Well, I suppose there were several reasons, really.'

'One would be a start.'

'Well, I panicked a little, to be frank. Don't forget I've never been involved in anything like this before. I suppose I thought that if you knew we'd been together in the coven, I'd become a murder suspect.'

'Which you did, as soon as we found out that you'd known Annie Clark quite well and specifically denied the fact to us.'

'Yes. I see that now. But there was another thing that influenced me. When I spoke to you on Wednesday, my wife didn't know anything about my involvement in the coven. She didn't even know that I'd taken up witchcraft. I've told her since then, but at the time I was trying to conceal it.'

Peach looked at him steadily. Without uttering a syllable, he contrived to give Dermot Boyd the clear impression that he found this a very feeble explanation of his conduct. Eventually he said, 'Tell us about the coven and its activities, please.'

'There is no secret about it.'

'And yet you chose to keep your membership of it secret, even from your wife.'

'Yes. People tend to regard witchcraft as something of a joke. They think we make models of people and stick pins in them to kill them, or cast evil spells to make people ill.'

'But you don't do that?' Peach's tone was studiously neutral, his words as much a statement as a question.

'No, of course we don't. We believe in the harmony of nature. We are also neo-pagans: we distrust the demands of traditional religions and eschew their doctrines and creeds.'

He looked rather nervously from Peach's impassive, attentive face to the younger one beside it, searching for some sort of reaction, fearing derision.

Lucy Blake looked genuinely puzzled as she said, 'But isn't your witchcraft itself merely a different sort of religion?'

'No. We practise magic, not religion. Our emphasis is on opening ourselves up to hidden powers. We use rites and chants and charms to do this, to bring ourselves into touch with ancient natural things, to put ourselves into alignment with what has always been and always will be, so long as man does not destroy it. We Wiccans have strong ecological and environmental concerns. We worship the Goddess and the Horned God, and other ancient deities that the established religions have tried to obliterate.'

He had spoken with passion for the first time. Peach watched him and thought, as he had often done before, that the man with a dull life who acquires a belief in the supernatural is the most extreme believer of all. Despite Boyd's protestations, this sounded to him rather like another religion, with less in the way of evidence to support it than some of the established ones; but he wasn't here to get into arguments of that sort. He said, 'And did Annie Clark agree with you on these things?'

Boyd, who had been staring past his visitors to the light behind them as he spoke with a missionary zeal, narrowed his vision and came reluctantly back to the real world and his immediate problems. 'She did, most sincerely. She didn't know much about us when she first came along, but she seemed as fervent as any of us by the time she disappeared.'

'And what was your own relationship with her?'

'There was no sexual liaison between me and Annie Clark.'

125

'I didn't suggest that there was, Mr Boyd. It's interesting that you should interpret my question in that way. As is the fact that you chose to conceal her existence from your wife. I'd simply like to know how closely you knew Annie Clark.'

'We knew each other well. When you are fellow members of a small coven, that is bound to be so. And Annie was very enthusiastic, very anxious to learn about witchcraft and everything Wiccans can offer to the world. I'd say we had quite a close relationship, because of our common interests and beliefs.'

'Closer than that between Annie and Katherine Howard, or between her and Jo Barrett?'

Dermot looked at Peach suspiciously, suspecting again that he was implying a sexual relationship; but the round face beneath the shining bald head was inscrutable. 'No, not closer. I'm aware that I'm currently the only man in the coven, but that was irrelevant. Annie asked me lots of questions, because she was anxious to learn about Wiccans – perhaps even a few more than she asked others, because I was the most recent recruit before her, and she knew I must have gone through the same process in acquiring belief.'

Peach nodded his satisfaction, as if the reply was exactly what he had expected. Dermot was learning that the chief inspector had an annoying habit of turning straightforward replies into what seemed like acknowledgements of guilt. 'Did you meet with her in other places than Katherine Howard's house?'

'I've already told you that there was no sexual aspect of our relationship.'

'Straightforward question, Mr Boyd. Needs a straightforward answer.'

Dermot told himself to control his anger, understanding that any loss of control would be playing into this man's hands. He forced himself to think before he spoke. These two would be talking to the others; perhaps, indeed, they had already done so. And they'd begun this meeting with the reminder that he'd already lied to them once. 'I had a drink with her a couple of times, after our meetings at Kath's house. These occasions were at her request, because she wanted to talk about aspects of our belief. She knew I was

126

an enthusiast and well informed: there was no more to it than that.'

'Have I suggested there was, Mr Boyd?'

'No. I think it was because of the very fact that there was no sexual link between us that she chose to talk to me. She felt that I was able to be dispassionate about these things.'

That implied certain things about the two women. Lucy Blake said gently, 'And what did Annie feel about the other members of the coven, Mr Boyd?'

'I think she got on very well with them. She was quite a lot younger than any of us, remember. You're asking me to speculate about what a girl who was eighteen years younger than me felt – a girl who had a boyfriend of her own age at the time of her disappearance. I might be quite wrong about her emotions, mightn't I? I spend my working life dealing with figures, not people. I'm not even a teacher, used to dealing with younger people and following what they feel.'

'As Jo Barrett is.'

'I was thinking of my wife,' he said stiffly.

Peach studied him for a moment, wondering if there was something here that Boyd was holding back, before he said, 'I want to go back to the day you discovered the body of Annie Clark. Nine days ago.'

'You've had all I can tell you on that. I know you asked me to go on thinking about this, but nothing further has occurred to me.'

'I see. That's a pity. Because we've talked to other people since then.'

That sounded ominous. Who did they mean? They'd talked to Ellie, but as far as he'd been able to ascertain, she hadn't said anything damning about him. He looked at his watch and said, 'Is this going to take much longer, Chief Inspector? Because I told the office that I'd be in by—'

'Not long at all, Mr Boyd – if you are honest and co-operative.' Peach's smile implied that he considered that unlikely.

'I am being very cooperative, Mr Peach. But I've said all I have to say about that Saturday afternoon on Pendle Hill. It wasn't a pleasant experience. It was one I'm doing my best to forget.'

'Well, that's understandable, I suppose, sir. All the more reason to ask you one or two questions, then, before your recall of things fades. First of all, why did you try to steer your wife away from that building where the remains were found?'

The question dropped like a grenade into the quiet room. Dermot told himself to take his time, not to be rattled by this man and his manner. 'I didn't. Simple as that.'

'Really? That is not the impression we have.'

'Then you have the wrong impression, Chief Inspector. The lace in my wife's boot broke. We looked for the nearest opportunity of shelter in a blizzard. That ruined building was the only one in sight.'

'Yes. DS Blake and I have been up there, and looked at the scene. We would agree with you that that derelict stone place was the only shelter available. All the more surprising, then, that you should seem reluctant to enter it.'

It could only be Ellie. Blast her, with her damned broken boots and her insights and her bloody detachment! 'If you're saying that my wife told you this, then I'm telling you that—'

'It was more what she didn't say than what she said, Mr Boyd. Are you denying that you tried to avoid going into that building?'

Dermot's instinct was to deny it, to tell them their suggestion was ridiculous. But he couldn't know exactly what Ellie had said, and they'd caught him out in one lie already. 'All right, I didn't want to go into that place. I had a bad feeling about it, that's all.'

'A feeling that it might house a four-month-old corpse?'

'No, of course not – nothing as tangible as that. A feeling of evil hung about the place, for me, that's all. I knew we were in the country of the Pendle witches. Perhaps that suggested something, I don't know. But Wiccans are in closer touch with nature and the elements than most people. It's what we are about.' He had no idea whether they believed him or not.

Peach let him go on, hoping he would offer them something significant before the words dried up. When they did, he said quietly, 'And when you went into that outbuilding, you scarcely looked at what your wife saw in the corner. You knew that it was a body. Knew that it was Annie Clark, didn't you, Mr Boyd?'

They expected him to fly into a denial. Instead, he said with quiet insistence, 'I didn't *know*, Chief Inspector. But my feeling of something evil increased as we went into the place. When Eleanor found a body in there, I was certain without looking at it that it was my friend Annie Clark – my fellow Wiccan.'

Peach studied him for what seemed to Dermot a very long time. Then he said, 'You can go to work now, Mr Boyd. Thank you for your help.'

Fifteen

The district nurse wished heartily that there were more people like Alan Hurst. She visited several chronic invalids in the course of her week, and none of them was better cared for than Judith Hurst.

Multiple sclerosis is a cruel disease, not least because of its unpredictability. No one had expected Mrs Hurst to deteriorate as fast as she had. Modern drugs and treatments had not worked as well for her as for most other people of her age. Before long, now, she would be permanently confined to a wheelchair, which always seemed especially hard when the victim was a younger woman; Judith Hurst was only forty-one.

Judith was patient and uncomplaining, invariably cheerful when the nurse called, though of course like everyone who suffered as she did she must have her moments when she railed against a cruel world, and those nearest to her caught the flak. That was par for the course, a necessary therapy for those stricken with illnesses like Judith's, and any other of the medical clichés you chose to use.

The only thing in which Judith had struck lucky was her carer.

Alan Hurst carried his loving care for his wife into practical deeds and had sustained it over years, in a way which the district nurse didn't see very often. No doubt it helped that he was younger than most of the people in such situations: too often she saw age getting the better of love, saw the carer borne down by the brutal realities of caring, and the spouse collapsing earlier than the invalid he or she tended. An overstretched National Health Service exploited carers much more than any of its paid employees.

The nurse had helped Judith with her bath, talking cheerfully through the small indignities that dependency brought, knowing that there would be greater ones over the next year or two. She helped Judith to dress and then left the exhausted invalid slumped in her chair, summoning up the energy to comb hair that still had a little of its original lustre.

Alan Hurst was waiting for the nurse, as he always did, in the spotlessly clean sitting room. That was where they conducted their weekly assessments of Judith's condition.

'She's getting worse,' he said, as if he divined that this was easier for his visitor than if she had to make the announcement. 'She's already looking forward to the spring coming and being out in the garden. But she won't be able to do anything there. Won't even be able to walk round, the way things are going.' He gazed through the window and down a lawn white with frost, his eyes moistening with the thought of the joyous springs that would not come again.

'How are you managing with the stairs?'

Alan gave her a grim smile. It was good to be talking to a professional, good not to have to pretend that things were better than they were, as he did all the time outside the house and some of the time when he was with Judith. 'With increasing difficulty, I'm afraid. She lets me help her now, which she wouldn't do at one time, but I'm always afraid of her falling. It's getting more and more difficult for her to keep her balance.'

'You might have to consider a stair lift. I know Judith didn't want it last year, but I think she'd accept it now.'

'She does. But I've got other ideas. Better ones, I hope. I'm planning a major extension on the ground floor – out from this room into the garden: two rooms, plus an en suite bathroom and a walk-in bath. A little purpose-built flat of her own.'

'That would be ideal. It won't be cheap, though.' Better to be realistic now than later: too many of her patients and their carers had ideas which collapsed when they found what it would cost to implement them.

'I know that. I've had a builder friend in to give a preliminary estimate. We'll manage it. The building society will extend the mortgage provision: they say it would make an excellent granny flat when the house is eventually sold. I'll find the rest, somehow. And it will be an investment, you see, adding to the value of the house. I've already sold it to Judith on those lines.'

Alan knew how he was going to raise the money, but he couldn't talk about that, not even to this helpful, supportive woman. Not to anyone.

She said, 'Well, that would be ideal, if you can stretch to it. Life isn't going to get any better for Judith, physically, as you obviously realize. The best we can do is to help her to enjoy the life she has.'

He went out to her car with her, saw her out into the lane. The district nurse was aware, as he waved to her cheerfully, that he could scarcely wait to get back into the house to his wife. She wished again that all her carers were like Alan Hurst. But the world wasn't like that.

Alan went back into the house to find that Judith had moved her wheelchair into the sitting room. He went and gave her a little kiss on the forehead, alarmed by how tired she looked at the end of the morning. 'Nice woman, that. I told her about our plans for the extension. She thinks it's a great idea. I might have the plans ready to show to her when she comes next week.'

'Are you sure you can afford it?' Judith's brow wrinkled in the way it had when he had first known her as a pretty, high-spirited nineteen-year-old.

'Yes, I'm sure. Don't you worry your pretty little head over it!' That was the phrase he had always used when they were first married and setting out on life together, and she smiled her recognition of it. Alan thought what a good thing it was that she had always trusted him about their finances. She would never know where the money was coming from to build this extension.

He went to the airing cupboard and got out the travel rug he had washed and dried on the previous night. He tucked it carefully round her hips in the chair, tried not to notice how wasted her thighs were becoming beneath her skirt. 'You'll need this. It's still bitterly cold outside. But you might want to go into the conservatory this afternoon, if the sun comes out.'

'Yes. I like looking at the frost on the trees. You notice

more detail, as your horizon gets narrower. That's good.'

He didn't suggest that she took up her painting again. They had endured a terrible hour a month ago, when she had found that she could not control her hands and fingers as she wanted to, had flung the brushes and her paints against the wall and screamed out her frustration with her failing body. Judith knew now as she often did exactly what he was thinking. She said, 'You'd better get off to work. You've been away for too long already.'

'Oh, don't worry about that. Anna Fenton will cope.'

'Good girl, is she, your new one?'

'Anna? Yes, I should say she is.' Alan nodded a couple of times, as if he had not considered the matter before. 'She's interested in the travel business and she's learned quickly. I'm quite happy to leave her in charge for short periods.'

One of the many frustrations of being in a wheelchair was that you couldn't look into people's faces when you wanted to; people spoke from above you or behind you. Unless you had them sitting in a chair opposite you, you couldn't study their faces, and, even with Alan's familiar voice, she needed to see the face as well. She often wondered exactly how close he got to the succession of girls who worked in the shop. He was still a handsome man, and he took a lot of care of his appearance, always checked himself in the mirror before he went out. Well, if he was having a bit of fun where he could get it, you couldn't really blame him, Judith thought sadly. And he was very good to her. It was better not to speculate about that other life he had outside, the life she never saw nowadays.

Alan was glad to get out of the stifling heat of the house and into the cold, clean air of the middle of the day. He drove carefully into the town, adjusting himself slowly to this second life he lived, slipping into the persona that was Alan Hurst the businessman. The transition was complete by the time he parked the car in the little yard behind Hurst Travel. He went breezily into the office and apologized for having taken so long over the visit of the nurse.

'That's all right. First things first. There was nothing I couldn't cope with. There are some very good offers coming in this morning for late bookings.' He went and stood close behind her chair, stooping a little to peer at the screen. He let his hand rest experimentally on the back of her chair, lightly touching the point where her sweater met her neck. She must surely have been conscious of it, but she did not move away, even leant back a little against his fingers, as she went methodically through the best of the bargains on her screen.

Alan said enthusiastically, 'Yes, we can certainly sell a few of those!' He moved his head closer to hers, still staring at the screen, catching the scent of her perfume. How young she was, how firm and wholesome was her flesh! He put one hand lightly on each of his assistant's shoulders as he stood behind her, gave her a little squeeze and said, 'I don't know how I'd ever manage without you, Anna Fenton!'

Heather Shields found that everyone who worked in the packing department wanted to talk to her about Annie Clark. It gave her a certain local celebrity for fully a week; people were much more interested in her as the flatmate of a girl who had been brutally murdered than they had ever been in plain Heather Shields.

When her companions heard that the CID were coming to see her at two o'clock on Monday afternoon, her status was heightened even further. The news ran round the whole works at lunch time, and she had to endure a succession of jovial but unoriginal remarks about her importance to the police. It was an eminence Heather could well have done without.

As she had feared, her inquisitor was to be Chief Inspector Peach, the man whom she had not liked at their first meeting. But he didn't bring the girl with him this time. He introduced the man who came into the works with him as Police Constable Northcott. He was tall, lean, inscrutable, and his police uniform fitted him as if it had been tailor-made. He was also very black, with close-cut black hair, and he looked as hard as nails. Heather looked as nonchalant as she could as seven pairs of eyes followed the trio into the supervisor's office, which had been volunteered for this meeting.

It was Peach who conducted things, whilst the black man noted her replies and looked at her as if she were already behind bars. It became an unnerving experience very early in the proceedings.

Peach said, 'We know a lot more about Annie Clark than when we spoke to you on Thursday. I told you that we would.'

'That's good, then. Have you found out who killed her?'

'No.' He smiled, as if she had amused him. 'We haven't come here to arrest you. We can set your mind at rest about that.'

'I don't know why you are here, though. I told you everything I knew about Annie last time I saw you.'

Peach nodded almost affectionately at her on that, as if he appreciated her spirited response. 'Not everything about yourself, though. Let me enlighten you a little about our procedures, Miss Shields. When a serious crime like murder occurs, we check up on the backgrounds of those closest to the victim. Not to put too fine a point on it, we check if they have criminal records, if they have been questioned by the police in connection with any previous incident or incidents.'

She told herself that she had known this would come up, that it didn't really mean a thing, that this was Britain, not Stalinist Russia, that they couldn't pin this on her because of her record. But she found she had lost a little of her confidence when she said, 'So I'm damned for ever because of things that happened years ago, am I? I'm never going to be let off the hook because of some stupid little quarrel which happened in my teens?'

Peach smiled the smile of a man with all the aces in his hand. 'Stupid, perhaps, Miss Shields: all crime is stupid, as far as I'm concerned. But hardly little. And not so very long ago, after all. You were nineteen at the time: although still technically a teenager, as you say, an adult as far as the law is concerned.'

'I wasn't myself at the time – wasn't fully responsible for my actions.' She fell back on the phrases her counsel had produced in court.

This time it was the black man who weighed in upon her. 'No defence, that, Heather. Being high on drugs is no defence in law, as you're well aware – not for a violent act such as assault with a dangerous weapon, to wit, a knife.'

There was no point in denying it. They'd have read all about it, probably even seen the psychiatric reports which had got her out of it with a probationary sentence. Perhaps they'd come here to arrest her now, to pin this one on her because she'd got away with that other crime. They were like that, the pigs: they didn't like you getting the better of them. She said, 'I don't deny that I was drug-dependent at the time, that I'd got into the wrong set, was going down-hill rapidly.'

The black face studied her inexorably. 'You were dealing.'

'That was never established. I was never charged with dealing.'

'No. But you were dealing.' PC Northcott was grimly certain, watching her with just the suggestion of a smile at the corners of his broad mouth.

'You can't be certain of that. You shouldn't come in here making allegations that you can't—'

'You sold cocaine to me.'

For a moment she thought it must be some sort of elaborate joke. But Clyde Northcott wasn't laughing. She said, 'I'm not admitting to anything. And I don't see what this has to do—'

'Outside Mullards. I used to work there. And I rode a three-hundred-and-fifty-cc Yamaha. You sold cocaine to me and to one or two other bikers.'

She remembered him now – a wild, feral boy whom no one had been quite at ease with, whose eyes had always looked manic, the whites of them glistening hard against the black of the rest of him. He looked very different in the police uniform, with his cap with the black and white squares laid carefully on the table beside him. The dark-blue uniform might have been made for him as a fashion suit, so absolutely did it become him. He smiled as he saw how disconcerted she was. Then he said quite gently, 'So we all have our skeletons in the cupboard, Heather. Even policemen.'

Peach took over again, bathing her in one of his broader and more dangerous smiles. 'And all of this is off the record, Miss Shields. You are at present a citizen helping the police in the course of their enquiries, as a citizen should. But the fact that you once flew at someone with a knife is bound to interest us, when we're looking for a killer. Incidentally, our forensic people have informed us that Annie Clark could well have been killed by a woman. Taken unawares, you see. No great strength would have been required. Especially if some sort of ligature was used. You didn't do that, did you?'

It was asked as casually as if he were enquiring whether she wanted sugar in her tea. Heather found that her mouth had gone dry when she said, 'No. And when I stabbed that boy, I was drug-dependent. When I look back at that period now, I feel that I didn't know what I was doing half the time.' She looked hard at Clyde Northcott, remembering what a wild, unpredictable, dangerous creature he had been three years ago, wondering how much of that temperament he had carried with him into the police service. 'They got me dealing because I was drug-dependent myself at the time. That's how they get you to work for them. You get your own supplies as part of your allocation.'

Clyde Northcott nodded. 'I know that. How did you kick the habit?'

'I took a rehabilitation course – after I'd wielded that knife. I was injecting heroin then, but I hadn't been doing it for long. And I didn't know who my supplier was, so I managed to give up dealing without being rubbed out. I wasn't important enough for them to kill me off.' She was silent for a moment, as they both contemplated that grim criminal industry, where anyone who knew too much was likely to be quietly eliminated by a professional killer. 'The social-services people got me on to the rehabilitation course in Manchester, after I'd got away with the probationary sentence.'

Northcott nodded. For a brief interval, the two of them were back in that other life they had shared, the nightmare world of addiction, which he had never quite reached and which she had survived. He smiled at her and said, 'I was a murder suspect, you know. There was a time when they thought I might be the Lancashire Leopard.' He was referring to the region's most infamous serial killer of the last decade. 'When the real killer was arrested, DCI Peach suggested I might consider a career in the police service. I thought he was joking at first, but when—'

'When you two have finished your pretty picnic down memory lane, we're in the middle of a murder investigation!' said Peach abrasively. 'In connection with which, we'd like to know your reason for attacking your victim with a knife four years ago, Miss Shields.'

She glared at him, trying to refocus her mind to what she must do now; for a minute or two, the black man had almost made her feel that pigs could be the same as other people. It was no use trying to deceive them. They'd have read the court case, would know all about the damning circumstances of her attack. 'I didn't fly at him, as you said earlier. And I didn't come prepared to stab him, with a knife in my pocket.' She was desperately going through the arguments her counsel had put to the jury in his summing-up at the crown court. That seemed to her now like a different world, with herself as a different person in the dock. But there was no point trying to explain that to the filth.

'That man said awful things to me. Hurtful things. And I was high on heroin. I picked up a kitchen knife from the table and stabbed him. As it happened, I only got him in the upper arm, but it bled a lot.' Despite herself, she could not contain a little grin of pleasurable recollection.

'And what was your relationship with the victim?'

'You know that. He was my boyfriend.' She felt a little spurt of real fear as she said it. She knew where this was going now, where this bald-headed tormentor was leading her.

'But he was no longer your boyfriend at the time of the incident.'

'No. He'd ditched me. Shacked up with someone both of us knew. Thrown it in my face.' She wanted to justify herself, to repeat the vile, obscene things he had said to her, the taunts he had thrown into her face about what he proposed to do with her friend. But there would be no point in that, not with this man. She made herself take a deep breath. 'It's over, all that. It went through the court and I was sentenced. You might think I got away with it, but you can't alter the verdict. And I'm a different person now.'

She glanced away from Peach's remorseless dark eyes to Clyde Northcott, and the uniformed man said involuntarily,

'That's true, Heather. You seem to have made a good job of picking up the pieces, getting your life back together.'

'Yes. All very admirable.' Peach's tone softened for a moment, after he had glanced at the lean figure beside him. 'But what we have to consider is facts. And one of the facts now appears to be that you deceived us when we met you on Thursday at your flat.'

'I didn't. I don't lie to the fuzz. I might like to do it, but I've got more sense.' But she knew now exactly where this was going, and she couldn't see a way out of it.

Peach knew it too, and he gave her a broad smile. 'You might not have lied, love, but you chose to deceive us. Quite deliberately. About your relationships with a murder victim and a murder suspect.'

She wanted to deny it, but she could summon neither the words nor the energy. It was hopeless. She remained silent, staring at the supervisor's desk in this office she never entered, biting her lip with bitter resignation.

Peach's voice resumed, steady and implacable. 'You told us on Thursday that Annie Clark had acquired a serious boyfriend – that his name was Matt Hogan; that they had only been together for a few days.'

'All of that was true.'

He smiled again. She wondered if this man always did that when he was going to hurt you, if he was like a matador giving the *coup de grâce* to a bull. 'That is true. That is why I said you deceived us rather than that you lied to us. You chose to conceal information, Miss Shields – including the information that for several months previously Matt Hogan had been your boyfriend, not Annie's.'

'Yes.'

'You didn't part amicably, did you?'

'No.' She was in no state now to distinguish between what was established and what might be mere speculation on Peach's part.

'So we have to consider that in the light of your previous record. Which indicates to us the possibility that you might have taken some violent revenge.'

'I didn't.'

'Miss Shields, did you kill Annie Clark?'

'No. I didn't kill her and I don't know—'

'Then why were you so certain that she wasn't coming back?'

She looked at him with widening eyes, trying to take in this switch of tack. She hadn't even prepared herself for this. 'I wasn't.'

'But you relet the flat from the beginning of October – only nine days after Annie had disappeared. We've checked that.'

'I didn't know what had happened to her. I suppose I presumed she'd be off somewhere with Matt. I didn't see how we could go on sharing the flat, with Matt Hogan coming between us like that.' She wanted him to believe her, but once he had exposed her deceit about the way Matt had ditched her, nothing she said seemed to carry any conviction.

'You'd had a row, just before she disappeared, hadn't you, Heather?'

It was the first time Peach had used her forename, though the other man had done it from the start. She wondered if there was any significance in that. But she no longer had the will to resist him now. 'Yes. I accused her of being a snake in the grass, of plotting all along to take Matt from me.'

'And what did Annie say about that?'

'She denied it. She said that she'd just been part of the group, that she'd had no idea that Matt even fancied her until a fortnight or so earlier, that she'd held back because of me at first.'

'But you didn't believe her.'

'No. I screamed at her, called her a scheming cow and lots of other things. Awful things. Now I believe that she was probably telling me the truth.' With that admission, she was suddenly in tears.

Peach studied her for a moment, as dispassionately as if she had been a specimen under his microscope. Then he repeated softly, 'Did you kill Annie Clark, Heather?'

'No. I'd have liked to kill her, that last Saturday, but I didn't.'

Peach glanced at Clyde Northcott. The uniformed man shook his head almost imperceptibly, then turned back to

Heather Shields. He said awkwardly, 'You don't want to go back to your mates in the packing room – not like that.'

She looked up, conscious for the first time of her tears. 'I'll go to the loo – put some cold water on my face.'

He smiled, showing her a set of very white teeth, slipping back with her for a moment into that twilight world where they had once existed. 'You did A levels. You were a bright girl, before . . .'

'Before the coke and the horse. Yes. And I'm back on track now. I won't be in the packing section here for much longer. I'm already processing orders.' She didn't tell him how earnestly she wanted to be a writer. That was far too exotic an ambition to be paraded before the police.

'That's good, then. You could do a really responsible job, you know.'

She thought he was going to give her arm a quick squeeze before he left, but he didn't touch her. He gave her another of his broad, surprising smiles and turned away. Then, when he got to the door, he turned and said, 'Always assuming that you didn't kill Annie Clark, of course.'

Peach reckoned as they went out into the icy afternoon air that PC Northcott should certainly make CID.

Sixteen

During the last hours of a bitter January, the three remaining members of the coven met at Katherine Howard's house.

It was a dark, clear night, with only the thinnest crescent of moon adding its light to the diamond-white stars in the navy sky. This wasn't their usual night, and this wasn't a normal meeting. They met for mutual reassurance, as minorities meet everywhere in the world. Kath had rung Jo Barrett and Dermot Boyd rather diffidently to suggest that they got together, but each of them had responded eagerly to her suggestion that they should meet and exchange notes about what the police had said to them individually.

When the trio had assembled in the familiar high room of Katherine Howard's house on that Monday evening, they found a comfort both in being together and in their beliefs. They felt it natural to worship together, to offer up their adoration and incantations to the Mother Goddess and to the male Horned God who was her consort. The moon was waxing, so they addressed the eternal Goddess as Diana and invoked her help, her assistance in bringing them into line with the rhythms which the moon and the sun brought to all things natural.

It was the Horned God they associated with the sun, and they uttered to him their prayers for a wholesome year, for the benefits of the spring and the summer which he would soon usher in for them. And they felt a consolation as they worshipped together, a strength that was anchored in their common beliefs. Their tiny community seemed to give them an effectiveness above what they might individually achieve.

In short, they behaved very much like followers of any of

the great religions which they found so mistaken and inadequate.

It was left to Dermot Boyd, as it usually was, to invoke the animism that is a pillar of the witches' world. He prayed that they might become a part of the 'Life Force' which is immanent within all creation, which would guide their actions benevolently, if only they could immerse themselves in the stream of its movement. All was sacred; all was to be cared for and revered – the entire earth and the tiny coven in this room as members of it. He invoked the life force which informed and guided all creation, then went through the familiar list of rocks and trees, deserts and streams, mountains and valleys, ponds and oceans, gardens and forests, fish and fowl; from amoebae to human beings, and all things in between. Dermot Boyd prayed that all in the room might be brought to live in harmony and to be psychically in tune with nature.

A tiny voice within him asked as it always did at this point whether this was not similar to what that other mystic William Blake had been crying out two centuries before, and what the bright young Wordsworth had been trying to say about nature at almost the same time. But that did not matter: Dermot knew that Wiccans were rediscovering the truths of the universe, not inventing them; and if Blake and Wordsworth had been alive now, they would surely have been Wiccans.

The three who were all that was left of a coven which had once numbered eight relaxed together afterwards, offering each other reminiscences of their exchanges with that awful man Peach, who was conducting this investigation.

Kath Howard said, 'They asked me about what we did, what we believed in. I told them what I could, without disclosing details. To be fair, I think they were only interested in witchcraft and our coven as they affected poor Annie Clark. They wanted to know about my relationship with Annie: I suppose that's natural enough. But they seemed more interested when I mentioned in passing that Annie Clark's boyfriend was a new one than in anything I had to say about what went on here. How did you find them, Jo?'

Jo Barrett crossed her long legs in her slim black trousers, studiously relaxed. 'I agree that the man Peach is a shrewd operator. I didn't take to the woman who was his detective sergeant, either. But I didn't hold things back. I told them all about the crush Annie had on me when she was at school, seven or eight years ago.' She was studiously avoiding eye contact, looking down at the backs of her slim hands as if they were suddenly of great interest to her.

'I didn't know about that.' The words were out before Dermot Boyd could check them.

'No reason why you should. It would only have embarrassed Annie. It was no more than the kind of crush on a teacher many girls get in early adolescence – something which was knocked firmly on the head at the time. It was well behind her. She was a young woman when she came to us.'

Kath Howard looked closely at the slim face beneath the dark hair, wondering why Jo was not looking at them in her usual bold way. 'Annie must have got a shock, when she came here and found you in the coven.'

Jo smiled. 'She did. We both did, I suppose. But we got over it.' A small, reminiscent smile flickered about the corners of her mouth. 'They asked me if I thought one of us killed Annie. I told them the idea was ridiculous. But I suppose they had to ask.'

Dermot Boyd said, 'They asked me that as well. I found the notion as ridiculous as you did.'

But there was something wrong, he thought, that they should even need to offer each other such assurances. He decided to tell them the way in which Peach had embarrassed him; better that they should hear it from him than from that mischievous chief inspector. 'If Peach suspects anyone, it's probably me. I discovered the body, remember. And when they'd been given an identification and came to see me again on Wednesday, I didn't admit to them that I'd known Annie Clark. I think they found that suspicious.'

'I should think they would,' said Jo Barrett. 'Why did you conceal that?'

Dermot forced a rueful grin, trying to dispel the tenseness he felt in his companions. 'My wife didn't know about the coven, about Wiccans. She didn't know I was coming here.

She does now. I was foolish ever to conceal it from her.' He had no idea whether they found it a convincing explanation; he felt them both watching his face, which he was sure was reddening.

Jo said, 'Not a good idea, lying to the police. I expect that man Peach has got you in the frame for his murderer now. That's what they call it, isn't it?'

'I expect he has. It's my own fault. But things conspired against me. I didn't know I was going to find Annie's remains in that awful place up on the side of Pendle, did I?'

But no one answered him. Normally, once the formal prayers and incantations were concluded, the exchanges among them were lively, even humorous. They were usually a group of people full of the confidence in each other which comes from a shared set of beliefs. But tonight, the spirit of the departed Wiccan Annie Clark seemed to hang heavily upon them, deadening their exchanges, making them more cautious with each other than they had ever been before.

Each of the three was struggling with the awful realization that there might be a murderer amongst them.

'Looking for a spring holiday, sir? We have some excellent offers in Spain and Portugal at the moment. They're booking up fast, though!' Anna Fenton produced a smile which, even in one of her tender years, was remarkable for nine o'clock on the morning of the first of February.

'No sale, I'm afraid, love.' Peach flashed his warrant card in front of her disappointed face. 'We're here to see the boss.'

Alan Hurst, hearing the exchange, came out and ushered them through into the storeroom behind the main office, shutting the door carefully behind them. He turned and gave them a smile which was much more strained than Anna Fenton's professional welcome. 'We won't be disturbed in here.'

'Good.' Peach looked quickly round the small room, taking in its closed doors and its single small window. 'We'll need a bit of privacy, for this.' He managed to make even his introduction sound menacing, thought Lucy Blake, with a mixture of deprecation and admiration.

'I can't see why it should take us very long. I'm pretty

sure I gave you everything I knew about poor Annie Clar when we spoke at my house on Saturday afternoon.'

'Are you, sir? Interesting, that – because we've been talkin to a lot of people, some of whom you don't even know during the last week. We have a team of thirty people in al doing house-to-house enquiries, questioning shopkeeper; talking to bag ladies, drunkards, vicars and tarts. Even th odd witch, believe it or not.' He smiled at the recollection 'Most of it is a total waste of police time, of course. Bu that's the trouble with this job: it's not until after our lad and lasses have made all these enquiries that we can se what's useful and what isn't – that we are able to pick ou the little nuggets of gold amongst all the gravel we put throug our riddles.' He gave his man a broad smile, as if please with his metaphor, and then looked around the room agai

It was a crowded and untidy place. Piles of brochures fror various travel companies occupied all four corners of th room. A filing cabinet with one drawer open and a sma desk occupied most of the rest of the floor space, so tha there was barely room for the three upright chairs occupie by the players in this odd little drama.

Alan Hurst caught his glance, said nervously, 'It's neve very tidy, this place. We have to store a lot of brochures you'd be surprised how quickly we get through them.' H tore his eyes away from the bottom drawer of the filin cabinet, which he knew was securely locked. 'There's a littl kitchen through that door there. I can make you a coffe easily enough if you'd like one.' He was aware that he wa saying more than was necessary, talking for his own sak not theirs, filling the silences, which he was already findin oppressive.

Peach gave him the understanding smile which told hir that he comprehended all of this. 'Coffee won't be neces sary, sir. Too early in the morning for that. We wanted t explore again your relationship with the murder victim, M Hurst. To give you the opportunity to revise some of th information you volunteered to us on Saturday afternoon.'

'I can't think why I should want to do that.'

'Can't you, sir?' Peach's eyebrows arched up into the white ness of his head, which he then shook sadly, as if surprise anew by the foolishness of humanity. 'Well, not to put too fine a point on it, and speaking strictly off the record, of course, I'd say you'd been telling us porkies.'

'Porkies?'

'Porky pies, Mr Hurst. Lies. Ugly word. But lying is an ugly thing to do, when you consider what's at stake. Which might be your liberty.' He was perfectly calm and quiet, but he wasn't smiling any more.

Alan didn't know what to do. If he admitted it, how much should he say? He couldn't be sure how much they really knew and how much this Torquemada of a man was bluffing. He said with draining conviction, 'I told you that I found Annie Clark a good worker. I told you that she was very willing to learn and entirely trustworthy.' The phrases sounded in his ears like the references he had written for some of his other girls, when he had decided that it was time they left. 'I felt confident enough of her abilities to leave her in charge of the shop, whenever it was necessary for me to be away.'

'When you felt it necessary to be at home with your wife, I think you said, sir.'

Alan understood now that phrase about your heart missing a beat. His own heart seemed to do that quite literally, and then to resume with a much faster rhythm. Was Peach hinting that not all of the time had been spent with his wife, that the police were on to that other and more productive side-line, which had proved so lucrative for him over the last year? He made himself speak slowly. 'Yes. Judith needs a lot of my time. Unfortunately, I can only see the situation getting worse over the next year or two.'

Peach nodded sympathetically, then turned to the watchful woman beside him. 'And how did Mr Hurst describe his relationship with Annie Clark to us, DS Blake?'

Lucy made a play of consulting her notes. '"Professional", sir. That was the word he used.'

'And that was what I meant.' Alan couldn't stop himself coming in promptly on the end of her sentence.

'Indeed, sir. You reiterated it, I believe. When I asked you if you were sure that your relationship hadn't moved beyond the merely professional, you were quite definite that it hadn't.'

'Yes.' Alan knew now that things had gone badly wrong,

but he had no idea what to say. He couldn't see any way out of this. Damage limitation would be all that he could attempt.

'I have to tell you that the team's enquiries have thrown up a rather different picture, Mr Hurst.' Peach enjoyed being pompous, delaying his moment of revelation, watching his man's discomfort increasing with every second. Some people would have said he was a sadist; he merely believed that this lying bugger deserved everything he got. 'You were seen, Mr Hurst – seen with Annie Clark. In a variety of situations, by a variety of people. Not professional situations, in my opinion.'

'If you're going to take gossip as evidence, there won't be much hope for any of us.'

'I'm not speaking of evidence, Mr Hurst. We're not in a court of law. Not yet, anyway. Are you still denying that your relationship with Annie Clark went beyond the professional?'

He tried to work his brain furiously, to out-think this man. But it wasn't an equal contest. Peach held all the cards, and Alan was never going to learn exactly how much he knew and what his sources were. The man seemed very confident that he could substantiate what he was saying. Cut your losses and run, Alan Hurst's furiously working mind told him. Admit to a bit on the side and keep him well away from the criminal sideline that is making you a rich man.

He forced a smile, glanced for a moment at the girl who looked so innocent beside the chief inspector, and said, 'All right, I was attracted to Annie Clark. No doubt people with nothing better to do have told you how they saw us in some of the pubs of the Ribble Valley. Everything I told you about the excellence of Annie's work is correct. She was also a very attractive young woman. I used to take her out for a drink occasionally.'

'And also took her to bed.'

It was a statement, not a question. He could deny it, but he sensed that that would only land him in deeper trouble. He smiled ruefully. 'All right. It's not a crime, is it? I suppose you could say I was a little flattered when she found me attractive. You wouldn't blame me for that, perhaps, if you had seen what an attractive twenty-three-year-old Annie Clark was.'

'She wasn't the first, was she? Annie was one of a succession of young women with whom you consorted.' Peach savoured the word and apparently found it to his liking.

'I can't see that it's really any business of yours to hound me over this.'

Peach produced one of his smaller smiles and shook his head sadly. 'We're not here to take moral stands over who sleeps with whom, Mr Hurst. It's not a crime, as you say. But neither was it a crime on Saturday, when you chose to lie to us about it. It's the lying that we're here to investigate. Lying to us when we're trying to trace a murderer is very serious indeed. It is also very foolish, because it makes us ask ourselves why you did it.'

Alan forced himself to take his time. 'I can see that. Hindsight is a wonderful thing.' He took a deep breath, nodded slowly, and spoke as evenly as he could. 'You've seen my house and the way I have to build my life around my wife's illness. Judith is a permanent invalid, getting worse each year. I am only forty-one and I have my sexual urges, like most men of my age. I'm not proud of the fact that I've indulged myself elsewhere, which is why I tried to conceal it from you. To use your word, it was foolish. I lied to you, held back the full story, because I was ashamed of my weakness. But there was nothing vicious about it. I wasn't concealing anything which had a bearing on Annie Clark's death.'

'Really, sir.' Peach managed to convey a weight of cynicism in four syllables. 'So how long had you been sleeping with Miss Clark at the time of her disappearance?'

'You make it sound like a full-blown affair. It was less noble and more furtive than that. And quite sporadic. We took our chances wherever we could.' Alan tried a self-deprecating, man-of-the-world smile, but couldn't quite bring it off.

There was no answering smile from either of the contrasting faces which were so close to him in the tiny, crowded room. Peach merely said, 'You haven't answered my question.'

'What? Oh, I suppose the first occasion when we had sex was about six weeks before she disappeared. And for what it's worth, I think whatever there was between us was over by that time. She'd acquired a new boyfriend and she seemed quite serious about him.' He tried to imply that they would be better investigating Matt Hogan than him as a killer, but he had more sense now than to put that idea into words.

Peach said, 'It would be interesting to have Annie Clark's version of her relationship with you, but of course we cannot have it.'

Alan Hurst was well aware of that. He allowed himself a small, bitter smile. 'I'm sure that if she were here, Annie would confirm what I have told you.'

'Were you the father of her child?'

It came like a blow across the face because of its abruptness. Alan had known from the moment they had found out about his bedding Annie that Peach would ask that question, but the suddenness still threw him off balance. 'No! Of course I wasn't!'

'No of course about it, is there, Mr Hurst? You've got to be a likely candidate for instigating Miss Clark's pregnancy. Particularly as you chose to conceal the affair from us.'

'Well whatever you think, that foetus had nothing to do with me. You'll need to look elsewhere for your father. I didn't even know she was pregnant until you told me on Saturday.'

'So who do you think was the father?'

'I don't know. How should I know?'

'You were in daily contact with the girl. As well as taking her to bed. Sporadically.' Peach managed a huge contempt as he dwelt on the five syllables of the word Hurst had given him. 'You're as likely as anyone to have been the recipient of Annie's confidences.'

'Well I wasn't! I told you: it was a complete shock to me to find that she was pregnant at the time of her death.'

They left him then, without any of the social niceties of a leave-taking, with a gruff direction to get in touch if any further recollection about Annie Clark came back to him. Alan thought that Peach lingered a little in the public part of the building, looking assessingly at Anna Fenton, who fortunately was serving a customer at the time.

In that moment, Alan Hurst decided that he had better go

carefully with Anna, had better take things slowly until this Annie Clark thing was out of the way. They'd exposed what he'd been doing with Annie, as he now realized he should have expected them to do. But they didn't seem to have a clue about the way he was now making big money, the way in which he was going to finance poor Judith's new luxury quarters back at the house.

Seventeen

'So who've we got in the frame?' Chief Superintendent Tucker leant back in his chair and assessed his chief inspector. 'Do sit down, Percy, and give me a full report.'

It was always a sign of danger when Tommy Bloody Tucker used your first name. Peach positioned his chair with extreme care, as if an inch out of place would lead to some undefined disaster, and sat very upright on the edge of it. 'We have several possibilities, sir.' Tucker, he noted, was like a golf caddie: it was always 'we' when the man sensed a success, always 'you' when things were going wrong.

Tucker smiled benevolently. Management was all a matter of carrots and sticks. Today he would use the carrot on Peach. He might detest the man, but on this day he would encourage him, show his skills in man-management. The fact that he knew that his own success was carried on the back of his enigmatic chief inspector was quite incidental. 'You'd better give me the full picture. Take your time, Percy. Murder is too important to hurry.'

Peach realized with a sinking heart that his chief had time on his hands. No meetings with the Chief Constable; no regional crime conferences; no media briefings. Tuesday was usually a quiet day for Tommy Bloody Tucker, however busy his underlings might be. Percy said carefully, 'No father has been identified for the foetus found in Annie Clarke, sir. I'm not certain that forensic will be able to do a DNA match on the foetus, because the corpse was so badly decomposed.' Privately, he was pretty certain that DNA matching would be possible in due course, but they would need strong evidence against a suspect before they could demand a DNA sample.

'Let me know if I can be of any help with forensic. I'm

quite willing to add the weight of my rank, if it helps.' Tucker shifted that weight in his chair, as if preparing to throw his body into the lists. He apparently had some vague idea that the laboratories were being deliberately obstructive.

Peach said, 'It's not easy, either for them or for us, when a body isn't discovered until four months after death. Scents go cold. People disappear. People with something to hide have ample time to cover their tracks.'

'If I didn't know you better, I'd say that sounded defeatist, Percy!' This was Tucker's attempt at impish humour; it crashed to the carpet with a thud when it met Peach's uncompromisingly inscrutable face.

'Well, sir, we still seem to have six possibilities for this crime. Not equal possibilities, sir: I'd say some of them would be much shorter odds than others, with the bookies.'

'Well, give me your leading suspects, and I'll give you my opinion, Percy.'

Again that first name. Percy Peach expected it, even welcomed it, from almost everyone else in the station, but he didn't like it at all from Tommy Bloody Tucker. He said, 'I think it would be best if I ran all six of them past you in no particular order, sir. Then you could give me the benefit of your expertise and insights. Your detached overview is often the most valuable thing you contribute.'

Tucker looked at him suspiciously. 'Very well, if you think that's necessary. But I'd much rather you gave me your leading candidates to start with. We haven't got all day, you know.'

'Yes, sir. I must have been deceived by your suggestion that we should take our time over it, that murder couldn't be hurried.' Peach's sturdy frame became even more upright on his seat; Tucker thought with irritation that this was the only man he'd ever met who seemed to be able to *sit* to attention.

The chief inspector now spoke stiffly, through lips that scarcely moved. 'Well, there's the boyfriend, sir – always a good place to start. Lad of twenty-three who goes by the name of Matthew Hogan. Some people would say not a lad, sir, but when—'

'A strong candidate, as you say, Peach. Didn't you say that the girl was pregnant?'

Even his short-term memory's going now, poor old soul, thought Percy. 'I did, sir. About two minutes ago.'

'Well, there you are, then. Irresponsible young man, like most of them nowadays. Puts her into the club, then refuses to accept his responsibilities. Probably wanted her to have an abortion, and the poor girl was refusing that. Very strong candidate, I'd say.'

Tucker's ability to jump to conclusions was surpassed only by his talent for leaping on to bandwagons, in Percy's view. He enunciated now like one trying to get through to a very old person, 'Matt Hogan says that he didn't know that Annie Clark was pregnant, sir.'

'And you believe him?' Tucker smiled his superior smile and shook his head. 'For an experienced detective, you can be very naïve at times, Peach.'

Percy noted with satisfaction that they now seemed to be firmly back on surname terms. 'I don't believe or disbelieve him, sir. But it appears that he had only been the boyfriend of the girl for about a week when she disappeared.'

'So he says.'

'So other people say, as well, sir. He'd known her socially for a few months, but she only became his girlfriend about a week before she went missing.'

'Ah! But without having a serious relationship these young people are quite capable of leaping into bed with each other, don't you think? He might have given her a bun in the oven, and then she comes on to him wanting marriage, you see. And he doesn't want to accept his responsibilities, so he strangles her and dumps her body up on Pendle Hill.'

Percy wondered what a lawyer would make of the chief's capacity to predict the behaviour of a whole generation from what he read in his *Daily Mail*. 'It's an attractive theory, sir. It will take a bit of proving.'

'Well, get out there and get the proof, then. That's your job, you know, Peach.' Tucker stared past him and out of the window, his chin jutting in what he regarded as his Churchillian mode.

'Yes, sir. Annie Clark's flatmate was an ex-girlfriend of Matt Hogan's, sir.' He looked at Tucker's uncomprehending face and decided that this time the man needed to be led. 'She

154

let the flat very quickly after Annie had disappeared. Almost as though she knew Annie Clark wouldn't be coming back.'

'And she was probably very jealous of her. The girl who'd snatched away her boyfriend. She might very well have killed her in a mad fit of revenge.'

What a loss to the romantic-fiction market the chief was. Percy said, 'Yes, sir. That sort of thing had occurred to us. But it's wonderful to have the benefit of your oversight, sir. Gives us a lot more confidence.'

'*Cherchez la femme*, Peach. Always a good principle.'

Peach reflected sadly that the feminists would never hear this conversation. 'Then there is the girl's employer, sir. That's if you think we need to look any further than her flatmate.'

'No, let's hear about him, Peach, by all means. You have to remain objective, you know. When you've been in this job as long as I have, you'll find that objectivity must be a watchword.'

'A watchword, sir. Objectivity. I'll remember that.' Peach furrowed his noble brow as if making an immense mental effort.'

'Dodgy character, is he, this employer?'

'Not on the face of it, no, sir. Alan Hurst. Hurst Travel Services: you probably know the shop, on Southgate. He has an invalid wife. She suffers from multiple sclerosis, which is now quite advanced. Everyone says that he's a saint in the home. Cares for her admirably. He's even planning a major ground-floor extension because she won't be able to manage the stairs for much longer.'

'Doesn't sound like a murderer.'

'Indeed not, sir.'

'And Hurst's a respectable businessman. Running his own firm. Very successfully, by the sound of it.'

'Very successfully indeed, to judge by what he's spending and planning to spend. And he's not a Mason, sir. Which, as you know from my research, would increase his chances of being involved in serious crime by a factor of—'

'Peach, I'm not interested in your ill-advised attempts to blacken the reputation of a fine body of men! It seems that you're wasting your time in giving this degree of attention to a respectable man like Mr Hurst, so—'

'Even though he was bedding Annie Clark at the time of her disappearance, sir?' Percy's face was full of innocent surprise, his eyebrows arching like black slugs into the furrows of his forehead.

'You didn't mention that. You should have begun with it.'

'Sorry, sir. Well, he denies it has anything to do with either Annie's disappearance or her death. Confesses that with an invalid wife not able to give him the bedroom excitements he desires, he snatches a bit of rumpety wherever he can get it.' Percy thought that this was a fair and succinct summary of what it had taken Alan Hurst twenty minutes to confess.

Tucker was torn between his prejudice in favour of business success and the emergence of a very obvious motive for murder. He said doubtfully, 'Some men do manage to take young women to bed outside their marriages.' He stared bleakly past Peach at the picture of the Queen on the wall, as if trying to come to terms with such marvellous philandering. His own wife Barbara, a thirteen-stone Brunnhilde, did not even indulge fantasies of that kind, let alone permit the real thing. He strove to emulate Peach's mastery of the vernacular. 'It's possible that he was giving her the occasional poke without actually having killed her, you know.'

Percy nodded sagely. 'There's your objectivity again, sir – your ability to take a properly detached view. I was thinking that it was possible that he might be the father of the foetus the girl was carrying, that he might have panicked about that and decided to get rid of her.'

'I don't say that that isn't a possibility.' Tucker hastened to cover his tracks. 'You must proceed as you think fit. I was only pointing out that a respectable businessman might have his little weaknesses without being a murderer.'

'Very true, that, sir.' Peach furrowed his brow as if trying to compel his mind to accept a memorable and original human insight. 'Hurst tried to convince DS Blake and me that that was exactly the case. We were a little sceptical, but it will clarify our minds to know that you agree with the thesis.'

'Now, I didn't exactly say that, you know. I—'

'And then there's the witches, sir.' Percy smiled happily at this new complication of Tommy Bloody Tucker's happy day.

'Witches?' Tucker flicked a hand over his brow, as if trying to banish a vision of crones dancing round a cauldron. 'You did say something about that when you interrupted me on the golf course on Saturday. You're surely not serious about black masses and Satanism being involved in this death?'

'Not Satanism, sir. And no black masses or curses, they assure me.' Peach shook his head sadly, as if a few broomsticks and black cats would have been a welcome addition to a humdrum day. 'White magic, they say. Bringing themselves into line with nature – with the world and all things in it. And beyond that, with the sun and the moon and the stars.'

'And you're telling me that you take this seriously? That you really think these women might—'

'Warlocks, sir.'

'What?'

'You gave me the word yourself, sir. From the benefits of your oversight. When you were struggling a little with your swing on the golf course.' He took pity on his goggling master. 'Male witches, sir, as you were kind enough to point out to me. Witches aren't exclusively female. There's one male in this coven.'

Tucker sighed deeply. You'd better tell me about these witches, if you think they have a bearing on this case.'

'Wiccans, sir.'

'Wiccans?' Tucker's perplexity was wonderful to view.

'That's what they call themselves, sir. They worship the Universal Goddess and the Horned God.'

Tucker tried condescension. 'Well, I'm sure this is all very interesting, but I shall be very surprised if—'

'Annie Clark was one, sir. A Wiccan. A member of this coven.'

'I see. Then I suppose I'd better hear all about them.' Tucker spread his arms stiffly outwards for a minute, a gesture which was meant to indicate the intense magnanimity of his attitude to his inferiors.

Peach relaxed visibly, pulled his chair six inches nearer to his chief's desk, and prepared to impart confidences. 'Katherine Howard, sir.'

'I've heard that name before.' Tucker donned his mien of shrewd intelligence.

'Yes, sir. Victim of violence, I believe. Henry VIII's fifth wife. Had her head chopped off for sleeping around, for putting it about a bit, in a Tudor sort of way. Things were simpler in those days.' He looked at the wall behind his chief and shook his head wistfully. 'But I don't think this Katherine's any relation to that one; I'm not even sure she spells her name the same way.'

'Sinister woman though, is she?'

'Seems very normal, sir, in most respects. Widow lady. Runs her own business, since the death of her husband. Very competently, from all the accounts we've had. The firm supplies temporary workers for a whole variety of office situations.'

'She doesn't sound like a murderess.'

Peach noted the disappointment in Tucker's tone. 'Head of the coven, she is, sir. Leader of their devotions and incantations.'

Tucker said rather helplessly, 'What exactly do they do?'

'Bit secretive about the actual form of their incantations to the Mother Goddess, sir. But I gather this lot aren't devotees of naturism, sir. They don't worship naked. Apparently most covens discarded that practice thirty or forty years ago.' He shook his head with a great sadness.

'So you think this head of the coven might have killed Annie Clark?'

'It's a possibility, sir, no more than that. It's one of those occasions when we need the dead girl's account of things, and can't have it. Katherine Howard admits that it was she who instructed Annie Clark in the ways of the Wiccans, that it was she who got Annie excited about the cult. She admits that they've lost two members of the coven in the last few months. If Annie Clark was a third and Kath's protégée, Mrs Howard would have felt her own position seriously threatened by another defection, especially when it was a girl who seems to have been her acolyte.'

'You mean that this Howard woman might have had a fierce row with her if Annie had said she wanted out – might even have killed her in a fit of rage.' Tucker, like most

158

unimaginative men, became excited when his atrophied creativity was given an unexpected outing.

'She might not even have meant to kill her, of course. It's a possibility we have to consider, sir – no more than that. We haven't been able to rule Mrs Howard out. She's an intelligent woman, and she seemed a little evasive, even guarded, when I spoke to her.'

Tucker didn't fancy the idea of an intelligent woman. He said sagely, 'It will pay to keep an eye on her, if you want my view, Peach.'

'Oh, we do, sir. Then there's the warlock in the enterprise: Dermot Boyd, accountant and company secretary.' He was curious to know what Tucker might feel about those callings.

The chief superintendent said, 'Professional man. Seems unlikely. But then, we can't disregard him, if he's a – a male witch.'

'No, sir. And he does other odd things, for an accountant. He reads books, sir. Even poetry, it seems. His wife confirmed that, sir.' He shook his head, as if this literary strain was a damning thing in a man.

Tucker nodded sagely. 'Good that you spotted that. He may not be as sound as he appears.'

'Especially as he lied about Annie Clark, sir. Said he didn't know her, at first. Persisted in it, until we confronted him with his lies.'

Percy thought that Tucker was about to yell 'Eureka!', such was his animation. But the Head of Brunton CID controlled himself and said with suppressed excitement, 'And why did he do that, Percy?'

The first name was back again. Peach said rather stiffly, 'Apparently his wife hadn't been told that he was going off to join the coven every week.' He relaxed and leant confidentially towards his chief. 'Do you know, sir, he'd actually told her he was going off to the local Masonic lodge?' He allowed himself a sudden, disturbing peal of laughter at this deception.

'And he was really sneaking off to meet Annie Clark!' Tommy Bloody Tucker had rarely shown such buoyancy.

'Well, yes, sir. Along with the other Wiccans in the coven, according to his account.'

159

'But don't you see, he could have been conducting an affair with Annie? He might have been the father of this foetus. And when, for whatever reason, it all went wrong, he might have killed her.'

By Jove he's got it, thought Peach. He said, deliberately low-key to counterbalance Tucker's excitement, 'Boyd and his wife found the body, of course; and there seems to be some evidence that he wanted to prevent his wife from going near that derelict building where the corpse had been dumped.'

'It fits, you know. By George it does!' Tucker leaned across his desk towards his subordinate. 'What would you say was the state of this man's marriage, Percy?'

'Lukewarm, I'd say, sir.' Peach had the word ready, because he had given the matter considerable thought himself over the last few days. 'They haven't any children, and they don't seem very close to each other – as is evidenced by the fact that Dermot Boyd felt he wanted to conceal his participation in the coven from his wife Eleanor.'

'More likely wanted to conceal his relationship with Annie Clark, you mean!' Tucker had the exhilaration of a man who has made a decisive breakthrough.

Percy nodded slowly. 'Another of your insights, sir. Most valuable.'

'Well then, I suggest you get about your business, DCI Peach. Get about the task of—'

Peach coughed softly, deferentially, happy to hear his surname once again ringing round the walls of authority. 'There is one other possibility, sir. One other person in the frame, as you put it.' He pronounced the phrase as if it were a Tucker original, rather than one of the commonest in the police argot.

'Well, who is it?'

'Another witch, sir. The third of the trio of Wiccans whom we have to regard as suspects.'

Tucker put aside his excitement over the previous candidate. 'Another woman, eh?' The gender seemed to rekindle his interest.

'Yes, sir. A lady who makes no secret of her gay background. Teacher at the same school as Dermot Boyd's wife, as a matter of fact. Name of Josephine Barrett, sir. More usually known as Jo.'

'I've heard that name before, you know.' Tucker looked as if he thought he deserved a gold star.

'Athlete of some renown, sir. Olympic standard eight hundred and fifteen hundred metres runner, I think. Geordie in origin, but she's worked in our area for eight years now.'

'And a lesbian! That might be more relevant to this investigation, you know.' Tucker believed in wearing his prejudices upon his sleeve.

'Yes, sir. Another interesting fact about Jo Barrett is that she taught Annie Clark years ago at school. As a matter of fact, Annie apparently had a teenage infatuation for her at that time.'

'Ah! Good work, Peach, digging that out.'

'As a matter of fact, sir, Ms Barrett volunteered the information herself. At our first meeting with her.'

Tucker was cast down for a moment. Then his face brightened. 'But that may be the cleverness of it, you see. This woman may have been shrewd enough to realize that we'd be on to her, that we'd find out about her past.'

It's become 'we' again, thought Percy with a frown. 'The girl's crush was dealt with by Miss Barrett and the head teacher at the time, sir. They had Annie's mother in and discussed it with her. Apparently such passions for teachers are quite common in adolescent girls.'

'Significant, though, in this case.' Tucker nodded sagely, with the air of one acknowledging a decisive intervention. 'You may well find that this Barrett woman had a thing going with Annie Clark at the time of her death.'

'Yes, sir. Annie did have a boyfriend, though. As well as being a bit on the side for Alan Hurst.'

Tucker's features clouded, then lightened again; he was as changeable and uncertain as an April day, thought Percy. 'But you said a *recent* boyfriend, Peach. This fellow Hogan had come on the scene and put Ms Barrett's nose out of joint, I expect. So your schoolteacher had a hell of a row with Annie Clark and killed her in a fit of rage.'

Percy contemplated that theory. 'Yes, sir. Like Alan Hurst when she wouldn't get rid of his baby.'

'What? Oh yes, I suppose so.'

'Or Katherine Howard, when Annie announced that she was leaving the coven.'

'Well perhaps, but—'

'Or Dermot Boyd when—'

'Now look here, Peach; you came here to get the benefit of my expertise, not to be obstructive.'

'Yes, sir. Sorry, sir.'

'It's my job to throw out ideas, yours to weigh them and implement the necessary action. I've given you plenty of ideas. It's time you were off and investigating things.'

'Indeed it is, sir. May I say that your overview of the case has been every bit as useful as it always is.'

'You may, Peach, you may.'

Tommy Bloody Tucker waved his hand benignly as Percy Peach backed out of his presence.

Eighteen

Wednesday morning, the second of February, and Judith Hurst was being stubborn. 'I know it's cold. It won't hurt me. I've still got quite good circulation: the nurses all tell me that. And I'll wrap up well.' Her lips set in the determined, half-humorous little pout which had been one of the things that had attracted Alan to her when they were both twenty, in that time which seemed at once only yesterday and part of a vanished and very different era.

He said, 'I know the sun's out, and it always feels quite warm through the glass in the conservatory. But it's still below freezing in the shade.' They were both happy because they knew he was going to lose the argument, because they understood each other so well that both of them realized how this would turn out.

'The snowdrops are beginning to come out. The harbingers of spring. I'm not going to miss them!' She stopped speaking suddenly on that, and both of them comprehended in that instant that she was wondering how many more springs she would have to savour.

Alan Hurst said, 'I suppose if you wrap up really thoroughly and don't stay out long, we might get away with it. All right! I'll get the coats and scarves. I'll show you where the new extension will be going. We'll need to move a rhododendron and some perennials. You can show me where you'd like them to go.'

He wrapped her in her thickest coat and the woollen bobble-hat she had used in happier days, when they had walked on the local hills and skied in Austria. Then he wound the long scarf round her giggling face so that it concealed most of it, and with his forefinger touched the tracery of fine lines that was beginning to furrow her temples. Then they went through the window of the conservatory and out into the frozen garden.

She leaned on him more heavily than she had ever done before, once almost losing her balance as they moved in clumsy unison down the lawn, like some old-time dance played in slow motion and imperfectly performed. It was difficult to believe that they were only forty-one. Her body was frailer than he could remember it ever being before, but its dependence on him was greater; the awkwardness of their movements stemmed partly from the fact that neither of them wanted to acknowledge either of these things.

'The extension will come to just about here.' He traced a thin line with his heel in the frost.

'You're sure we can afford it? I've been looking at the plans again. It seems a very grand conception. I'd be perfectly happy with something less ambitious, you know.'

'We can afford it. It's an investment, really. It will add very considerably to the value of the property. And in the meantime, it will be very useful to us for many years!'

Both of them feared that it would not be so, and again each of them divined what the other was thinking. But they had to deal with thoughts like this at least once a day, so they were easy with each other as they waited for the shadow to pass. Judith said, 'The business must be doing very well.'

'Well enough.' He would be making his deliveries tonight, in that other, secret activity which brought in the real funds. The travel business limped along, but he would get the money he needed for the extension from the trade he could never discuss with Judith.

He felt a shiver run through the ailing body which leant against his side, and this time she raised no objection as he led her back into the oppressive warmth of the house. She took a final longing glance back at the borders she had planted and would now never tend again. 'I must have a cautious temperament, you know. I can never help worrying a little bit about money.'

Alan Hurst fell back once again on the chauvinist phrase he had used to tease her all those years ago, when the world had been such an exciting place, and they had been innocents beginning the great adventure of life together. 'Don't you worry your pretty little head about it, Judith Hurst!'

*   *   *

'The dead woman's boyfriend is always a suspect. It's a fact of life. Regrettable, from your point of view, but there it is.' DCI Peach seemed to find it a very satisfactory situation.

Matt Hogan thought it a very unfair one. 'I've told you all I know. Done everything I can to help you to find who killed Annie Clark. Even came into the police station at Brunton to tell you that I thought the corpse you'd found on Pendle might be her.'

'Yes. You did exactly what a good citizen should. About four months too late, of course. Being an experienced detective, and thus a nasty, suspicious sod, I have to point out if I'd been the murderer, I think I'd have come in exactly as you did. Knowing that once the body was identified, the boyfriend would be the first person the local rozzers would want to see, I'd have taken the initiative and a deep breath, and come in all bright-eyed and bushy-tailed and innocent to say I was terribly worried about my missing girlfriend and terribly afraid that this might just be her body – whilst hoping against hope that it wasn't, naturally.'

'It wasn't like that. I tried to explain it at the time, to that DC Pickering that I spoke to then.'

'Yes. I heard all about that. Though to my mind, you never came up with a satisfactory explanation of why you hadn't come in at the end of September when she disappeared.' Peach shook his head in happy confirmation of that.

Matt Hogan thought furiously, trying unsuccessfully to disguise both his dislike of this man and his gathering panic. He could hardly say that it was his habit to avoid the police, that his previous dealings with them had left him without a criminal record but with a couple of cautions. He said, 'I can see with hindsight that I should have reported Annie missing much earlier. It doesn't seem as clear at the time, when you're in the midst of things. I just thought she'd abandoned me and gone off somewhere else. Perhaps with someone else.' It didn't sound convincing, even to him. He said rather desperately, 'We'd only been an item for about a week at the time when she disappeared.'

It wasn't quite the explanation he'd offered the first time they'd seen him, when he had come into the station a week earlier. He'd said that he'd kept expecting Annie Clark to turn up.

Lucy Blake studied him for a moment, then put her dagger in very quietly. 'Forgive me for saying so, Matt, but you didn't seem to be absolutely devastated by Annie Clark's death.'

'I'd had four months to get used to the idea, by then.'

'Really? But you just said that you thought she'd abandoned you and gone off somewhere else, rather than been murdered.'

'Well, I'd had four months to get used to the idea of being without her, then.' Matt didn't dare look at either of them. He was sure that the two very different faces would both be looking sceptical.

And then the man Peach, who seemed to enjoy seeing him squirm, was at him again, leaning forward as though imparting a confidence. 'It seems to us, Matt, that Annie's pregnancy is likely to be at the centre of this killing. You're quite sure you weren't the father?'

That again. Matt said wretchedly, 'No. I told you last time: I didn't even know about it, until you told me.'

'Yes. Surprised us, that did. So who do you think *was* the father?'

'I don't know.' He sought despairingly for something that would get him off the hook. 'I bet it was something to do with those witches. They were leading her into all sorts of things, that lot.' He let his revulsion come out as he said it; it surely couldn't do him any harm.

'Bit vague, though, isn't it? – if all you can come up with is a vague accusation against a group of people you don't understand and don't like?' Peach managed to give the young man the impression that he'd put himself even further into trouble by flailing about like that. 'What about Annie's flatmate, Heather Shields? Do you think she knew about the baby?'

'I don't know.'

'Girls together, like? Don't you think Annie might have confided in her?'

'I don't know. I don't think so.' Matt was sure Heather hadn't known. But he couldn't tell them why. That might put both of them even deeper into the shit than he felt now.

Peach studied him for a moment in a cold silence. There was something here, something that the sullen, childlike

166

set of the young lips told him he wouldn't get out of Hogan today – something that he would take up in due course with Heather Shields. The chief inspector stood up and looked round the shabby bed-sit, noting the cheap prints of a jungle scene and a spaniel on the walls, the absence of any photograph of Annie Clark. 'Pay you to open a few windows, you know, if you're going to go on smoking that pot. Cloying pong, you see. Better still, give it up altogether!' He went through the door without another look at his man.

DS Blake gave Matt Hogan her sweetest, most understanding smile as she followed. She turned suddenly when she reached the doorway, so that her face was within a foot of Hogan's. She inspected his forehead unhurriedly. 'I see that knife wound is healing up nicely now. Hope you've changed your pub!'

PC Clyde Northcott was pretty sure that he was in trouble.

His uniformed sergeant did nothing to mitigate his fear. He had a jaundiced view of CID, who in his view got all the glamour, took on only the most interesting cases, and left the uniformed boys and girls to do the thankless day-to-day policing work. The sergeant was, in fact, a creature of convention in such matters. And when one of his newest, toughest and most reliable recruits was constantly in demand by CID, it did not improve the sergeant's temper. So he now said to Northcott, 'Percy Peach wants to see you in CID: I don't know what you've done wrong, but don't come running to me to bail you out.'

DCI Peach was uncharacteristically uncertain. He was much happier exercising the rough edge of his tongue, with his juniors as well as the criminal fraternity of the town. When he had good news to dispense, praise to offer, or favours to bestow, he was much less sure of himself. He said gruffly, 'I suppose you'd better sit down. You make me uncomfortable, prancing about like a Christmas decoration.'

Clyde Northcott glanced down at the gleaming buttons on his immaculate uniform. You got compliments for being smart on parade in one place, insults from the most respected man in CID in another. He wasn't resentful; he had quickly grown used to the contradictions of police life and he did not question them.

It was over two years now since Clyde had finally abandoned his reservations and entered the police service. In the months before that momentous decision, he had been dabbling with cocaine and keeping the kind of company that was going to lead to trouble. It had culminated in his involvement in a murder investigation. There had been two awful days when he feared that Peach and Blake had been planning to pin the crime on him.

Instead, they had cleared him. And then, in a turn of events he still found it difficult to believe, they had suggested he consider a career in the police service. He had resisted, of course: the decision ran against everything he had thought he believed and against everything his former friends had told him. But Clyde Northcott had always been something of a loner: being six feet three inches tall, lean and intensely black had been unusual on the Brunton council estate where he grew up. Violence had not been at all unusual, and Clyde had learned to handle himself early in life.

He had found that he did not have to apologize for being tough in the police force, but rather to channel his hardness into the right areas. To his delight, the police service did not even object to his riding his Yamaha 350cc motorcycle, which had once seemed the centre of his very existence; he was just rather more careful now about the places where he broke the speed limit on it.

Clyde Northcott had found that he even enjoyed the police training. He had felt quite guilty about that, at first. He was fitter and stronger than all the others in his intake, so that the physical demands had come easily to him. And he had found to his surprise that in the area where he had thought he would be most at risk, that of dealing with the public, he was really rather effective.

When he passed from cadet policeman to probationer and finally to the real thing, Clyde enjoyed a camaraderie he had never experienced before in his sporadic working life. It was quite new and unexpected for him, and thus all the more welcome. At Brunton, he met none of the institutional racism which he had been warned about in the police service. Where he came across individual and generally unthinking examples of it, he dealt with them with an effortless and ruthless efficiency.

PC Northcott was afraid of very little. But there are limits, for all of us; and when Clyde found himself invited to sit down in the office of the fearsome Percy Peach, he felt that he had reached those limits.

Peach studied him with that dispassionate, unblinking gaze which had unnerved many a criminal. Then he said, apparently with regret, 'You seem to be doing all right in the job. Everyone says so. Even your superintendent says so.'

'Thank you, sir.'

'Clever bugger, then, aren't you?'

'I wouldn't say that, sir.'

'But I would. And it's my opinion that counts in this.'

'Yes, sir.' Clyde waited for him to go on, and then, like many a man being interrogated, found that he was thrown off balance when the chief inspector remained silent. He said defensively, 'It was you who encouraged me to apply for the police service, sir. You and DS Blake.'

'Aye. We've a lot to answer for, one way and another.'

'Yes, sir.' PC Northcott divined for the first time that he might not after all be here for one of Percy Peach's right royal bollockings. But he had more sense than to relax; his ebony features remained alert but impassive.

'And the fact that you're black gives you a head start, with the shortage of coloured officers. Better if you were female and homosexual as well, of course, but I don't recommend you to take any steps in that direction.'

'No, sir.'

'Because the facts that you're young and a big bastard and can handle yourself when the shit's flying are also in your favour, in my book. Not that anyone works from my book, nowadays.' Peach shook his head at the aesthetic deficiencies of his profession.

'Yes, sir.' Northcott finally allowed himself the ghost of a smile. Whatever this was going to be – and he still couldn't for the life of him work out where it was going – it didn't have the makings of a bollocking.

'You've done all right, when we've needed a uniform man.'

'Thank you, sir.' This was praise indeed, from Percy Peach.

'And hopefully you've learned a bit about serious crime. You're not as stupid as you make out.'

Clyde wasn't aware that he'd ever pretended to be stupid. 'Perhaps you've mistaken my modesty for—'

'Not mistaken owt, lad, so don't get above yourself.' Peach was more at ease now.

PC Northcott actually grinned, showing the regular and complete set of very white teeth which was testimony to his ability to handle himself. 'No, sir.'

'And because I'm soft-hearted, and because you're a big bastard, and because I've got this silly suspicion that you might be a bit brighter than you look, I want to know if you'd like to join CID.'

Clyde Northcott's brain reeled. 'But I haven't even been a policeman for that long, sir. I'm still playing myself in as far as most people are concerned, I'm sure, and it would cause a certain amount of—'

'You saying you don't want to join CID?'

'No, sir. I'd love to join CID.'

'Right. Leave it with me. And keep your trap shut.'

'Yes, sir. Inspector Hughes won't like it.' He mentioned his uniformed chief officer.

'No. That's another advantage, then.'

'Yes, sir.' Clyde Northcott could feel the elation surging through his lean frame. He was finding it difficult not to laugh out loud now.

'You leave Bert Hughes to me. You'll be officially responsible to Tommy Bloody Tucker once you're transferred, but only officially, so don't think you can swing the lead. You'll be working for me, which means that you'll get away with bugger-all. Understood?'

'Understood, sir.'

'Once it's arranged, you'll be able to put that bloody uniform in the wardrobe. Save it for formal occasions.' He looked with some distaste at Northcott's model's physique and immaculately pressed uniform. 'You'll be working in what's laughingly called plain clothes, once you're with us.

But I don't want any technicoloured kaftans or limbo-dancing.'

'No, sir. I was born in Manchester and haven't lived outside Lancashire at any time during my life, sir.'

'I know you haven't, you daft sod. You'd better go and grab a shoplifter and get out from under my feet. I'll have you under them soon enough.'

Percy Peach allowed himself a grin. He was much happier, now that the uneasy business of communicating good news was out of the way.

Matt Hogan felt thoroughly disturbed after Peach and Blake had left him. He moved restlessly about the squalid little bed-sit, looked out of the small window at the distant view of the hospital on the skyline, and made the decision which seemed inevitable.

He thought at first there was going to be no reply; but the receiver was picked up after four rings and the familiar voice said, 'Brunton two three five one. Heather Shields speaking.'

'It's Matt.'

'Matt who?'

'You know who! Matt Hogan.'

A little snigger. 'This is indeed an honour. What do you want, Matt?'

'The CID people have been to see me. Again.'

'Lucky you.' But she wasn't sniggering now. 'So why are you ringing me?'

'I'm going to tell them about you and Annie. I'm going to tell them you knew she was pregnant. I've got to, Heather.'

'But we agreed that you wouldn't.'

'I know. But they've got me in the frame for this. They're pressing me hard. They'll be back, I'm sure. If I'm going to get them off my back, I've got to give them something.'

'So you're giving them me.'

'It won't matter.'

'You'll tell them that, will you?'

He could visualize her at the other end of the line, see that expression on her face which always made him quake. He was glad that she wasn't here in the room with him. 'I'm sorry, Heather. I don't want to tell them, but I've got to.

They'll have me for withholding information if I don't.'

'And they'll have me for murder if you do.'

'No, they won't. Not if you didn't do it, they won't.'

It was the first time he had ever voiced that thought to her. He could hear her breathing heavily at the end of the line. He wanted to ring off, but he knew he couldn't, that he couldn't just leave it like that, with what had been between them.

She said, 'I've got a record, you know. A record of violence. I flew at someone with a knife. They've already reminded me that they know all about that. That I nearly killed someone, once before. In circumstances very like the ones in which Annie Clark died. They've reminded me all about that.' Heather Shields tried not to let him know how important this was to her, but she could hear the hysteria rising in her voice as she appealed to him.

'I'm sorry. I don't feel I have any alternative.' He stood by the phone, feeling his left fist clench with determination, knowing that his resolution would not hold out if she were here in the room with him.

'You'll destroy me if you do this. I'm begging you to keep it to yourself, Matt. It's what we agreed. It will make both of us look like liars if you blab it out to them now.' As soon as she said it, she wished she hadn't used that phrase, hadn't shown the flash of the contempt that had come between them once before. She should never have begged him to relent like that, either. Begging wasn't her style, and no one was in a better position than Matthew Hogan to know that.

He did know it. He didn't feel proud of himself, but her desperation made him feel stronger, more confident that this was what he must do. He said, 'I'm sorry, Heather, but I've got to tell them. They've driven me into a corner. And you've nothing to fear. Telling them you knew about the pregnancy won't make much difference, will it? Not really, not if you didn't kill Annie.'

It was the second time he had made that provision. As he put the phone down, he wondered what she would make of that.

Nineteen

Katherine Howard ushered them into what in its Victorian heyday had been the dining room of the spacious, high-ceilinged house.

She normally took her visitors into the room at the front of the house, with its long blue velvet curtains reaching to the floor in the bow window, but these were not normal visitors. And something told her that she did not wish to speak to her CID questioners in the same room where the coven held its meetings and she held easy sway among them.

It was that little bantam cock of a chief inspector again, the one who seemed to exude energy, who seemed likely to break at any moment into a bout of shadow-boxing to relieve his tension. The man who went by the incongruous name of Peach; the man she most feared in the whole of this sorry mess. And with him that pretty but sturdy Detective Sergeant Blake, with her very striking chestnut hair, who said little but observed and noted all; a woman whom Kath now knew that she must not underestimate.

Kath had dressed in the formal grey suit she wore for important business meetings, in the hope that it would enable her to keep the initiative in this unaccustomed context. She was aware even before they had begun to speak to each other that it was not going to work, that these two would determine the agenda of what went on here.

They refused tea or coffee, but did not seem to be in any great hurry. They positioned themselves carefully in the armchairs she had planned for them and she herself sat down, rather self-conscious and upright, in the high-backed green leather armchair which had once been her husband's. Kath became aware that they were watching her every movement.

Peach eventually said, 'We now know a lot more about

Annie Clark and her life than when we last spoke to you, Mrs Howard.'

'Good. You probably have some idea of who killed her, then.'

He smiled. 'If we have, Mrs Howard, you wouldn't expect us to relay those thoughts to you. When we make an arrest, I'm sure you will learn of it very quickly.'

Kath wondered if there was an insult or even a threat in there somewhere. Was he suggesting that the Wiccans had perpetrated this and would be in contact with each other about what was happening? She returned his smile and said, 'Of course I don't expect you to tell me everything you've learned.'

'One area which is still a little foggy for us is the nature of Annie's relationship with you. We're hoping to clarify that this evening.'

Kath's first instinct was to resist. But she overcame that, thrust down the tension she felt rising at the back of her throat. 'I'll be as frank as I can. I don't think it will be as exciting as you would hope.'

'We hope for nothing, Mrs Howard. All we expect is a series of honest answers to our questions.' Peach gave her the impression that he rather enjoyed this verbal fencing. That was not surprising, she thought, when everything was in his favour: she had no idea exactly how much they knew, how much knowledge a week of questioning had brought them about the last days of Annie Clark.

She paused, then went into the speech she had carefully prepared but had hoped not to have to deliver. 'I suppose my public life is on the face of it very successful. I run what until a few years ago was my husband's company and it is very prosperous. Over the last ten years or so, conditions have favoured a business like ours, which provides efficient temporary replacements across a range of fields, and we have made the most of those conditions. The people who work for me see little or nothing of my private life, and that is the way I prefer it.'

It was Lucy Blake who now said, 'It is that private sector of your life which interests us. I am sorry that we have to intrude, but you must surely see that it is necessary.'

'I do. It has taken me some time to accept that: I have never been involved in a murder investigation before. But I expect you hear that from people all the time.' She made herself pause and measure her words. 'I have only one child. My son is now twenty-nine and he lives and works in Canada. I have never had a daughter.'

Lucy Blake, sensing her difficulties in speaking about this, prompted her gently. 'And did Annie Clark in some ways seem like a daughter to you?'

'She might have done, with time. I think I was certainly something of a mother figure to her. She had only just left her own mother, and like a lot of women of her age she was not as confident as she pretended to be. We had our belief in witchcraft to unite us. That was a powerful bond.'

'And you were her instructor.'

'Instructor and protector. I was well aware that that gave me a privileged position, which I did not want to exploit. Annie was twenty-three, but she was in some respects younger than that. She was still very impressionable. But we developed a close relationship. I think she came to rely on me, and I don't deny that in some respects I was beginning to look upon her as the daughter I had never had.'

Katherine Howard found herself touching her neat, well-cut blonde hair, as if to reassure herself that it was still in place. It was a gesture she recalled from her past, but one she had not made for years. But then it was years since she had talked to anyone about herself; now she was being made to confront the loneliness in her own life which she had always concealed from the world at large. She stared down at the dark-red carpet, as if afraid that eye contact with these strange confidants would break the spell of her intimacies.

'I taught Annie about witchcraft, removed some of the misconceptions she brought to her new beliefs. She was almost pathetically grateful to me, at first. I made her laugh a bit about some of the people I met in business, to lighten things up. And the laughter brought us closer together. She used to come and ask me about the big events which had happened in my life, as well as hers. I'd never been able to talk to anyone about such stuff before, and it brought us much closer together.'

Peach said, 'It has been suggested to us that Annie Clark was planning to leave the coven – that you resented that.' He wouldn't tell her that the only person who had suggested it was Tommy Bloody Tucker, superintendent in charge of CID and prize wanker.

'That isn't true. Of course Annie found that her contemporaries poured cold water on the Wiccans and witchcraft: both her flatmate and her new boyfriend had very silly ideas about us. But I'd warned her that that was sure to happen, and her belief was secure.'

Peach nodded slowly. 'In view of the close relationship you have outlined, it would have been rather devastating for you, wouldn't it, if Annie had chosen to go off with her boyfriend to pastures new and abandon the coven?'

'It would. I'm not disputing that. But that wasn't going to happen.'

There was a determination about the set of her mouth which made them wish once again that they could have Annie Clark's version of these things. Peach, as usual introducing his most dangerous darts most gently, said quietly, 'You mentioned that you were Annie's protector. What did you mean by that?'

Kath forced a shrug, feeling in that moment how stiffly she had been holding her shoulders beneath the smooth grey material of her suit. 'No more than what we've been talking about, really. I warned her about the misconceptions the public at large hold about modern witchcraft. I helped to clarify her beliefs. I acted sometimes as a confidante for her. Sometimes it's easier to talk to an older woman about emotional matters.' She looked instinctively to Lucy Blake for confirmation of that idea, but found that the young, intelligent face was on this occasion professionally blank.

Instead, DS Blake nodded slowly and said, 'I'm sure you can see that you need to reveal to us any secrets which Annie confided to you. You owe it to her and to yourself, if you want us to find out who killed her.'

'These things sometimes affect the living as well as the dead.' Kath knew that she had led them into the area she had determined to keep to herself before they came. The human brain works with amazing swiftness: she had time

176

even in her dismay to wonder whether her psyche had led them deliberately there.

'And that is the very reason why we need to probe these things. If they prove to have nothing to do with Annie's death, your confidences will be respected and we shall not pass on your thoughts.'

Kath looked into the young, earnest features and found herself smiling – an unexpected, involuntary smile – at the thought of roles reversed. Here was the younger woman leading the older one gently into revealing the secrets of her heart, a strange role-reversal from her time with Annie Clark. She tried to speak calmly. 'I've nothing very profound to tell you. I warned her gently about Jo Barrett. Then, later, I talked to her about her new boyfriend and tried to warn her against getting too excited too early about the relationship.'

Lucy nodded, using even that small physical movement as an outlet for the excitement she knew she must conceal. Katherine Howard obviously didn't realize that she'd given them new information, and she was much more likely to give them more if they did not react too eagerly. Lucy left the Jo Barrett reference for a moment, moving to the area they already knew something about. 'Was Annie excited by getting together with Matt Hogan?'

'Very excited. I tried to keep her calm, to tell her it was early days. She seemed pretty sure that it was going to last.'

'Do you know Matt Hogan?'

'No. Annie said she was going to bring him to meet me, but she disappeared before that ever happened.'

'He didn't approve of her involvement with witchcraft and the Wiccans. I fancy he would have tried to prise her away from you, from what he tells us. Is that the impression you had?'

'Yes. I wanted to talk to him, to show him that we were really quite normal people. But I never got the chance to do that.' She stared bleakly past them, looking out at the frost on the lawn of her front garden, which the sun did not reach until the afternoon.

Lucy Blake nodded her understanding, trying to make sure Katherine Howard would see nothing very remarkable in her next question. 'And Jo Barrett? I think you said you warned Annie gently about her.'

'Yes. Jo makes no secret of her sexual preferences. She would no doubt feel that she is honest and open in these things. But she was far more experienced than Annie was. And I sometimes think there is – well, a predatory streak in Jo. She wouldn't see it that way, but I did.'

'You didn't approve of her advances to Annie?'

Kath smiled. 'I didn't. No doubt Jo would tell you that I was the old-fashioned mother hen – that Annie Clark was a woman of twenty-three, perfectly capable of making her own decisions. On the face of it, she's right; of course she is. But I saw an inexperienced and vulnerable girl who'd previously led a very sheltered life being conducted into new areas by a much more experienced woman.' She smiled ruefully. 'I was being the protective mother, wasn't I? But no doubt Jo Barrett has called me that and worse to you.'

Lucy smiled. She could feel the tension in Peach beside her, but he kept quiet, trusting her to handle this. 'We don't reveal what people say to us, Mrs Howard – just as we shall respect your confidences, unless they seem to have a direct bearing on our investigation.'

Kath knew from the woman's inflection that this was a standard reassurance, probably one that she had uttered dozens of times before. Yet it was in that minute that she divined that they had not known about Jo Barrett and Annie before today. Even as she felt the pain of her unwitting treachery to her fellow Wiccan, a tiny part of her mind was asking why that should be so, why the normally scrupulously honest Jo should have concealed something that she should have known was bound to come out. She said woodenly, 'I shouldn't have told you about Jo Barrett and Annie. I thought you already knew.'

Peach could restrain himself no longer. 'On the contrary, Mrs Howard, it was your duty to speak about this. You have told us only something that Ms Barrett should have told us herself. What was the nature of their relationship?'

Kath shrugged, feeling a need despite his words to play this down, to try to mitigate the damage she had done to her friend and show loyalty to the coven. She picked her words carefully as she said, 'I don't know the details. Annie told me that she'd had a teenage infatuation with Jo as her teacher, many years before they met when Annie came to the coven. Perhaps Jo thought that gave her a right to some sort of intimacy with Annie.'

'So Jo Barrett made a bid for sexual favours from Annie?'

Kath tried to show a contempt for such a simplistic question in her smile. 'She plainly fancied Annie Clark, who was an attractive young woman. Would you find it so sinister if we were talking about a man who was ten years older and who had tried to get her into bed with him?'

'I wouldn't regard it as sinister at all. But in a murder investigation, I should certainly investigate both the man's feelings and the girl's reaction to them. Which is what we shall do in the case of Ms Barrett.'

'Then you should take it up with her.'

'That we shall certainly do, in due course. At this moment. I'm asking you how you saw the exchanges.'

Kath wanted to tell him to go away, to refuse to discuss the matter any further. But she was a logical woman, who had trained herself to take logical, dispassionate actions. And she could see the argument that murder made its own rules, that the woman who had been at the centre of this affair was not here to give her version of it. She owed a loyalty to Jo, but a greater loyalty to the girl who had been so close to her: these two saw that, and she must behave accordingly.

Kath tried to choose her words carefully. 'Jo Barrett "came on strong" to Annie, in the week after she had been initiated into the coven. That was Annie's phrase for it.' For a moment her face carried a sad, reminiscent smile. 'To be honest, I think Annie was flattered by Jo's feelings. She should have knocked the idea of a lesbian affair on the head from the start. But perhaps she didn't know Jo well enough, didn't realize that she wouldn't have committed herself without being intensely serious about it.'

'So there was a big row between the two of them?'

Kath's lips set in a firm line. 'I can't tell you that. I only know what Annie told me.'

'Which was what?'

He wasn't going to give up. Perhaps he was right: she was

the only remaining mouthpiece that poor Annie had left. And a small, unworthy voice within her said that at least this was taking his thoughts and his suspicions away from her own part in Annie's last days.

'Annie said it was pretty grim. Jo called her a lot of unpleasant names, said that she'd led her on, lured her into making a fool of herself.' Kath paused. 'She's a very proud person, Jo. A very private person, about her own feelings. I can imagine how hurt she might have been. But of course, I only had Annie's version of events. I've never spoken to Jo about what happened.'

'But Ms Barrett is aware that you know about this?'

'I imagine she must be. We've never spoken of it, as I say, but Jo knows that Annie used to confide in me, both as a mother figure and as leader of the coven.'

They asked her a little about the other people in the case. They questioned her about Dermot Boyd and whether he had been attracted to Annie, and she was carefully non-committal about that. Then they asked about the dead girl's relationships with her flatmate and with her employer, Alan Hurst. She replied carefully, telling them that she did not know these two people herself and that Annie had scarcely spoken of them to her – not that she could remember, anyway, after all these months. Annie had been very excited about her new boyfriend, but Kath was pretty sure that she hadn't mentioned any dispute with him. But that could have come after her last meeting with Kath, of course.

Kath wondered if these experienced questioners realized that she was waiting for them to come back to her own part in this. She felt the tension rising in her as they checked again when she had last seen Annie Clark, but they didn't ask her any more questions about that last day.

Lucy Blake said, as they drove away from the tall Victorian house, 'She was mortified when she found she'd let the cat out of the bag about Jo Barrett, wasn't she?'

'She was, but she recovered herself very quickly and went back to telling us just as much as she wanted to about things. She's a cool one, Katherine Howard. It makes you wonder what she's still concealing about herself.'

Twenty

Heather Shields was enjoying her breakfast.

She had been to her writers' circle on the previous night, and they had talked about the importance of bringing your personal experiences to your writing, of using events in your own life to bring immediacy to what you had to say. Heather had been happy as she listened to the earnest talk, but she had kept her thoughts to herself. She was the only person in the room who was involved with a murder, who had lived with the victim and been close to her – the only one who had known what the victim's thoughts were; the only one who had seen the very souls of herself and Annie Clark exposed, in that raw, elemental quarrel they had flung at each other on the day before Annie had died.

It was her secret, one she would use to inform her writing, to give it individuality. She was still musing about the advantages it would give her when she got the phone call.

A smooth, dark-brown voice, which in other circumstances she would have found very attractive. A Police Constable Northcott, he said, at Brunton CID. The man who had interviewed her last time with that Rottweiler of a chief inspector. He had seemed sympathetic to her then, but she had not recognized his voice on the phone today: it had seemed darker and deeper than she remembered. They needed to see her again, he said, in connection with the death of Anne Marie Clark. New information had come to light, and they needed to speak with her in connection with that. It would be better if it was in private.

Heather phoned in to the works and explained that she would be a little late on this Thursday morning. The impersonal voice on the other end of the line did not ask why, and she thought it better not to tell them. She threw away her half-eaten slice of toast and tried to drink her coffee black. Her appetite had suddenly disappeared. She told herself that she would remember what happened today, because it would be material for the writing she planned. But on this occasion, Heather failed to convince herself.

PC Northcott was even taller and blacker than she had remembered him. He had Detective Sergeant Blake with him, the woman who had come here with Peach after the news of Annie's death had broken. They wanted to talk to her again about that day in September when she had last seen Annie. She had known it would be that: it was almost a relief to her when they said it. She said, 'I know that Matt Hogan has told you that I had a big bust-up with Annie on that day. He phoned me.'

DS Blake frowned, wondering exactly what had taken place between the duo, whether they had agreed upon what she would now say. She shrugged. 'We'd rather he hadn't done that.'

Heather smiled, trying to play this easy, to make herself a spectator rather than a participator in that drama these two and others were trying to unravel. 'Matt meant well. And I've nothing to fear, have I? I told you all about my big row with Annie Clark when you were last here.'

Blake studied her dispassionately, noted how her fingers twisted in her lap, beneath a chest and shoulders which were rigid with tension. 'What we have to decide is whether you told us all about that last day with Annie, or whether you withheld something. We have to bear in mind, you see, that you denied all talk of any disagreement, when I first interviewed you, with Chief Inspector Peach.'

'At first I did, yes. That was foolish of me. But I have a criminal record, as DI Peach was delighted to point out to me when he saw me again on Monday. My first inclination was to conceal any disagreements I'd had with a dead girl or the man who used to be my boyfriend and was now hers.'

Lucy Blake studied the round, pretty face in its frame of abundant black hair. 'If I'd suddenly lost my long-standing boyfriend to someone who'd been sharing a flat with me, I think I'd have felt quite violent about it.'

'And if you'd been a druggie with a history of violence

182

you'd have attacked her and killed her. That's what you mean, isn't it?'

Blake looked at her evenly, letting the pause stretch. 'It's a possibility we have to consider.'

'I didn't kill Annie Clark. I felt like tearing her eyes out, but I didn't touch her.'

'But you lied about this – pretended there had been no disagreement between you, when in fact there had been a violent row.'

'But with no blows exchanged. Remember that, please. I'm not an addict any more, and I'm very conscious that I have a record. I can't afford to offer violence to anyone, and I didn't do so.' Heather was pleased with the quiet formality of her reply: like a much older woman, she thought.

'You knew Annie was pregnant, didn't you? In spite of what you've told us before.'

Heather wondered whether she should go on denying it. But Matt Hogan had said that he was going to tell them. Perhaps they already knew the facts, and were inviting her to stumble deeper into trouble. 'Yes, I knew. But it was only on that last Saturday, when we were screaming all kinds of things at each other. I can't see that it has anything to do with this.'

DS Blake looked at her for a long moment. 'Except that you've lied about it, until now, so you must have thought it was significant. Did Annie tell you who the father was?'

'No.'

'And you assumed it was Matt Hogan.'

Heather wondered if she could deny it, could scream at them that it was not so. But she had lied quite enough already, and each lie had got her further into trouble. 'Yes, I thought it was Matt. Perhaps Annie wanted me to think that, with the things we were flinging at each other at that moment.'

'It must have increased your fury with Annie Clark – made you wish you could be rid of her, once and for all.'

'Probably it did. I certainly wasn't thinking rationally. But I didn't kill Annie.'

The white, freckled, female face and the smooth, ebony male one studied her for seconds before Lucy Blake said, 'We can only consider the facts. And one of those is that you were very sure that Annie Clark was gone for good. By the end of September, no more than a few days after she was last seen, you'd got someone else to take on her share of the rent.'

'Because I knew there was no going back after the terrible things we'd said to each other. Because I knew she planned to set up house with Matt Hogan. Because I thought she was carrying his baby. Because I didn't want to see either of them ever again.' Heather threw all the vehemence she could muster into the phrases, aware that what they had said sounded very damning for her, that these were the police, looking hard to pin a killing on someone. She wondered if the desperation she felt was coming out in her words, if the wildness she felt raging in her head was visible to these watchful opponents.

It seemed to her a long time before PC Northcott, speaking for the first time since they had come into the room, said softly, 'You were one of the last people to see Annie Clark alive. Did she tell you where she was going, when she left here?'

It was a lifeline, an acknowledgement that she might after all not be guilty of murder, and she grasped at it eagerly. 'We parted on such bad terms that I didn't know where she was going. We were just hurling abuse at each other, by then. But I'm sure she'd said something earlier about what she was planning to do. She'd mentioned going off the next day with someone for a long walk, trying to sort things out once and for all. Those were the words she used.' As the phrase came back to her over the months, her face brightened with hope, as if quoting the dead girl's exact words was some guarantee of her innocence.

Clyde Northcott knew that it was nothing of the sort, that even if Heather Shields was speaking the truth, it might be an irrelevance, a mere cul de sac leading them away for a time from her guilt. Or it might, of course, be very important. He tried to make himself sound almost bored as he said, 'And whom do you think Annie was planning to meet on that Sunday, when she said that?'

'I don't know. I assumed she meant Matt Hogan. That's what started the big row between us: I thought she was

184

rubbing my nose in the situation. Now I think it may have been someone else she was planning to see. But I've no idea who it might have been.'

Dermot Boyd hadn't seen the man Peach introduced as DC Pickering before. He was a young man, lanky and a little uncoordinated in his movements, which somehow made him seem less menacing than the squat and pugnacious man beside him.

Unfortunately, it was DCI Peach who was doing most of the talking. Dermot had taken them into the inner office, the one he and his fellow professionals in finance used when they needed privacy with a client. He was uncomfortably aware that the place was not completely soundproof, that the exchanges in here might reach the curious ears of his colleagues if voices were raised. He found himself saying defensively, 'I don't know why you keep going over this. I've told you all that I know about Annie Clark and what went on at the time of her disappearance.'

'I expect you see it like that. But after ten days of intensive enquiries, we now have a fuller picture of this crime than do any of the individuals we have been questioning. Certain things have acquired added significance.'

'I don't doubt it. All I'm saying is that I have nothing further to tell you about the crime.'

'And yet you may have, Mr Boyd. Sometimes we unearth extra facts that people have been concealing – sometimes wittingly, sometimes unwittingly.' Peach's dark, penetrating eyes left Dermot in no doubt which adverb would apply to him. 'In your case, we keep asking ourselves why it was that you seemed to know that Annie's body was in that ruin on Pendle Hill; why you tried to steer your wife away from the spot; why you were not surprised when that decomposing corpse presented itself to you in that derelict place.'

'You've no reason to say that.' Dermot hissed the words like a conspirator, fearful that his denials would be heard outside the room if he raised his voice.

Peach pursed his lips, weighing the matter unhurriedly and dispassionately, enjoying the accountant's discomfort. 'I'd say we had quite good reason. Your wife certainly has the impression that you did not want her to go into that place, even to shelter from a blizzard. You have been evasive about it yourself. You are uneasy, even now, about the suggestion. In the light of what our team has picked up from a host of other people, your discomfort seems to us significant. Which is the main reason why we have taken the trouble to come to see you this morning, to allow you to pass on to us any further information or reflections you may have on the matter.' DCI Peach gave him a bland smile, which nevertheless seemed to Dermot full of menace.

He licked his lips, trying to make himself take his time. 'I didn't know Annie's body was in that place. It's probably true that I had an uneasy feeling about that ruined farm. It was probably because I associated Annie with Pendle Hill from the time when she disappeared. I knew she was planning to walk up there, on the Sunday when it now seems that she was last seen alive.'

'There you are, you see. Something's come back to you. Another fact falls into place. You knew that Annie was going to be in that area on the Sunday when she was killed!' Peach beamed his satisfaction.

'I'm sure I told you this before.'

'And I'm sure you didn't. I'm sure DC Pickering, who has diligently kept himself informed on the development of the case, will confirm that.'

'Yes, sir. First we've heard of this. No previous record of Mr Boyd knowing the whereabouts of the deceased at the time of her death.' Gordon Pickering, fresh-faced and eager, spoke as though flicking through the pages of his mental notebook, turning the screw competently on the older man.

Dermot Boyd wrenched his eyes away from the delighted detective faces in front of him. 'It was after the meeting of the coven. I was chatting to Annie about the weekend. She said she was going into the original witch country – going up on to Pendle Hill. She had a bit of a laugh with me about it.'

'I see. Shame this bit of a laugh should have escaped your recollection until now. So who was Annie Clark planning to have as her companion on this journey into witch country?'

'I don't know. I didn't ask her.' It sounded feeble, even

186

to him. 'I presumed she'd be with her new boyfriend, I suppose. That's probably why I didn't ask her about it. It was only a casual conversation, after the coven's worship and incantations were over.'

DCI Peach looked very satisfied as he stood up. 'New information, you see, Mr Boyd. Well worth our arranging this meeting, after all. Annie Clark almost certainly died up on Pendle on that Sunday. And so far you're the only person who has confessed to knowing she would be up there.'

It was five o'clock and the stars were already glittering in the clear navy sky. Alan Hurst left the tiny flagged yard at the back of his premises and went into the brightly lit shop. 'You might as well get off early, Anna. We're not going to have any rush I can't cope with now.'

He gave her the cheerful smile of the good employer, keeping their relationship close but not intimate. He wouldn't do anything about bedding Anna Fenton until this Annie Clark investigation was over and he could relax again. Curious that their first names should be so similar, but that must be no more than coincidence. He'd done the right thing, being frank with Peach about his philandering, about his situation at home; about the weakness of the flesh, and the little flings he indulged in. The man had seemed to understand, to accept that there was a huge difference between a little harmless lust and murder.

When his assistant had gone, he went and unlocked the bottom drawer of the filing cabinet, took out the video tapes and put them into his briefcase. He was glad of the winter and the darkness. The fewer people who were about the town, the better it would be for him.

From the age of about twelve, Lucy Blake had fantasized like most girls about this scene. She had never envisaged it happening across two pint glasses in a back-street pub.

She said automatically, 'I only ordered a half.'

'You might need a pint, to cope with what I've got to say.' Percy Peach set the big mugs of bitter and shandy down on the beer mats with elaborate care, as if any deviation from the exact centre would affect what was coming.

187

'Is it about the case?'

'No. Be easier if it were.' Percy took a long, speculative pull at his beer, then studied the glass intently, as if it could deliver to him the necessary words. 'You can blame your mum, if you don't like it.'

'I'm getting a bit old for that.'

He grinned suddenly at her. 'Th'art nobbut a lass, yet.'

'I'm twenty-nine, tha big daft lummox.' She warmed to him as usual when he thee'd and thou'd her, when they lapsed into the language that she had grown up with and still heard in rural Lancashire. Sometimes he did it in bed, and it became a comedy cloak for their passion, a reminder that even the greatest things in life should be treated with a certain levity. Now she knew that, in the quietly absurd setting of the back room of this dingy old pub, it was a humorous vehicle for something intensely serious.

Percy frowned at his beer. 'Tha must understand that I only want thee because I like thee mum.'

'I understand that, Percy me lad. Perhaps it's her thee should be talking to now.'

He smiled. He'd stopped himself just in time from saying that he'd already spoken to her. 'Aye. 'Er knows her cricket, does tha mum. 'Appen she only wants me for a son-in-law because I'm Denis Charles Scott Peach.'

'She tells me there's more nor that to it, lad. But it helps that tha were a decent cricketer.'

'Decent, yes. Never a Denis Compton, though.' Percy downed another two inches of his beer, and she wondered if they would be on the third pint before he got to the important bit, whether she would have to plunge the whole thing into the farce which was threatening by running for the loo.

Perhaps her man felt the same. He said suddenly, 'Will tha marry me then, Lucy Blake?'

She had always thought the man of her dreams would be looking soulfully into her eyes at this point. Instead of that, the stocky, bald-headed Peach was staring at the initials scratched into the top of the table by his beer-mat. But, amazingly, he was still the man of her dreams. She pushed out her small hand until it sat on top of his broad one and said, 'Aye, I will that, Percy Peach.'

'Bloody 'ell, Norah!'

He finished his beer with one swift swallow, bolted to the bar, came back with another pint and set it down beside the shandy she had scarcely touched. He looked at her now, and a smile of pure pleasure flooded into his round face. He put his hand back on hers, left it there for a full thirty seconds before he broke the spell. 'Best bum in Brunton. I never thought I'd get me 'ands on that.' He dropped his eyes towards that mercifully invisible part of her anatomy.

'Very capable hands. Sometimes I can't believe there's only two of them.' She ignored him as he held the skilful appendages up proudly in front of her. 'Mum wants grandchildren, you know. Don't let her pressurize you.'

Percy couldn't remember when he'd last been pressurized. He took a more relaxed and meditative pull at his second pint, contemplating the vision of a small, sturdy, red-haired boy with a cricket bat in his hand. 'She has some good ideas, your mum.'

'I want a long engagement, though.'

'Perhaps we should discuss that with your mum.'

'And have the two of you ganging up on me? Not likely. I can hold my own with most, but not with an alliance between Agnes Blake and Percy Peach.'

'Aye. But tha must remember that the best bum in Brunton is flanked by child-bearing hips.' He allowed himself a low groan of pleasure, at once reminiscent and anticipatory, which ran round the walls of the shabby room. 'Shame to waste either the bum or the hips, I'd say.'

Lucy Blake found that she was enjoying her shandy now. 'All that's for future discussion, Percy lad – between the two of us, without third parties. It's time that we were on our way.'

She stood up, reached for her coat, leaning across him and putting the best bum in Brunton within eighteen inches of his widening eyes.

'Bloody 'ell, Norah!' said Percy Peach.

Twenty-One

Alan Hurst watched Judith anxiously as she struggled into the sitting room after their evening meal.

He had already put the television programmes and the remote control on the little table next to her chair. Now he brought her the morning paper and her ballpoint pen and put them neatly alongside the remote control. He didn't want to seem too much like the mother hen, but his wife liked to do the crossword while the television was on in the evenings, and he didn't want her falling over trying to reach things whilst he was out.

He went and stacked the pots methodically in the dishwasher, with an expertise born of much practice. He put on his coat and gloves before he went back into the sitting room. 'I'll be as quick as I can, Jude,' he said cheerfully. 'I don't expect to be much more than an hour, but don't worry if I'm delayed. Do you have everything you need?'

'Yes. I'm sorry you have to go out again, on a bitter night like this.'

'Needs must. You'll think it was worth our while, when you see our new extension taking shape!'

'You never needed to work in the evening in the old days – the days when I used to be able to help you in the business.' She had meant it to be sympathetic, but it sounded in her own ears like a petulant complaint, and she regretted her words as soon as they were out.

'Business is very competitive these days. You have to be quick on your feet to stay alive. But we're doing all right, aren't we, Jude?' He bent and kissed her lightly on the forehead, then turned towards the door, feeling the weight of his coat already in the oppressive heat of the room.

She wondered what other, younger and healthier, flesh

those lips would touch before the evening was over, whether the real reason for his venturing out on a night like this was to meet some female. She never mentioned his girls, and she tried not to resent them. It was just the situation that did it: you couldn't blame a man for his needs – not when he was as good to you as Alan was. 'Be as long as you have to,' she called after him bravely. 'I'll be perfectly all right here.'

She didn't know in that moment quite how long it would be before she saw him again.

Alan Hurst tried hard not to feel relieved as he shut the front door of the house carefully behind him. He unlocked the boot and took out his bulging briefcase, setting it down in front of the passenger seat in the car. It was good to be out in the cold, clear air after the stifling heat of the house. He breathed in slowly and deliberately several times, the way his father had taught him to do as a child, feeling the welcome coolness drawn into his lungs, putting off for a moment the journey of deliveries he had to make.

He didn't like doing this. Some day, when Judith and he had built the extension they needed, he'd give up this lucrative sideline, which was threatening to become more profitable than his proper business. Some day. But he put away all thoughts of a distant future, because he was conscious at the base of his brain that it would not contain Judith.

He made his first delivery to the house of the circuit judge. He usually went there first, having an obscure feeling that this client from the high ranks of the legal world could somehow give legitimacy to his enterprise.

The judge lived alone with a manservant, the only example of the species whom Alan had encountered in his entire life. If he came here in daylight, as he rarely did, he left his package in the garden shed. But at night, he delivered it into the manservant's hands. This man always appeared to know when Alan was coming, so that he never had to ring the bell. The wide and heavy oak door eased back on well-oiled hinges as Alan walked between the laurels and up the drive. The old man with the immaculate silver hair took the envelope with the two video tapes from him with a wintry smile and the briefest of nods, and the door shut as silently as it had opened.

It was much the grandest of the houses that Alan visited. The other properties demonstrated what an estate agent would have called a comprehensive price range. Vice, like its great antagonist virtue, knows no social boundaries, and Alan Hurst was in no position to be choosy about his customers.

He knew exactly where he was going, having rehearsed the route in his mind several times during the day. Most of these people had become regular customers, and neither he nor they wished to linger over the transactions. He felt confident. Now that he had got used to the trade and his particular niche in it, one of the tricks was to appear self-assured, not shifty, to behave as though the idea that you were doing anything against the law was preposterous. Alan Hurst walked brisk and erect, and he did not glance back nervously over his shoulder, as he might have done in the early days.

He did not like going into the new block of flats: he always felt more at risk in this luxurious rabbit warren of a place, where the lift and the corridors were brightly lit and there were inevitably people about. But he managed on this occasion to get to the fourth-floor apartment without meeting a single person, and the door opened as he reached for the bell, just as that very different door had done at the judge's house. The occupant must have been watching the car park from the window as Alan had driven in. He was a youngish man, with unfashionably long hair: he took the videos without a word and did not respond to Hurst's hesitant smile.

Alan was away from the place without a word spoken, without anyone other than his client having remarked his presence, as far as he was aware. Nevertheless, he did not like the place. Perhaps he would make some arrangement for the customer to meet him in the car park in future, or even in some spot far removed from those eyes, which gave him the feeling of claustrophobia whenever he set foot into that modern, functional block.

He did not take long with any of his deliveries, for this was not a trade where many words were exchanged, where there was even the pretence of social niceties. Most of his clients were even more nervous than he was. Perhaps as he despised himself for his involvement in meeting this demand, they despised themselves for their weakness. People who are full of self-loathing often divert their self-contempt on to the messenger who brings to them the things they crave, so that Alan Hurst was seen by them as both necessary and despicable.

Without conversational exchanges, each transaction was swift. Yet as always the journey, with its frequent stops, took longer than he had expected. He glanced at his watch as he left the house on the edge of the Asian quarter of the town and prepared for his last errand of the night. It was almost two hours since he had left home. He pictured Judith, sitting with her crossword in the overheated room, half-watching the television, waiting patiently and uncomplainingly for his return, and his heart filled with an immense tenderness and sadness.

Not long now before he was home, and at least the streets were mercifully deserted, even in this section of the town, which was so often brimming with people. That was not surprising: the cold here was intense, and most of these old terraces had their cheap brick frontages shut tight against it. He was glad to slide himself back into the warmth of the car. The frost on a few scrubby bushes of privet glittered in his headlights as he eased the car away towards his last delivery.

This final sale was one of the easiest and least dangerous. He drove some three miles to the outskirts of the town, where an estate of comfortable semi-detached houses built in the nineteen-fifties sat solid and ordinary, beside a pub called the Hare and Hounds and several football pitches. He could see the playing fields white with the frost as he swung his car into the road he wanted.

He passed across his merchandise as quickly and as silently as with any of the night's other terse exchanges. The man who came to the side door of the house seemed even more anxious to be rid of him than his predecessors, even less prepared to look into his face as he muttered the meaningless phrases of acceptance. That suited Alan well enough: the more anonymous these things could be kept, the better it was for him.

He had no idea that anything was wrong until the car at the end of the road switched on its lights and pulled out to block his path. It was only when the police sign on its roof was suddenly illuminated that his heart stopped for a moment, and then began to race.

They were big men, seeming even bigger as they stood at the window of his car and asked him politely to switch off his engine. He heard words which were familiar, but which had never in his life been addressed to him, about not needing to say anything, though it might harm his defence if he failed to mention when questioned something which he might later rely on in court. He was informed politely and formally that he was being arrested on suspicion of purveying pornographic videos of children.

Alan Hurst listened dumbly for what seemed a long time, letting the seconds elapse even when the words had finished, watching the man's breath curling away into the freezing air above the bright buttons of his uniform and the black and white squares of his cap. Alan said dully, 'I've an invalid wife at home. She needs attention.'

'That will be taken care of,' said the officer. Alan wondered that one who was so young and so ignorant of life should speak with such confidence about things of which he knew nothing.

They took him into Brunton police station, its lights unnaturally white against the clear and freezing night.

And even in the stifling heat of the room where he had left her, Judith Hurst shivered a little, as she glanced at the clock on the mantelpiece and waited for her husband's return.

Twenty-Two

Jo Barrett led them into the lab assistant's room behind the laboratory. 'We won't be disturbed here,' she said. 'Our assistant doesn't work on Fridays.'

'Just as well, that,' said DCI Peach. He looked round the little room, with its shelves tightly packed with bottles, its single window high in the wall, its scents of chemicals which he didn't know and which were probably lethal. 'I'm sure you wouldn't want anyone listening in on what we have to say today.'

'That sounds bad. I'm trembling with apprehension, now.' Jo tried to pass it off as a joke, which was uncharacteristic for her and a sign of her nervousness. It brought no response from Peach. She turned her attention to Lucy Blake. 'Move those lab coats and sit yourself down. It's hardly the Ritz, but I'm sure you've been in worse places.'

Jo wasn't used to exchanges like this. She always said that she enjoyed conversation but was no good at small talk. Now, when she tried to summon those meaningless phrases that help to grease the wheels of communication, she found them falling unnaturally from her tense lips.

Peach studied her without a word, for seconds that seemed to Jo to stretch endlessly. She was dressed in her usual contrast: an immaculate white polo-neck sweater, with its sleeves rolled up just a little on the slim arms, topped well-cut black trousers and low-heeled black shoes. He'd liked this woman, had responded immediately to her love of her family and her sturdy independence when they had interviewed her in her own flat. Now he was dispassionately weighing the idea that she might be a killer.

She would certainly have the nerve for it, and the raw physical strength to see off a sturdy young woman in the

195

prime of life, especially if she had taken her by surprise. It seemed that after their meeting thirty-six hours earlier, Katherine Howard had obeyed his injunction that she should not make contact with Jo Barrett, her fellow Wiccan. He said, 'You haven't been completely honest with us, Miss Barrett. Perhaps you haven't been honest at all.'

'I can assure you that I have.'

'Not only have you concealed things. You have deliberately attempted to mislead us.' He had ignored her denial and continued as if she had never spoken. 'We have to take a very serious view of that.'

'I don't know what you're talking about. I resent the implications of what you're saying. I told you everything I knew about other members of the coven and their relationships with Annie Clark.'

'But not about your own dealings with a murder victim. That was the most important relationship of all.'

'I don't know what you're talking about.'

But she was no longer meeting his eye, and that was very significant in the case of this most direct of women. 'I think you do. You tried to establish a close relationship with Miss Clark. A sexual relationship.'

'I told you. She made a bid for intimacy with me eight years earlier. I couldn't reciprocate then, because she was under age. Indeed, she was a schoolgirl and I was her teacher. I believe I behaved in a proper professional manner in the way I handled her infatuation at that time. But I told you all about this when we spoke on Sunday morning.'

'Indeed you did. You gave us what I have no doubt was a frank and accurate account of that adolescent episode in Annie Clark's life – in what now appears to be an attempt to divert our attention from your real and more recent feelings for Annie Clark, the woman of twenty-three.'

'We were friends at the time when she disappeared. And fellow Wiccans. Whoever has told you that we were anything more is making mischief. Perhaps you should be taking account of this in your assessment of that person, rather than trying to make trouble for me.'

It was spirited enough to make them wonder for a moment about just that – about Katherine Howard's motives in setting this particular hare running. But Jo Barrett's eyes were switching quickly from Peach's face to the younger and softer female one beside him and back again, and there was a kind of desperation in the slim features beneath her very dark hair. It was Lucy Blake who said quietly, 'You speak of the time when Annie disappeared, Jo. We have to be interested also in what went on in the months before her disappearance.'

'I'm not sure what you mean by that.'

But she was very sure. She had been truthful, in her straightforward, literal way, about the relationship at the time of Annie's death. There was nothing between them then. Except for a smouldering resentment on her part, a sense of betrayal that she could not dismiss. She found herself saying reluctantly, as if the words had formed themselves without any direction from her brain, 'I was attracted to Annie Clark when she first joined the coven. She had a freshness, a kind of natural innocence, about her, which was quite captivating.'

Lucy felt as she often did nowadays that she was prying into a private grief and reopening old sores. But in a murder investigation, privacy is the first casualty. 'And I expect you presumed, because of what had gone on eight years earlier when she was your pupil, that she would have certain feelings for you – that there would be a sexual attraction of a more adult kind; one you could now feel free to indulge.'

Jo Barrett's dark eyes flashed a look of hatred at her, and Blake realized at that moment that this woman would be capable of a swift, instinctive violence, when passion took her over. But Jo controlled herself, took seconds to do so, before she spoke. 'There was something of that in it, I suppose. I don't care to delve too deeply into my own psyche. But I'd felt no attraction at all for Annie Clark when she was at school. She was just another adolescent with acne and a steamy and stupid infatuation for one of her teachers. I just felt very unfortunate and embarrassed to be the object of that infatuation. Because I'd made no secret of the fact that I was a lesbian, it was more dangerous to my career than it might have been otherwise. I could cheerfully have strangled the little minx at the time!' She stopped, realizing what she had said, wanting to take it back, or make a joke

197

of it, but feeling too tense and brittle to be able to do that.

It was left to Lucy Blake to say with soft insistence, 'And last September? Is that what happened then? Did you strangle the adult Annie Clark?'

'No! It's a preposterous idea!' But even as she said it, she knew that it was not.

It was Peach who now said, 'Miss Barrett, you strike me as a woman who does not commit herself lightly. I don't think it was a casual attraction that you declared to Annie Clark. I don't think you're the sort of woman who makes a pass at just anyone she fancies.'

She forced a smile. He was her enemy now, but she must make the best terms she could with him. 'I suppose that's a sort of compliment. And you're right: it was quite unexpected when Annie came along and I fell for her. It took me by surprise as well as her. It was at least a couple of weeks before I told her what I felt for her.'

It wasn't a long time, for someone as serious-minded as Jo Barrett. But everyone said that Annie Clark had been an attractive young woman, and any lover is desperately afraid of other suitors stepping in. Peach said quietly, 'And what was her reaction to your declaration?'

'She pretended to be shocked. But she must have seen it coming. She must have known something at least of what I was feeling for her!' Jo felt her voice rising on the tide of her resentment. She mustn't allow that to happen. She must keep calm, if she was to persuade them that this dispute was more trivial, more run-of-the-mill, than it had been. 'An older woman declares her love for a pretty and inexperienced younger one. The younger one says, "Thank you very much but I'm not that way inclined. What happened at school was part of a vanished world for me, so don't presume that I want to get into bed with a woman now. In fact, the idea revolts me. So go away and don't suggest anything like that again." I can't give you the exact words, but it was something like that.'

She had spoken in a curious hollow monotone, as if seeking to squeeze all emotion out of her words. Lucy Blake said, 'And that's how it was? There was no attraction on her side?'

Jo smiled bitterly. 'That's a fair summary of it. I can see now that it was no big deal.'

'Not for her, perhaps. But for you, it was a very big deal indeed.'

Unexpectedly, Jo Barrett squirmed. It was a manifestation of her tension. The lithe, athletic body convulsed like that of a child who desperately wants to be anywhere rather than confronting what she has done. She was a private person: the last thing she wanted to do was to talk about her personal passions and her humiliations, but this was out in the open now and the pain of revelation must be endured. But she wanted this over with quickly and her punishment out of the way. She said dully, 'Annie said the idea disgusted her. She said she was as straight as a die and didn't want to know about my "perversions". She had a mature man who delighted her, and plenty of boys who wanted her. The last thing she wanted was a woman pawing her.' She produced each of the wounding phrases with a little wince of renewed pain at the memory.

'Who was the man, Jo?'

'I don't know. I thought perhaps she'd just made him up to hurt me, at the time.'

She meant Alan Hurst, in all probability, if this was in the months before her teaming up with Matt Hogan. DS Blake said, 'And how did you react to this rejection, Jo? It doesn't sound as if Annie was very tactful.'

Jo Barrett tossed her dark head of closely cut black hair, perhaps as much in annoyance at herself and her having laid herself open to the humiliation as at the remembrance of Annie Clark's dismissal. 'I went away and wept, if you must know everything. But I didn't lay a finger on Annie Clark.' She was breathing hard now, taking in great lungfuls of air, as if she had just sprinted at the end of one of her runs. But the air was stale in here.

'And her new boyfriend?'

'Matt Hogan? She went on a lot about that, saying she thought it was the real thing, thrusting him into our faces at the coven.'

So others as well as her might have been inflamed by that. Lucy said sympathetically, 'That must have been very hard for you to take.'

'It was. As you said, tact wasn't part of Annie's make-up.' She controlled herself, then declared with an anticlimax that was almost comic, 'She was still very young – younger than her age, in many respects.'

It was Peach, fastening her dark eyes with his even darker ones, who asked her the final question. 'Did you kill her, Jo?'

'No. I felt like killing her, on more than one occasion, if you want to know. But I never laid a finger on her.' She repeated the phrase carefully, as if she could give credence to her tale by its repetition.

'Are you close to an arrest?' Chief Superintendent Tucker jutted his chin masterfully across his big desk at his chief inspector.

'I think we are, sir, yes.' Peach, sensing that Tommy Bloody Tucker was in bollocking mode, deflated him skilfully with his unexpected reply.

'That's good to hear.' Tucker didn't sound as if it was. He'd prepared a stern pep talk about the necessity of results, and he wasn't good at the improvisation which now seemed to be indicated. 'How quickly can we expect someone to be under lock and key and facing a murder charge?'

'Wouldn't like to commit myself on that, sir. I hope events will become clearer later today.' Peach drew himself up to his full five feet eight inches and crossed his fingers firmly behind his back.

'I'll call a media conference for tomorrow morning.' Tucker stroked his silvering hair automatically: he might need a visit to the hairdresser, if he was to be at his avuncular best under the lights of the television cameras.

'I'd rather you didn't do that just yet, sir. I may be barking up the wrong tree altogether – chasing entirely the wrong hare.' He considered the next in the extensive range of clichés he reserved for Tucker. 'The investigation is at a rather delicate stage, sir.'

'But we two senior officers have no secrets from each other, Percy. Pull up a chair and tell me the name of the man you are planning to arrest.'

Peach noted the use of his forename as a danger signal. He made great play of positioning the chair exactly the distance from his chief which would combine intimacy with deference. 'Man, sir?' The black eyebrows arched impossibly high into his forehead. 'You're plainly ahead of me, sir. You've got your own candidate for this nasty little business lined up, haven't you? Well, I suppose I should have anticipated that. I was only saying to the lads and lasses at the team briefing this morning, "Chief Superintendent Tucker will be down with the results of his overview any time now." One or two of them were a bit sceptical, but the experienced ones knew just how much they could rely on you.'

Tucker glared at him suspiciously, but found Peach's gaze as usual rooted on a spot three inches above his head. 'Well, that's as may be. Let's have the name of our murderer.'

Peach shook his head firmly. 'Couldn't do that, sir. Might make a complete fool of myself to my superior officer. Matter of pride, sir. And more interviews to conduct. Of course, if you'd like to add your expertise to the questioning, I'm sure you'd spot our killer faster than anyone.'

Tucker was, as usual, horror-stricken at the thought of direct involvement with crime. He said stiffly, 'You know that I never interfere, Peach. It is only by remaining detached that I can give you the overview which you claim to value so highly. You must play this your own way. And I shall as always give you every support.'

'Yes, sir. Most gratifying, sir. Your support, I mean' – which will, as usual, disappear like shit off a hot shovel if I get anything wrong. 'Perhaps I'd better bring you up to date.'

'Brief me as you see fit, Percy. I am as always at your disposal.'

Peach noted that the threat of real police work had succeeded as usual in bringing his man to heel. But he'd got more urgent things to do than pandering to this high-ranking fool. He'd give him the picture quickly and get out of this office. 'Three men and three women, sir.'

'In the frame?'

'Still in the frame, sir. As of this minute.' Peach glanced at his watch as if anxious to record this key moment of enlightenment in his day. 'First woman, Katherine Howard. Local businesswoman and witch, sir. Head of the coven of

which Annie Clark was a member at the time of her death.'
He enjoyed Tucker's glassy-eyed stare of incomprehension.
'Admits to being a mother figure to the deceased. Admits
that Annie Clark was in some respects the daughter she never
had. Introduced her to the complexities of modern witchcraft in the Wiccan mode and to the mysteries of life generally. Took it badly when Miss Clark found herself a new
boyfriend and proposed to desert both witchcraft and Mrs
Howard.'

'Hardly a strong case for murder, is it?'

'Could be manslaughter, this, sir. Quite possible that
whoever attacked Annie Clark did so in a fit of temper and
didn't intend to kill her. I can see some defence counsel
arguing on those lines, unless we get a confession to murder.'

'Bloody nuisance, you know, these damned lawyers.'

Percy reflected once again on his chief's weakness for the
blindin' bleedin' obvious. 'Yes, sir. Second female suspect
is the deceased's flatmate, sir. Heather Shields. Apparently
knew Annie Clark wasn't coming back when she disappeared,
because she re-let the flat pretty well immediately. Had a
blazing row with Annie Clark on the day she disappeared,
over the boyfriend whom she thought Annie had stolen from
her. Former druggie, with previous history of violence in
similar circumstances.'

'I must say, when you put it like that, it really does sound
as if this Heather Shields is—'

'Just come from interviewing the third female suspect, sir.
Schoolteacher by the name of Jo Barrett. Also an Olympic-
standard athlete, in the past. Made lesbian advances to the
deceased and was rudely rebuffed. Didn't take kindly to that.
Strong woman, sir, capable of violence. Newcastle United
supporter.' Peach allowed himself a glance at Tucker out of
the corner of his eye to see how he perceived this connection.

'Lesbian, eh? Well, as you know, I'm not one for prejudices, but—'

'Then there's Alan Hurst, sir. Employer of Annie Clark,
in the months before she died.'

'And a prominent local businessman. It really does seem
most unlikely that—'

'Had a bit of a fling with the deceased, sir. A possible

candidate for the father of the foetus found in the dead woman, like the other men in the case. Admits to being a serial philanderer. Has an invalid wife, sir. Treats her very well, by all accounts.'

'Well really, you know, it hardly seems—'

'Has plans for an ambitious extension to his house to make life easier for his invalid wife Judith. Where's the money coming from? Modest travel business seems unlikely to be making huge profits.'

'Now Peach, you can hardly hold it against a man if—'

'Answer: the money is coming from a criminal enterprise. Mr Hurst has been purveying child-pornography videos to a variety of eager clients in the district. The National Child Pornography Unit has been tracking him for some time. He was arrested last night.'

'He's been trafficking in pornographic videos?'

'Exactly, sir.' Peach sounded as if he was congratulating a clever five-year-old. 'His clients are being interviewed and there will no doubt be charges brought against many of them. They include a judge and several local luminaries. Probably one or two Masons among them.' Peach had no idea who these people were as yet, but it seemed an opportunity for one of his ritual snipings at Tommy Bloody Tucker's favourite pursuit.

'So Mr Hurst is in custody?'

'Yes, sir. I shall be interviewing him myself presently, in connection with the murder of Anne Marie Clark. I thought I'd let the Child Pornography Unit soften him up a little first.'

'Well, from what you say it does seem—'

'Then there's the boyfriend, of course, sir. Matt Hogan. Always a likely candidate, as I think you indicated yourself in one of our previous meetings. Rather a devastating insight, that was. Says he didn't know about the pregnancy: that seems unlikely. Also says he wasn't the father. That seems more likely, since he wasn't the regular boyfriend at the time of conception.'

'Well, in the light of—'

'Either way, the pregnancy gives Hogan a motive. If he was the father, the pair may have disagreed about whether to keep the baby. If he found she was carrying another man's baby, he might have attacked her in a fit of jealousy.'

Tucker leaned forward happily. 'I've said all along that the boyfriend was the likeliest candidate, you know.'

'There's good news about the foetus, sir. Forensic are pretty certain there's enough left for a DNA match, once we have enough evidence against someone to demand a sample.'

Tucker nodded sagely. 'Well, if that completes the list, I must say—'

'And then there's Dermot Boyd, sir. Only man who admits to knowing Annie Clark was going to be in the Pendle area on the Sunday when she died. Fellow member of the witches' coven of which the dead girl was a member: the only male participant in that coven. Thoroughly unhelpful to us at the beginning of our investigation. Tried to steer his wife away from the building where the body was found four months later. Certainly seemed to be half-expecting that the body would be found there.'

Tucker shook his head dumbly at this welter of information, most of which he should already have known. Then he suddenly brightened. 'But you said that you felt you were close to an arrest, Percy?'

Again the forename. Be careful, Percy old lad. 'Just a hunch, sir. I don't aspire to your remarkable insights, but I have the occasional gut feeling.' He stared down at that part of his anatomy, as if it might suddenly voice a Delphic prophecy. When it remained obstinately silent, he said, 'I'll let you know as soon as I have anything more definite. Then you can arrange your media conference.'

He'd managed to produce the phrase without even a curl of his expressive lips.

'So you're engaged, our Lucy.'

It was warm and intimate in the sitting room of the old cottage where Lucy Blake had spent the first twenty-two years of her life – just the setting for a mother to put a little gentle pressure on her daughter. Lucy took a deep breath and prepared herself to be firm.

'Yes. Percy proposed last night.'

It seemed he'd taken notice of her, after all. They needed

pushing along, these men. He was a bright lad, Percy Peach, but not where women and their emotions were concerned. 'Your Dad would have been pleased. Especially with Percy being a cricketer.'

'Ex-cricketer, Mum. He's a golfer, now. Quite good, they tell me.'

'Golf!' As she had done with Percy himself five days earlier, Agnes managed to compress a lifetime of contempt into the monosyllable.

Lucy contrived to keep her face perfectly straight as she said, 'I thought I might take up the game myself, Mum.'

'Tchah! You want to keep a proper sense of proportion, our Lucy. When are you getting married?'

There it was – the question she had known would come, thrown in on the back of her teasing about golf, catching her unawares. She said defensively, 'We haven't fixed a date yet, Mum.'

'It had better be soon, at your time of life.'

'I'm barely twenty-nine, Mum, not fifty.'

'Plenty old enough to be getting wed. Plenty old enough to be having childer.' The old word she had not used for forty years had surfaced from Agnes Blake's subconscious, as she tried to disguise her emotions.

'Women have children when they're much older, nowadays. The maternity units are well used to dealing with older mothers.'

'What about older grandmothers? I'm going to be in a wheelchair by the time these kids are running around. That's if I'm not pushing up daisies.'

'You're good for many years yet, Mum, I'm sure. You'll be chasing around with a toddler when you're eighty, if I'm any judge.'

'Well, you're not any judge, our Lucy. And I certainly don't want to wait until I'm eighty. I want to teach my grandson how to hold a bat and play straight, before you get hold of him and start talking about bloody golf!' Agnes Blake never swore, but it seemed right to make an exception for that stupid game and this obstinate daughter.

'It's not as simple as you make out, Mum. I've a career to think of, for one thing. And then there's Percy. We have to take into account his opinion on these things, you know.'

'Yes, I do know. And I fancy he's likely to be a sight more sensible about a family than you seem to be! He's a good lad, our Percy – more amenable to reason than some I could name around here!' She gazed into the glowing coals of her open fire and nodded thoughtfully.

'Now don't you start pressurizing Percy, Mum. These things have to be settled privately, between husband and wife.' Lucy had never spoken of Percy and herself like that before: she found that she rather liked the expression.

'Pressurize? Me? You know I'd never do any such thing.' She sniffed her contempt at the idea. 'All I'm saying is that your Percy Peach has his head screwed on right. He's likely to see the sense of these things a lot more clearly than a slip of a girl like you!'

Lucy reflected on how a mother's prejudices could turn her from a woman in danger of being left on the shelf two minutes ago to a slip of a girl at the end of this conversation.

And Agnes Blake thought that the solution to the problem was now clear. She'd talk to Percy about the issue of grandchildren. He'd listened to her about proposing, and he would surely see the sense of fathering a new line of English batsmen.

Twenty-Three

Judith Hurst swivelled herself with difficulty in the passenger seat of the Jaguar car. She took the strong female hand as firmly as she could into her two emaciated ones and hauled herself stiffly upright. 'You've been a good neighbour, Jane. I don't say that often enough. You've not just been kind; you've been a good friend as well.'

The plump, cheerful woman looked up at the high, modern walls of Brunton police station and did not know what to say. 'I hope it's not as bad as it seems. I expect they'll let Alan out soon.'

'Don't come in. I can manage, with my stick. I hope they don't think I'm playing for sympathy.' But Judith knew that all the sympathy in the world wouldn't make any difference to this. She wanted to scream out to the world that her husband wasn't into child pornography, that he would never harm a child. She wanted to storm into this impersonal modern building and scream at these stolid policemen that Alan Hurst was into young women, not children – that he had the normal healthy lusts of the flesh, not this awful perversion of them.

But her days of storming anywhere were over. She hobbled carefully towards the big doors, easing herself over the single step with slow, careful effort; she didn't want to begin this by losing her balance and falling. The station sergeant was sympathetic, as most people were to this woman of forty-one who moved as if she were eighty-one.

At seven o'clock on a Friday night, there were plenty of empty rooms in the place, and he found her a vacant office and a chair with arms to support her. The rules said that a young constable would have to sit in the room with them, but he'd sit at the back and not interfere with their conversation.

The station sergeant implied that he would hardly be listening at all, that this was just a tiresome formality.

Judith was shocked by Alan's appearance when they brought him to her. This man who was usually dapper, even a little vain, about the way he looked, had hair that looked as if it had not seen a comb for days and buttons undone on his shirt. He caught her glancing down at his shoes and said with a sad smile, 'They take your shoelaces away. And the belt from your trousers. So that you can't hang yourself in the cells, that is.'

He looked as if they had also taken away every shred of his self-respect. She didn't know what to say; it was almost like sitting beside a hospital bed. She said, 'Have they been treating you properly?'

'Properly? He looked as if she had introduced a foreign word. 'Yes. I suppose so. You don't seem to have many rights, when you've done what I've done. But they've been kind enough to me, yes. They've given me drinks, and what little food I could eat. They've told me I'll need a lawyer. Apparently you should have a lawyer, even when you're pleading guilty.'

They were both silent for a little while, while the implications of his words sank in for both of them. Judith could not contemplate life without him. She did not want to ask what sort of sentence he would get. But she could not prevent herself saying wildly, 'Why did you do it, Alan? Why on earth did you do it?'

'We needed money – for the extension. I wanted to make life a little easier for you. For both of us.' It was at once the absolute truth and the most abject of excuses. 'A man came into the shop and said he could supply the materials to me. He said it was easy money. And it was, until this happened.'

'But you're not – not . . .' She couldn't frame the words that would complete the question.

'Not into sex with children? No, of course I'm not. The idea revolts me. Don't ever think that.' With that last phrase, he acknowledged that he wasn't going to be with her for long months, perhaps years, and left both of them staring into a bleak and separated future.

'Then why get involved with this? I need to understand, Alan.'

'It was easy money. The people who like this stuff were going to buy it from someone, so why not me? That was the way it was sold to me, and I believed it.'

'You knew people who bought these vile videos?'

'I knew one. He gave me the names of others. It was as if he wanted to prove that he wasn't alone, that there were lots of others who liked child pornography. And there are, Judith. That's one of the awful things. The man who supplied the tapes was right: it was easy money.'

She was silent for a moment, wondering how you could live with someone for so many years, could love him and be loved by him, without knowing him properly and fully. 'But why, Alan? Why take money for something like this? Why get involved with anything as squalid as this?'

He wanted to say that it was for her, that he would do worse things even than this, for her. But that might be the most wounding thing of all. He said dully, 'We needed the money. The business isn't doing as well as it used to, when you were more involved. I had to get the money from somewhere, to do what we planned to do to the house.'

She had no tears left. A great weariness was coursing through her frail body. She mustn't collapse. Not here; not with only strangers' hands to lift her and carry her outside to her neighbour's car. She forced out the words she had not wanted to voice. 'Will you be coming home?'

'Of course I will. I don't know when. Soon, I hope. There'll be formal charges. They'll let me out on bail, I expect. The lawyer will handle it for me. I never intended that it should come to this, Jude.'

Judith Hurst stood up then, before either of them could collapse into tears. She put her hands briefly on top of his, then turned carefully, staggering a little, steadying herself quickly with her stick and a hand against the wall, as the young constable hurried to help her. She crippled her way out of the room without another look at the wretched man at the table.

Alan Hurst sat with his head in his hands where she had left him, feeling his eyelids still dry against the palms of his hands. He told himself that at least he had gone through the horror of confronting Judith, that things could certainly

209

not get any worse now. He found no consolation in that.

And he was wrong to think that the worst was over. Five minutes later they led him with surprising gentleness from this room to another, starker one, and told him that Detective Chief Inspector Peach wished to speak with him.

Peach stood for a moment looking down at the handsome, ravaged face. Alan Hurst looked ten years older than when they had seen him three days earlier. Peach decided to forsake his normal aggression: if this man was to reveal everything he knew, they might need to coax him rather than bully him.

'We need to ask you some questions, Mr Hurst. There may be formal charges, in due course. You may wish to have your lawyer present for this interview.'

Hurst looked up, seemingly conscious for the first time that Peach had entered the room. 'I haven't got a lawyer. I don't want one, not yet.'

Peach looked at him for a moment, sizing up his condition. He wanted to be certain of his reliability, not just his vulnerability. Then he set the cassette turning silently in the recorder and announced that it was seven twenty-three p.m. on the evening of the fourth of February and that Alan Charles Hurst was about to be interviewed by DCI Peach and DS Blake.

Before he could speak, Hurst said, without raising his head, 'I'm concealing nothing. But that other inspector has already had all I have to offer.'

Peach nodded. He said to the top of the head in front of him, 'The officer from the National Child Pornography Unit says that you have been entirely cooperative. I'm quite prepared to believe that you've told him everything you know about those child-pornography videos.'

'Then why this?' He lifted his arms, then let them drop back helplessly to his side; the gesture took in his abject state, the criminal charges which were pending, and this sterile, green-walled box of an interview room. 'Why can't you leave me alone now? I need to be with Judith. My wife needs me, and I need to be with her, if she's ever going to understand why I did this.'

It was Lucy Blake who now said softly, 'We don't need

to go over that ground again, Alan. The specialist detectives from the National Child Pornography Unit are handling that. As DCI Peach has just told you, we're quite prepared to believe that you've been completely frank with them.'

'I have! I wish I'd never got involved in that vile trade and I want to do everything I can to damage it.'

It was the first time since they had come into the room that he had spoken with energy. But he could not hold his moment of conviction. His eyes fell back to the surface of the square, scratched table and the cassette tape moving silently through the recorder.

Lucy Blake's instinct was to be compassionate to a broken man. But she was a CID officer, and she knew by now that suspects are at their most defenceless when they are either in the grip of passion or in the atrophy of despair. She said softly, 'We don't want to talk to you about the videos, Alan. We're still pursuing our enquiries into the death of Annie Clark.'

Alan Hurst raised his eyes, looked in turn at each of the contrasting faces on the other side of the table. He felt an immense weariness, an overwhelming desire to let lethargy take him over. He knew that he must rouse himself, must stir his reluctant brain into action against this new and even greater threat. But his mind refused to obey his will. He said dully, 'I've told you everything I know about Annie Clark and the way she disappeared. You've questioned me twice before and you've had all I know.'

It was Peach who said, almost apologetically it seemed, 'We don't believe that, Mr Hurst. We believe you've both concealed the truth from us and lied directly to us.'

Alan felt an intense urge to give them what they wanted, to capitulate quietly and have it over with. But he heard himself saying, 'You must be mistaken. I don't know what happened to Annie on that last weekend.'

'On the first occasion when we saw you, you concealed the fact that you had been having an affair with the dead woman in the months before her death.'

'I shouldn't have done that. But I wasn't proud of my behaviour with Annie. I was scared that if I told you about it Judith would get to know of it. I didn't want that.'

'You also denied any knowledge of Annie's pregnancy and said you had no idea who the father could be.'

'Yes. I wasn't completely honest with you when you came to the house that first time. I've already admitted that.' The trouble with lying, Alan thought, was that you had to remember exactly what you had said and on what occasion. He was too battered by the events of the last twenty-four hours to remember anything very clearly.

The DCI seemed to know exactly what his problem was, which was disconcerting. Peach now said, 'When we saw you for the second time, on Tuesday, you admitted to having an affair with Annie Clark.'

'Yes. I realize now that I should never have tried to conceal it. But you were interviewing me in my own house on that first occasion, with Judith in the next room. I wasn't proud of my adultery.' He'd never used that word before, never admitted to himself that it had been that. He dragged a hand wearily across his forehead. He kept thinking of Judith, when he needed to have all his attention on the contest with this determined opponent.

'Miss Clark had been working for you for four months when she disappeared. You told us on Tuesday that you had been lovers for six weeks. But I believe that you had been sleeping together for most of those four months.'

'Probably.' He found that he wanted, absurdly, to tell them how quickly Annie had fallen for his charms. Even in his exhaustion, some tiny sediment of vanity tried to assert itself. He thrust away the idea and said with some of the revulsion he felt for himself, 'Annie Clark was asserting her freedom when she left home and started a new life. Perhaps I took advantage of that, but I didn't see it like that at the time. I saw a chance of bedding young, healthy flesh, and I took it.'

'And before too long, she became pregnant.'

'No!' The word came unexpectedly loud, echoing round the walls of that sterile box of a room. But it was an automatic, unthinking denial, an assertion of the way he wanted things to be rather than the truth. He could not muster his thoughts to follow it up with any convincing logic.

Peach saw all this and said quietly, 'The foetus found

212

inside what was left of Annie Clark was severely damaged. But the forensic laboratory assure us that there will be no difficulty in establishing a DNA match with the father. We shall be requiring a DNA sample from you in due course, Mr Hurst.'

Seconds elapsed, during which he tried to gather together the rags of his resources to make a final, hopeless defence. 'I'll deny it. There won't be enough left to make a connection. You'll never make this stick.'

Lucy Blake said almost gently, 'We have a statement made this morning by the secretary at the Gold Hill Convalescent Home, which is primarily an abortion clinic. On September the fifteenth of last year you made an appointment for a termination for Anne Marie Clark.'

'You'll never be able to prove it was me. I never gave my name!' He was careless now of the way he phrased things. The prizefighter was on his knees, with nothing left to offer save the urge to resist, listening to the count and unable to get to his feet.

'The appointment was for Thursday the twenty-first of September. It was cancelled on Tuesday the nineteenth by Annie Clark herself, who said that she had decided to keep the baby and was ringing to cancel the appointment made by a Mr Hurst.'

'She said she wanted to keep her child – that she wanted me to acknowledge that I was the father and help to bring it up.' His voice seemed to be coming from a long way away; he felt as if he were a medium for someone else's thoughts.

More to take him forward than anything else, Lucy Blake said firmly, 'She had every right to do that, Mr Hurst.'

He lifted both hands a few inches, then let them fall back heavily on to the table. 'I couldn't let her do that. I couldn't let Judith see another woman carrying my child.' He sobbed, suddenly and hopelessly, without producing the tears which might have brought some sort of relief. 'Jude always wanted a child. We never managed it, and then she was ill.'

Lucy Blake thrust away the thought of those other, putative children, the ones her mother was so anxious for her to conceive, and said remorselessly, 'So you killed Annie Clark.

She died because you couldn't face the consequences of what you had done.'

'I took her out to the Ribble Valley on that last Sunday, to explain to her that I couldn't let her go ahead with this. I thought that now that she had a boyfriend, she'd want to get rid of our baby, to start a new life with him. She said her religious beliefs wouldn't allow it.' Hurst said it with an exhausted bitterness, as if a moral argument had been the final irony for him.

'And you climbed Pendle Hill.'

'That was her idea. There was cloud on the top and a cold wind, but she was always full of energy, was Annie. I went along with it because I knew it would take hours. I felt that if I only had enough time I could convince her.'

'But it didn't work.'

'No. We climbed all the way to the top. The wind got stronger and stronger, but she kept saying how much she was enjoying it. I teased her about her Wiccan beliefs and having Pendle to herself for a witch's sabbath. Once the weather worsened, we seemed to be the only ones up there, and she liked that.' He stopped, and for a moment all three of them were visualizing the last, exhilarating hours of a pretty, unsuspecting girl. 'I was afraid that we'd get lost in the mist, but Annie ran in front of me along the ridge to the top, shouting and throwing her arms into the air. We were on the way down when it happened.'

'Near that deserted farmhouse.'

'Yes. I suggested that we rest for a minute – said that I was tired out; that she had too much energy for me. Really, I just wanted to go over the arguments with her again, to make her see reason. I don't think I was planning to kill her, even then.'

'But you did.'

He nodded, all resistance now long gone. 'We sat on the wall by that ruin and argued. I went over everything I'd said before about Judith and the impossibility of Annie keeping this baby. She just kept shaking her head, more and more vigorously, as if she wanted to shut out my words, to stop listening to me. It was then that I took her throat into my hands. I think I was just trying to shake some sense into her,

214

at first.' He spoke wonderingly, as if he still did not understand how it had happened. 'And then she started to scream, louder and louder. I had to stop that.'

It was Peach who said, 'And you found you had a corpse in your hands.'

He nodded, seemingly grateful to them for their understanding. 'There was no one about. It was evening by then. I put Annie in the outbuildings of the farm, against the far wall. I was almost out of the place when I remembered that I should empty her pockets, remove all traces of who she was. So I turned back and did that. And I removed the cheap ring that her new boyfriend had given to her from her engagement finger.'

A curious smile crept over his exhausted face at the memory. Lucy Blake said, 'Was that because you thought it would help to identify her?'

'Yes. I've still got it, though. I've kept it in the drawer of my desk at work.' With the charge of murder being prepared against him, Hurst was pathetically anxious not to be seen as a petty thief.

'And you got away from the farmhouse without anyone seeing you.'

He nodded. 'I didn't meet anyone until I was almost back at the car.'

Peach stood up and informed him that a charge of murder would be brought against him. Alan Hurst merely nodded meekly. He was told that he would now be taken back to his cell and he moved stoop-shouldered to the door. Then he turned a ravaged face back to them and said, 'You'll look after Judith, won't you? Someone needs to explain all this to Judith.'

It was Judith Hurst they were all thinking about. They had to remind themselves that poor, pathetic Annie Clark, the girl they had never known, had a measure of justice at last, as did the child she had never been allowed to bear; that Anna Fenton, that other innocent at large, had been protected from the attentions of a dangerous man.

Percy Peach dealt with the formalities of the charges. Alan Hurst would appear before the magistrates and be remanded to the crown court on Monday morning. Lucy Blake collected a uniformed constable and went off to the detached nineteen-thirties house on the fringe of the town.

She was relieved to find a nurse already with Mrs Hurst. As quietly and quickly as she could, Lucy gave her the worst news of all: that her husband was to be charged with murder. She left Judith Hurst staring at Alan's plans for the extension and contemplating a long, lonely journey into death.

DATE DUE

DATE DUE
08/28/13

Hempstead Public Library

Hempstead, New York

Phone: (516) 481-6990

APR 2 4 2006